Carter threw a sharp glance at the corpse. Elroy Brown had been directed to this room, and to his death.

In the hallway, Carter heard the sounds of heavy footfalls. Then voices. "Yeah, he was here. Checked in around six." The footfalls were getting closer.

Carter dared not move for fear the creaking floorboards would give himself away.

"Mr. Brown?" The hotel manager again.

Another voice, this one more gruff. "Open the door."

It was only three words, but Carter could have sworn he recognized the second voice.

"Mr. Brown," the manager said again. A key thunked into the lock. "The police are here and they need to speak to you."

Police? Carter's mind whirled, piecing together the familiar tone of the second voice with the word "police" and he arrived at a conclusion: the voice belonged to Bobby Anders, the policeman who had tried to beat answers out of Hiram Colby. But how in the world was Bobby here, at the St. Louis Hotel, at the same time Carter was?

When the key turned the lock, Carter made his decision.

ALSO BY S. D. PARKER

CALVIN CARTER: RAILROAD DETECTIVE

Empty Coffins

Hell Dragon

Aztec Sword

Brides of Death*

The Senator's Daughter*

Iron Knights*

WESTERNS BY S.D. PARKER

Mosaic Law

A Father's Justice

The Killing of Lars Fulton

The Box Maker

The Agony of Love

The Naked Con

MYSTERIES BY SCOTT DENNIS PARKER

Wading Into War

The Phantom Automobiles

Ulterior Objectives

All Chickens Must Die

*Coming Soon

AZTEC SWORD

Calvin Carter: Railroad Detective

S. D. PARKER

Quadrant Fiction Studio

Aztec Sword
Calvin Carter: Railroad Detective
By S. D. Parker

Copyright © 2019 by Scott Dennis Parker
A Quadrant Fiction Studio Book

Cover Design by Scott Dennis Parker
Cover Photos:
Top: jtanki03
Bottom: MaciejBledowski

www.ScottDennisParker.com

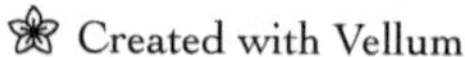 Created with Vellum

NEWSLETTER

Join my email list to receive updates on new books and videos, and get an exclusive **Catalog Sampler for 2019** with a special offer: *Buy One Book (of your choice) and Get a Second One Free.*

Sign up at ScottDennisParker.com

To my grandfather who loved westerns

❦ I ❦

OCTAVIA HENDRICKSON WAS one of the wealthiest women in Austin, Texas, so if she wanted to stage an exhibition of ancient Indian artifacts inside the brand-new museum that bore her name, the citizens of the state capital took notice and attended.

The Hendrickson Museum occupied a thin lot along West Pecan Street a block away from the bustle of Congress Avenue. The building itself formerly was a warehouse used to store goods being shipped back east. It was Gunter Hendrickson's first purchase in Austin twenty years ago, but it had laid dormant until his widow decided she needed a museum to display all the various things she had purchased with his vast wealth that now solely belonged to her. The ground floor had been completely renovated, the wood floor freshly cleaned and polished. Where the walls used to be rough and unfinished, now bright paint caught the lamp light and shone like the sun at noon. Lamps, hanging from chains extended from the ceiling, bathing everything and everyone on the ground floor with a warm glow. Various displays of artifacts dotted the area, and the high-end citizens of Austin had all turned out to pay their respects — some would say fealty — to Octavia.

The city elite milled around, murmuring their remarks about this artifact or that stone pottery. The men wore their finest tuxedos and formal wear. Shirts were starched stiff, ties cinched at the neck, and the finest of gold chains and cuff links were displayed. The women who accompanied the men — and some that were without a partner — were dressed in clothes so fine that a casual observer might have mistaken the party as being hosted in Paris or New York rather than the state capital of Texas. The finest of clothes and the latest fashions adorned every woman. Even their perfume, with various aromas, superseded the waft of cigar tobacco or the fresh flowers filling alcoves around the room.

In short, it was just the kind of fete Calvin Carter relished.

He wore his best tuxedo, which, as a former actor, was one of his favorite uniforms. His pants were neatly pressed, showing off a crease that could likely cut paper. His shirt was pristine white, his tie impeccably knotted, and the cuff-links at his wrists showcased silver and turquoise. The jacket was custom tailored to his form, and allowed for the presence of his shoulder holster situated under his right arm. As a current railroad detective, he once balked at carrying his weapon with him at all times, but after being caught without it one particular event, he relented and always carried the Colt .44. His insistence of a shoulder holster was to keep the gun hidden from any ne'er do wells. Carter's philosophy was that the gun was the last resort. He insisted he had the talent and joie de vivre to talk his way out of anything.

And, if not, he'd have his gun.

Carter wore his tux like a second skin. The same could not be said for his friend and partner, Thomas Jackson. The native New Yorker, who was raised on a cattle ranch in Texas, shoved a finger between his high collar and his neck and made more room. The fabric stretched and Carter heard a small tear.

"Careful, Tom. You'd hate to have to go back to Adena's and tell her the shirt and suit she specifically tailored for you was ripped on account of your thick fingers."

Jackson moved his chin up and down, trying to create even more space from the collar. "It's this damn collar. It's like being hogtied with fancy rope." Jackson was taller than Carter's six feet by a couple of inches. His thatch of blond air, usually barely kept in place, was nicely coiffed this evening. When Carter had arrived at Jackson's boarding house, he had fussed over his partner's appearance like a grandmother. Now, he beamed his smile out into the crowd.

"Get used to it, Jackson," Colonel Jameson Moore said. "This is as much a part of being a railroad detective as field work."

Colonel Moore was their commanding officer in the detective agency. A veteran of the Late Unpleasantness, Moore had made his way out west and helped found the detective corps for the railroad. He had recruited Carter and Jackson, pairing the mismatched men together a little over a year ago. The two younger men, initially unsure of the reason, nevertheless had come to rely and trust each other in the field and back at home.

Moore opted for a formal suit, eschewing any sort of military adornment. His bosses knew who he was, as did most of the people milling about and gazing at the ancient pottery and objects. But Moore preferred a low-key approach to his job. He directed all of his detectives from the comfort of his office. Field work was behind him, left in Virginia when Lee surrounded. There was likely never going to be a reason why an old man like him needed to strap on a gun. "That's why I have you two," he would often say to Carter and Jackson.

Next to Moore stood Catherine Moore his wife of thirty years. Adorned in a modest black dress that covered nearly all of her body save for her neck and hands, Catherine smiled gently at passersby, nodding to those she knew and some she didn't. "Don't worry, Thomas," she said, reaching around her husband and gently pulling Jackson's hand away from his neck, "when you meet a nice young woman and settle down, she'll be the one to fuss over you and how you look."

Jackson lowered his hand, but his brows remained furrowed in irritation. A waiter carrying a tray of champagne coupes, the bubbly liquid sloshing over the rims, approached. Jackson signaled for the man to stop. He plucked two coupes from the tray with the intention of handing one to Carter. But Carter had already plucked a coupe from the tray, so Jackson threw back the contents of the first coupe and replaced it on the tray. He kept the second.

"I may need more of these as the night wears on," Jackson muttered. He shot a glance over at Moore. "Do we have a new case?"

The colonel smiled noncommittally. "Surprisingly, most everything is quiet. For every incident, I already have detectives in the field." He raised his glass to Jackson. "Like my wife said, you can relax." He tinked his coupe to Catherine's and they both sipped the effervescent beverage.

Carter nudged Jackson and indicated the crowd. A woman strolled among the partygoers. Both detectives made way for her. She was in her fifties, but made up to look at least a decade younger. The most expensive make up available adorned her face. The rouge and the lipstick both a matching shade of brick red. Her dark hair had streaks of silver that she used to color and dye until someone told her it gave her gravitas. The full-length gown was of a splendid purple and velvet, with ruffles that cascaded down on each side of her hips. She carried a coupe of champagne, empty at the moment, and she searched for a waiter so should could pass off the glass.

"Our hostess," Carter murmured. "I'll introduce you."

Jackson arched an eyebrow. "You know her?"

Carter drained his glass. "Of course I know her. The colonel does, too."

"Actually, I don't," Moore said, a hint of annoyance in his voice.

Carter continued, undeterred. "You should always know the rich folks in town. They are the ones who can get things done." He signaled Octavia with a smile and a wink and beckoned her to come over.

With a ravishing face that beamed with joy at being the center of attention, Octavia Hendrickson glided over and came to a stop in front of Carter. The detective reached out and gently grasped her hand. In his peripheral vision, he could tell many people were watching, most notably his commanding officer and his partner. Fine, he thought, let them watch. It's all part of the performance.

He brushed his lips across her knuckles. Her delicate scent mixed with a little sweat and perfume. He didn't mind in the least.

"Octavia, my dear, your party is a rousing success," Carter said. He offered his best smile, partly for her, but mostly for the audience he knew he had. Ever the performer, Carter knew when to be in character, even if the character in question was a former actor turned railroad detective. He allowed her a moment to bask in the glow of his compliment, blushing almost on command.

As if on cue, the same waiter passed by, his attention

completely on his job. He never realized whom he was passing until Carter called out to him. Upon turning, he noticed Octavia and realized who she was. His eyes got bigger and he swallowed hard, his Adam's apple bobbing up and down over his tie.

"I'm sorry, ma'am, I didn't see you. Can I refill your glass for you?"

Octavia shot him the kind of look a royal gave a servant who had made a mistake but groveled in compliance. She sniffed at him, but traded her empty coupe for a full one.

He bowed, backed away, and resumed his job.

"You never can find the best help, can you?" She spoke to Carter conspiratorially, almost as if they were alone. Or she was testing him.

"I don't know, Octavia," Carter said, straightening his tie, "the man was just doing his job so well that his focus was elsewhere."

Another woman cut through the crowd and came to stand next to Octavia. She was much younger than the hostess, but still shared some of her mother's genetic traits. The woman's red hair, worn long, down to her shoulders, caught the lamp light and radiated like a red sun. The high cheek bones were prominent, none more so than when she smiled. Her strong jawline ended with a prominent chin with a slight cleft. The green eyes had the impression of softness but with an edge that rarely missed anything. The red dress was similar to her mother's, but cut lower, as was the style with the younger ladies.

"I don't know, Mother," Naomi Hendrickson said. "You could just fire him to make an impression on the other staff."

Unlike the introduction Carter gave to Octavia, to Naomi, he only nodded coolly. "That seems a little harsh, don't you think? The man was clearly just doing his job. In fact, he was doing it so well, he was intently focused on navigating the crowd and avoiding spilling any of his drinks. Now that might've been a true disaster, spilling champagne on the governor's wife or some other high society type. But he didn't." To Octavia, he said, "Maybe John could even use a pat on the back."

Octavia gave him a curious look. "You know him?"

"I do," Carter said. "I did a little work for him, looked into a situation he needed help with." The edges of his mouth quirked up. "It got solved." He decided to leave it at that.

With a subtle grunt, Octavia seemed to dismiss the incident without another thought. Naomi, on the other hand, gave Carter a stern look.

Carter deflected by turning to Jackson. "Octavia, I'd like you to meet my partner, Thomas Jackson."

"Pleased to meet you," Jackson said. He extended his hand, took Octavia's in his, and kissed her fingers. For all of Jackson's protestations of disliking to dress up, he possessed a certain grace and showed it here. It was nowhere near as polished as Carter's suavity, but it wasn't like he came off as a country rube. "You have a great party."

Octavia blinked, inclining her head. "Why thank you, Mr. Jackson. So you're the one who saves dear Calvin when the going gets rough."

Carter cleared his throat. "We're a good team. We help each other." He indicated Moore. "And this is out commanding officer, Colonel Jameson Moore, and his wife, Catherine."

Without missing a beat, Octavia turned her attention to the colonel. "I do hope you don't send dear Calvin away to anything very dangerous. I am hoping to catch him on stage again."

Moore smiled one of his public faces. "I only send my men out to catch the bad guys. It's not my fault they sometimes shoot back."

While Octavia spoke to Catherine, Naomi moved in her mother's wake. "I'm Naomi Hendrickson," she said to Jackson. She offered her hand, and he took it. "I guess I have to introduce myself since 'dear Calvin' isn't doing it."

"I was getting there," Carter said with a bit more irritation than he intended. "This is my partner, Thomas Jackson."

The look Naomi offered Jackson was one that carried multiple meanings. "I certainly hope you're not a sniveling bastard like Carter is."

Surprise registered on Jackson's face, but was soon smoothed over. "I most certainly am not. Tell me: what makes Cal a bastard?"

"How long do you have?" was Naomi's retort, complete with a pointed look at Carter.

Inwardly, Carter sighed. Ever since he had made the acquaintance of Octavia Hendrickson during his acting days, she had made herself something of a patron. Before his father was murdered and he opted to track down and bring the killer to justice, Carter had been a freewheeling actor, frittering around from role to role. Often he traveled with a company, and it was in this situation where he performed in Austin and came into the orbit of Octavia. She had taken a shine to him, and, despite their age difference, had taken him into her bedroom. Carter, never one to turn away the affections of a beautiful woman, had gone along with her. They had an understanding: she knew she couldn't own him and he knew the acting business brought him into contact with other ladies. This understanding, however, had one impediment: Naomi. She was generally miffed that her mother paraded her catch of

Carter in front of her daughter, a man closer to her own age.

Jackson grinned. "I have all night."

At that moment, Octavia signaled a man who stood off to the side of the small raised dais at the center of the room. The man nodded once, then rang a hand bell. The high-pitched sound permeated the room and quieted the crowd within seconds.

Octavia signaled Carter and he dutifully offered his hand for leverage as the hostess climbed the short steps to the top of the stage. She basked in the eyes and attention of all the assembled guests, turning around once to take in all she surveyed.

"Ladies and gentlemen, I'm so glad you could come to the opening of my new museum tonight." She waited for the polite applause to start and stop. "As many of you know, my dearly departed husband, Gunter, made a name for himself in the early railroad business. His generosity and prosperity made me able to pursue one of my lifelong passions of acquiring art from the savages who once roamed this land. And now, with the Hendrickson Museum, I am able to share some of these pieces with all of you."

More polite applause while Octavia sipped her champagne.

Next to Carter, Naomi had wedged herself between Carter and Jackson. Under her breath, she murmured, "As if the people even care about pottery and old tools."

Carter leaned over near her ear. "I wouldn't knock it. You can learn a lot about a culture from what they leave behind." His close proximity to her enabled her perfume to enter his senses. It was a delicious, musky scent that instantly captivated Carter.

In earlier encounters with Naomi over the months and years, Carter rarely found himself this close to Octavia's daughter. He had all but dismissed her when he determine she was generally irritated with him. Now, however, he surreptitiously gave her another appraisal.

She caught him. "What are you looking at?"

Momentarily caught off guard, Carter replied, "I have to say, you look very nice tonight."

Naomi masked whatever thought she truly had with a sarcastic sneer. "Don't look now, but I think you're about to be on."

At her comment, Jackson turned. "What does that mean?" He looked at Carter, concern registering on his face. "Oh no, are you going to speak?"

Carter gave the pair one of his lopsided grins. "Octavia has asked me to say a few words."

"For all our sakes," Naomi said, "say as few as possible."

From onstage, Octavia was still speaking. "And now, for part of this evening's entertainment, I would like to invite renowned actor"—Jackson rolled his eyes at that comment—"and current railroad detective, Calvin Carter, to come up on stage and speak. Calvin?"

Any time Carter got up on a stage, a certain part of him lit up. It never mattered if the stage was in an opera house, a gazebo in the center of a small town, or even this small dais in a museum. A stage was a stage. He rarely experienced what they called stage fright. In some ways, he longed for the stage more than he longed to wear a badge. But the badge brought with it justice, and after Carter's father was gunned down and he hunted down the killer, justice won the day.

Passing a hand over the front of his jacket to ensure it was smooth as possible, Carter ascended the stairs to mild applause. Some in the crowd knew him as a detective, but few likely knew him as an actor. Chances were that most of the folks here tonight didn't know him at all.

He came to stand next to Octavia, humble being the visage he presented. She had asked him to make a performance of a couple of his favorite Shakespeare sonnets or poems. He had selected a few, ran them by her, and she okayed them. She also had asked him to prepare a short little speech. "I just love the sound of your voice, Calvin dear," she had told him once. "You could read the train schedule and I would listen with rapt attention."

Calvin Carter had smiled at the compliment. Now, as he opened his mouth to thank her publicly, his words died in his mouth when the doors to the museum slammed open and five figures charged into the museum.

Each man welded a drawn pistol.

❧ 2 ☙

THE AUDIENCE TURNED and craned their necks to see who had caused the intrusion. Carter, from his vantage point on the dais, had a near unobstructed view.

Five men, all wearing wrinkled but dark clothes, stormed into the great room of the museum. They had bandanas around their faces and their hats of various sizes and shades were pulled down low on their heads. The only parts of their faces visible were their eyes. They were wild, darting this way and that, trying to take in their surroundings.

"Hold it right there!" called the man in the middle. He was broad shouldered, with a thick neck behind his red bandana. "This here is a hold up!"

From his position on the dais, Carter's hand shot into his jacket pocket and gripped the butt of his Colt .44. The wooden grip, taken from his father's own gun, was smooth under his palm. He was in the act of pulling the gun free from its shoulder holster when Octavia hissed at him.

"What are you doing?"

"Being prepared," came Carter's reply.

He slipped the gun out of his jacket and held down by his side, slightly behind his leg.

Thomas Jackson was the type of detective who preferred to wear his gun out in the open, slung to his leg in a low holster. The former cow puncher thought it best to announce to the world who he was and what he'd do if any owlhoot thought they could beat him. But tonight, Carter convinced his partner that wearing a gun on his hip would have been improper. So he had Jackson try out a shoulder holster. The Yankee had complained about the bulk of his pistol jammed up under his arm, but now, with the pistol already drawn and in his hand, Carter reckoned Jackson was glad to have put up with it for the night.

Jackson glanced up at Carter. With hand signals, Carter indicated that two of the bandits had fanned out to the left, two to the right, and one in the center in front of the main door. His partner nodded once, then eased his way behind Moore and edged closer to the right.

"Good evening, ladies and gentlemen," Red Bandana said. "We're here to make a withdrawal." He held his gun nonchalantly, almost as an afterthought of his arm. "If y'all would be so kind as to empty your pockets and purses of your belongings, we'll get this nasty business over with as soon as possible." He chuckled under the bandana, a muffled sound deadened by the tight cloth smashing his nose.

"And I'd hate to think that there is some valiant hero who thinks he might try and stop us." In a swift movement, he raised the gun and fired at the ceiling. Whether or not he was aiming at one of the oil lamps, Carter never knew. Nonetheless, his bullet slammed into a lamp, spilling broken glass down to the floor.

"My chandelier!" Octavia gasped. Her voice was a mixture of surprise and outright indignation. She called out to Red Bandana. "Just who do you think you are coming in here like this?"

Red Bandana chuckled. The dark gray hat he wore was round and it gave him the appearance of possessing a large head. He walked up to the dais, the crowd parting ahead of him. He stopped at the foot of the stage. "You must be the broad responsible for this little shindig." Red Bandana took the few steps easily, coming to a stop just in front of Octavia. "You're the woman of the hour."

At the direct mention of her mother, Naomi let out a short gasp. Carter caught her eye and subtly shook his head.

Red Bandana threw a glance at Carter. The detective, for his part, remained calm. There were still four other gunmen who could start shooting up the place at a moment's notice. But he got the impression Red Bandana was the head of this little band. Carter wondered what would happen if he cut off the head.

"Who the hell are you?" Red Bandana muttered.

"I'm tonight's entertainment," Carter replied. He kept his left hand with the Colt down by his side and slightly behind Octavia. "I've got a speech prepared. Would you like to hear it?"

In response, Red Bandana backhanded Carter. The blow wasn't too painful, especially considering the man thankfully didn't use his gun hand. The knuckles of the bandit's balled fist smacked into Carter's cheek, sending shooting pain down his face and neck. But it was one of the options Carter hoped the owlhoot would do.

The former actor rolled with the punch, exaggerating enough so that when he landed on the stage, his elbows clomped loudly on the wood. The sound had its intended effect. Red Bandana looked down, wondering just how much damage his punch had landed on Carter. The robber was met with the barrel of Carter's gun aimed directly at his face.

"I'll take that as a 'no,'" Carter said. His hand was rock steady. "Your loss. The speech was quite good." He made no move to stand.

Apparently, this wasn't the first time Red Bandana stared down the barrel of a gun. He actually chuckled again. "Boys, we got a hero here." His voice echoed off the spare walls. "What do we do to heroes?"

From his left, Carter heard one of the owlhoots yell, "We kill 'em."

"That's right," Red Bandana said. "We fill him with lead."

"Be that as it may," Carter said softly, "but I'm the one who's got the drop on you. You try anything, I pull the trigger. Any of your men try anything, I pull the trigger. They shoot me, I still pull the trigger as my last act on this earth. Now," Carter said, pausing for dramatic effect, "are you willing to take that chance?"

Red Bandana cocked his head, his eyes losing a little of their ferocity.

"There's something else, too," Carter continued. "Your mistakes. Normally I let my opponents know the number of mistakes they made right before I bring them to justice. I could list them for you, right now, but I'll settle on just one. This is a high-society party, I'll grant you that. But I have a gun. A friend of mine around here also has a gun. Who knows how many of the men—and maybe a few women— also have a gun. As soon as the shooting starts, many of the people here are going to scream or run around. But not all. And I suspect a few of the patrons here tonight who are armed have already sneaked their guns into a ready posi- tion. If shooting starts, they're gonna shoot back. Do you really think you'll get out of here alive if that happens?"

The room had become deadly quiet. The only sounds were the shuffling of shoes both from the other bandits as well as the gathered partygoers. From outside came the sounds of the city alive for the night: wagons and horses going up and down the streets, people walking up and down the boardwalks, oblivious to the action in the museum.

"What's it gonna be?" Carter prompted. In the ensuing moments, he never once tried to stand. He knew from past experience that any attempt to alter positions could lead to an opening not foreseen. So he stayed on the floor of the stage, resting on his elbow, gun arm extended up to Red Bandana's chest.

When Red Bandana hesitated, another one of his men answered for him. The other man reached out and grabbed a woman by the hair. His intention was to get her in a position where he could back away, keeping the woman as a hostage and a shield.

What he got instead was a bullet in the head from Thomas Jackson.

The loud report from Jackson's gun broke the tension. Most everything Carter had predicted came to pass. The men and women who had come for a good time screamed and started to scatter for the exits or some sort of shielding. Another gun blast sounded in the museum, causing another round of screaming. That blast was from Carter's gun. He had lowered his aim and fired at Red Bandana's gun arm. The slug bit into the bandit's bicep, spinning him around and onto the floor.

Carter leapt up in a single, fluid movement and swept Octavia down to the stage floor. He lowered her almost as if he were part of a performance, his hand guiding her head so she wouldn't knock it on the hard wood. In any other context, the action might have been considered romantic.

In this case, it was lifesaving. Her eyes were wide with fright.

"Stay down," he commanded her. He didn't wait for a response. He rolled over, got onto a knee, and smacked Red Bandana's gun out of his hand. The owlhoot held tight. Carter responded by slamming his fist down onto the bloody area on the man's shoulder. Red Bandana howled in pain and released the gun. Carter grasped it and threw it behind the stage.

"I'll be back for you later," Carter told the man.

He looked up and took stock of the chaos now unfolding inside the museum. The robber Jackson had shot lay upon the floor where he fell. Most of the other people, having no good option to flee, resorted to sitting or lying on the floor. The three remaining bandits, seeing their boss felled and one of their own killed, brought their guns to bear.

Carter and Jackson opened fire, Carter from a kneeling position on stage, Jackson from his position off to the side of the museum. True to Carter's earlier prediction, other men also had their guns out and in their hands, Moore included. Deadly flame blossomed from steel barrels. Hot lead slammed into the three would-be robbers, ventilating them from the outside in. Their bodies jacked back and forth with the impacts before each fell to the floor, dead.

The entire action had taken less than thirty seconds before it was all over. The sharp odor or gunpowder bit into Carter's nose. The thin stream of smoke wafted from the barrel of his Colt, which had again saved him. He realized after a moment that he was breathing heavy. He made a conscious effort to slow his breathing and calm himself.

Spontaneous applause arose from the survivors. Almost as one, they turned to face the stage, wanting to thank Carter as their savior. Octavia joined in the applause. Her dress had become disheveled, but, for the first time since Carter had known her, she didn't seem to mind. He stood and offered her his hand. She took it and got to her feet, her face beaming with relief and excitement.

"Oh my," she breathed. "That was quite something."

Naomi hurried up the stairs and came to hug her mother. The embrace was long and fierce. Carter noted the knuckles of Naomi's hands went white with the exertion. When Octavia patted Naomi's back to indicate her daughter could stop the public display of affection, Naomi complied. She threw a genuine smile Carter's way.

Red Bandana groaned. Carter turned his attention down to the foiled bandit. He yanked down the bandana and got a look at the man's face. It was grizzled, a couple days' worth of whiskers covering the man's cheeks and chin. The nose was askew, probably a sign of having been broken during some earlier fight. The yellowed teeth shown from behind dry and cracked teeth as the man's lip curled up in a grimace of pain.

Carter knelt beside the injured man. The detective regarded the criminal for a moment, trolling his brain to see if he knew the man. He came up empty.

Jackson came to stand next to the fallen criminal, his big bulk looming over the injured man.

"Well," Carter said, "I guess it's time we had ourselves a little chat."

❧ 3 ☙

THE MUSCULAR POLICEMAN emerged from the holding cell shaking his head. He flexed both fists, working out the kinks in his joints. His knuckles were red with the blood of the man Carter still thought of as Red Bandana.

"It's no use, sir," the policeman said. "Whoever paid him gave him enough to keep his mouth shut tight."

The man to whom the officer was talking nodded sagely. Leland Grooms, Jr., was the police chief for Austin, and if Carter were casting him in a play, he would have looked elsewhere. Grooms was a young man, likely less than a decade older than Carter. Every other officer on the force was older and wiser than Grooms, but none of them had the benefit of being the scion of a powerful local politician. Leland Grooms, Sr., was a state senator from the cotton growing region outside of Houston. He had been there before the Late Unpleasantness and beyond. His grip on power solidified after the Constitutional Conventions of 1876 and he never let go. He wrangled the job for his son more out of a desire to give Junior something to do rather than qualification.

It showed. Every day.

The younger Grooms sat imperiously behind his desk. The police station wasn't a large facility, but it still held room for numerous desks, lined in rows. The largest desk was Grooms'. It sat perpendicular to the rest and was ostentatious to the extreme. Stacks of paper lined the edges and, when Carter happened to glance at a few of them, realized that they were reports haphazardly written and incomplete. The other accouterments that dotted the surface of the heavy oak desk served more as props for a play than actual tools needed to enforce and uphold the law.

Grooms' feet were up on the corner of the desk. Carter could have given the police chief some lessons in acting. He would have started with this: leaders have to appear to care about what is being done in their name. Grooms was nursing the contents of a silver flask, smoking a cigar, talking with another policeman, the one who actually had arrived first at the museum and signaled a young boy to fetch Grooms who had been in a saloon.

The sound of the gunshots at the museum had alerted more than just the wiry policeman. Other people ran to see what had happened. They crowded into the museum, never once caring about the subject of the museum, but only interested in seeing the dead bodies of the would-be bandits and the braying of Red Bandana, the only living survivor of a shoot-out in the heart of the city.

In the immediate aftermath, Moore had scrambled to assess what had happened. He ordered Carter and Jackson to perform reconnaissance outside the museum and see if there were any more jackals waiting. At first, Octavia proved reluctant to let go of Carter's arm, but relented when Moore had reassured her that everything was fine and that he was in charge until the police arrived. The two detectives found only the five rider-less horses. They examined the saddles and saddlebags for clues as to the identities of the men, but found nothing. By the time they went back inside, the police had arrived and assumed jurisdiction.

Which was never a good thing. The police department in Austin wasn't a shining example of how to run a good law enforcement agency. Many an officer spent his days "enforcing" the law of the saloons, poker tables, and bordellos. When they could be bothered to work, their police methods left much to be desired. In murmured conversations behind closed doors, some said that the railroad detective agency was run with more professionalism than the local police.

Grooms' officers, eager to come to the scene and appear to be doing a good job, had taken over in time for the local newspaper men to arrive. Even the police chief himself, dressed in a black suit Carter could tell Grooms had tailored and cut to match his wiry frame, made time to address the crowd. In tones that sounded to Carter like a bad actor trying to play-act a police chief, Grooms had assured the gathering throng that all was under control.

And Red Bandana had been whisked away, not to see a sawbones, but to be thrown in a jail cell at the police station. And Grooms had ordered his largest policeman to beat the truth out of Red Bandana. Grooms wasn't stupid. Although he relied on his father's name and patronage, it would only go so far without any pushback. Just the previous year, local alderman tried unsuccessfully to remove Grooms from office. No one ever knew just how he avoided that fate, but avoid it he did. Now, with a shoot-out in his town, Grooms was out to reassure the citizens of Austin he meant business.

"That's okay, Bobby," Grooms said to the officer. "We'll give him a few minutes to think it over before we go at it again. Here," he said, holding up the flask but not removing his feet from his desk, "have a nip."

Bobby wiped his bloody knuckles on his pants and snatched the flask from the police chief's hand. He downed a good gulp and handed it back.

Carter and Jackson leaned against a wall near Grooms' desk. They had refused to sit, not wanting to appear like serfs paying homage to a lord. When Grooms had taken Red Bandana away, Moore ordered his detectives to follow the outlaw to the police station. They had complied, knowing full well the reason: Moore wanted answers and he know Grooms and his policemen were likely not to get them.

"Mind if we have a crack at him?" Jackson said.

Over countless hours and numerous cases, Carter and Jackson had developed a certain rapport. In certain situations, Carter's nuanced approach was the better call. In others, Jackson more rough-hewed version was the way to go. In this instance, Jackson's toughness was the way they went, hopefully, they reckoned, because all of Grooms' men were rough and tumble.

Grooms screwed up his face. "Listen," he said, his Texas drawl quite pronounced, "I let you boys in because my daddy is friends with your boss. I figured since you was the ones there, you ought to get a look. But I don't hafta let you see my prisoner at all. You think yer better'n Bobby here?"

Jackson shrugged. "I'm not saying that at all. It's just that I have a way of being more persuasive. My partner here, too."

Grooms set his eyes on Carter, looked him up and down, and came to the conclusion Carter expected and why Jackson was leading this little directive. "What's a pretty dandy like you think you can get outta him?" He snorted.

"You thinking of taking him out on the town?" He guffawed and Bobby joined him.

Carter rarely let anything bother him and he sure as hell wasn't going to give Grooms anything close to a last laugh. "I'm just here to watch." He tapped his temple. "And take notes. A second set of ears. So, shall we?"

Grooms' laughter stopped on a dime. He glared at Carter. "What if I say no?"

"I wouldn't do that, if I were you," Carter said.

"Why the hell not?"

"Because I'd hate to have my boss pay a visit to your father at this time of night. I'm not sure where the senator is right now, but I know my boss can find him and let him know that his son is impeding an investigation."

Grooms took his shoes off his desk and slammed them on the floor as he stood. "Listen here a damned minute." He stuck out his finger and aimed it at Carter. "This here is my station and I get to call the shots around here. I don't need no dandy telling me what I can and can't do." He gestured to Jackson. "You go on in, see if you can wring some answers out of him. But you stay here." This last he threw at Carter.

Carter had anticipated this. It was part of the unspoken play he and Jackson had concocted. In response, Carter parked himself behind a desk. He pulled out a small pouch of tobacco and papers. "I'll be here when you get back, Tom." He carefully rolled a cigarette and, with a Lucifer he brought to life by a strike along his boot heel, he set his feet on the desk in front of him.

Jackson grinned at Carter and moseyed back into the next room where the jail cells were housed.

Carter spun around and blew a smoke ring up to the ceiling. "So, gents, what's new in your world?"

* * *

IT TOOK Jackson nearly half an hour before he reemerged into the main room of the police station. In that time, Carter had managed to piss off every other man in the office, partly by his words but mostly because of his winning streak at poker. Bobby had challenged the detective to a poker match after Carter bragged that he could take five dollars from each man. The small pile of crumpled bills and coins in front of Carter served as a testament to his promise.

"Get anything?" Carter asked. He whisked the paper money into his hand and pocketed it. He left the coins over which the cops could haggle.

"Not a damn thing," Jackson professed. He appeared dejected. Of the two of them, Jackson was by far the stronger man. Carter was no slouch, but years spent on the Jackson family ranch had honed the taller detective's muscles and fists. They could actually be lethal, given the right set of circumstances. His strength could easily incapacitate any hombre, and Jackson had stopped many a fight with a single punch. He prided himself on being able to get any information out of any man, so his appearance now was a surprise.

Grooms and his men, their irritation at Carter momentarily forgotten, laughed at Jackson. "Told you that man was a hard case. He didn't give up anything did he?"

Jackson shrugged. "I got his name."

The laughter stopped. "He gave you his name?" Bobby asked. Incredulity creased his face. "How?"

"Not sure. Lucky, I guess." Jackson trundled his way over to Carter. He held his balled fists up, opened them, and then flexed them again. "I don't know what it is. I thought I was good."

Carter slapped Jackson's shoulder. "Don't worry about

it, Tom. We all have off days. Come on. I'll buy you a drink for your troubles. I'm suddenly flush with cash." To Grooms and his men, Carter said, "Listen, if he starts talking, would you mind letting us know. We certainly want to know why he and his men thought they could rob a room full of rich people."

Grooms woke himself out of his surprised stupor. "I'll do no damn such thing. And I don't care if you do call my old man. I'm the law around here. What I says, goes."

Carter opened his mouth to protest, but Jackson grabbed his shoulders, turned him, and steered him to the doorway. "We're done, Cal. Let's go. I want that drink."

Carter made to protest, but relented under Jackson's powerful grip. He threw off a merry wave and allowed himself to be marched to the front door. He pushed the door open and stepped outside. He waited long enough for the door to close before spinning on his heels. "Okay, what did he really tell you?"

"Not here," Jackson murmured. "Still too close to the station. Let's get a block away."

Carter relented, but the anticipation of the next piece of this puzzle nagged at him. He compensated by walking faster. When they rounded the corner, he stopped. "Okay, what did he say?"

"His name is Hiram Colby," Jackson said without breaking stride.

"Hiram Colby," Carter said under his breath. He fell into step with Jackson. He raked his mental files to see if he knew the name and came up empty. "I don't know him."

"I don't either."

"How'd you manage to get him to talk?"

He chuckled. "You would have been proud. I tried some Calvin Carter on him." He waited a few paces, registering Carter's perplexed look, before continuing. "I tried the soft touch. Colby was pretty bad off. Busted lip, black eye, cut on the cheek, missing tooth. That Bobby guy beat him pretty bad. And he still hasn't seen a sawbones. Despite him trying to kill you, I felt for him. Gave him a few swigs from my flask. That's kinda why I need a drink. He drained me dry."

Carter was surprised at Jackson's admission. Most often, Jackson was the one of them most willing to charge into the thick of things and sort stuff out later. "Did you get anything besides his name?"

"Yup. A location." He saw a cab approaching and raised his hand to signal the driver. The man, a grizzled old bat, hunched over, with a patch over one eye, pulled the reigns, and his mangy horse slowed to a stop. Jackson reached out and opened the door. He climbed inside, Carter right behind him. To the cabbie, he said, "Take us to the St. Louis Hotel, the corner of Lavaca and Cedar. On the jump."

The old man turned in his seat, the cracked leather squeaking under his weight. A lascivious grin etched on his face. "You boys know where that is, don't you?"

Carter nodded. "Yeah. It's in Guy Town."

$\maltese$ 4 $\maltese$

EVERY TOWN HAD A RED-LIGHT DISTRICT. Some towns or cities even tried to legalize the institution and regulate it. Austin was one of the latter cities. While not technically legal, most of the town aldermen looked the other way when it came to the frequent complaints by the law-abiding citizens about the goings on down in Guy Town. More often than not, those same aldermen as well as the members of the state legislature and not a few of the students at the University of Texas frequented Guy Town and all that it offered.

Which wasn't always to be desired. The facilities in Guy Town ran the gamut, from high-class bagnios to dirty, filthy bordellos little more than shanties. Often rotting garbage clogged narrow alleys. A putrid odor rose up in the air over certain areas. Saloons, gambling houses, and even some residential homes occupied the district. Officially christened the First Ward, Guy Town was located just to the southwest of the capital building. The Colorado River formed the south border, Congress Avenue the east, Pecan Street the north, and West Avenue completed the rough rectangle.

Over time, complaints arose about the activities down in Guy Town. Righteous citizens often thought the mayor's office would do something about the debauchery, but only token efforts were made. Those same citizens turned to the police as the enforcers of the law, but the cops, too, took a lenient view of what went on down there. They, like the politicians, had a vested interest in the region and partook of its charms.

The St. Louis Hotel sat just two blocks inside the east border. The farther west one walked, the trashier and dirtier the buildings and the people. Gas lamps lined the streets, the glows illuminating passersby and other denizens of the night.

Cabbies rarely shied away from taking patrons down into Guy Town, but even the most stern-hearted thought twice about going in there at night. The cabbie driving Carter and Jackson opted to take the more crowded Cypress Street than any other avenue. With the railroad tracks passing in the center of Cypress, the likelihood of any incident was lessened. He made the sharp turn north on Lavaca and brought the horse to a halt.

"This is as far as I go," the cabbie grunted. His voice rasped out of his throat. He spat on the ground.

"But there's still a block to go," Carter reminded him.

"Then y'all best be walking." He held out his hand, a dirty glove of cracked leather covering it. "I'll take my payment here."

Jackson stood and plopped a coin into the man's palm. "I don't know what you're worried about. You're on a wagon with a horse." He clambered to the ground. "If things go south, you can hightail it out of here."

"I plan on hightailing it out of here right now before something happens," the cabbie said. "You heard about Lilly Jane, didn't you?"

Carter nodded. The story had been in the newspapers all week long. Lilly Jane was a prostitute who lived down on Live Oak Street, a few blocks away. In the service of one of her customers, another man barged into her room at one of the low-class whorehouses. The man was a former lover, one who never knew she was a whore, likely because she never told him. This man, Evans by name, broke down her door. He had a pistol in his hand and a nearly empty whiskey bottle. He smashed the bottle over the head of Lilly Jane's customer. According to reports, the man went down, a huge gash on his head streaming blood. Evans, still holding the bottle, took it at Lilly Jane. He sliced her a few times before she managed to get out of the room. She fled through the house with barely a stitch of clothing on and outside into street. Evans followed her, all the while howling with rage at being duped. Once out in the middle of the street, he fired on her. The bullet got her in the back and she fell dead in the street. When the police came by soon thereafter, they hauled Evans away. But he was out the next day, having professed his sorrow, especially after sobering up. He was never charged with a crime because of Lilly Jane's profession. It seemed her lying about her job wasn't as bad as some citizens thought it should be.

"Yeah, we know," Jackson said. "Guy Town's certainly got its fair share of scum and villainy." He slapped the horse's backside. The horse jolted forward, the movement all but knocking the cabbie out of his seat. When he protested, Jackson just said, "Better get on to safety, you damned coward."

With a grunt, the cabbie adjusted himself and hurried away.

The streets were alive with activity. Shouts of joy and frustration emerged from various saloons and houses. From down Cypress came the sounds of a piano playing with some sort of band. Carter could make out a banjo and drums. He didn't recognize the tune. The street was hard-packed dirt, and plumes of dust rose up behind the feet of people walking by. The dust kept rising, the gas lamps illuminating it in, giving the entire panorama a gentle haze.

"Let's get to it," Carter said. He started walking north up Lavaca, approaching the St. Louis Hotel from across the street. The building itself was a two-story, frame-and-stone structure. The ground floor was slightly larger than the second floor, the end result was that part of the first floor roof was exposed to the air. It acted as a default porch on for the second floor rooms, but with no means of scaling from the outside. Carter though some architect should install exterior stairs and allow hotel patrons the opportunity to come in from the outside.

He stopped and studied the hotel. Even now, nearly ten at night, most of the rooms were lit from within. "You figure what's going on in there is sleeping?"

"Not a bit."

"Colby give you his room number?"

"He did," Jackson replied. "Twelve. On the second floor."

"Think we should just waltz in and announce ourselves?"

Jackson turned and took another look at Carter. "The way you're dressed, they'll likely charge you just to step foot inside." He pointed at the rear of the hotel. "I'm thinking stealth is the best way this time. Besides, Colby said a man hired him to pull this job. Not sure who that guy is, but he likely knows Colby got himself arrested and his gang killed. The time it takes us to explain what we're doing here to any manager could be time better spent just going in there ourselves. Come on."

Carter followed Jackson across the street, avoiding one

cabbie and a few dark piles in the dirt. Gas lamps didn't line this part of Lavaca so the detectives were able to use the shadows to hide their approach. This particular block didn't have many buildings, so the area behind the hotel was relatively sparse. They reached the rear wall of the hotel. Carter looked up. The first floor's roof was only about seven feet above them.

"Okay, I'll go first," he said.

"What? Why you?"

"I weigh less. And besides, I'm better at sneaking into places than you are. I have the gift of silence." Carter grinning in the half light.

"You should use your gift more often." Jackson shook his head, but nonetheless laced his fingers together, making a step for Carter. "I'll give you five minutes before I come through the front door."

Carter put a steadying hand on Jackson's shoulder while his partner lifted him up to the roof. Carter reached up and slipped over the lip. He heard one of the seams of his vest tear and his cursed himself. But, then again, when he put these clothes on earlier in the evening, he never expected he'd be sneaking into a hotel.

"Okay," he whispered down to Jackson, "I'll see if there's a way to get inside." Without waiting for Jackson's response, Carter stood. The roof of this part of the hotel was wooden, slightly raised to keep the rain from pooling and rotting the wood. He now realized why what looked like a great place for people to congregate when he stood on the ground was, in fact, no place to walk at all. He resigned himself to walking along the perimeter of the structure, where the wood met the stone. In this manner, he made his way to the true second story and the first window. Thankfully, this one was dark. So, either the room was vacant or someone was asleep. He lightly rapped on the window with his knuckle. Getting no response, he repeated the action. Still nothing. Smiling to himself, he pulled out a foldable knife, opened it, slipped it between the window and the frame, and worked the lock open. He replaced the knife in his pocket and opened the window.

A putrid smell met his nose. It surprised him that the hotel staff would let such a foul odor remain without cleaning it up. Nevertheless, he slipped inside, feet first, and stood in the room. The smell was stronger now. Carter reached inside his jacket and pulled out a match. With a fingernail, he lit a Lucifer, and what he saw in the meager flame chilled him to the bone.

On the bed was a body, the neck cut, blood having stained the sheets.

* * *

CARTER POSSESSED A STRONG CONSTITUTION, but even he momentarily gagged at the sight of the corpse. Involuntarily, he dropped the match and it fizzled out on the floor. In the sudden darkness, Carter's eyes readjusted. He fished out another match, giving his mind time to process what he saw.

The sulphur from the match went a small way to blot out the odor of the dead man, but not much. The second match added more sulphur to the room, and Carter's sense of smell relished the different aroma. He held the match up high to look for a lamp. The St. Louis was far from a fancy hotel, but he spied a small lantern on the bedside table. Carter walked to the table, the floorboards creaking under his weight, and put the match flame to the wick. Gradually, a warm light filled the room and he was able to get a better look at the corpse.

The man was partially undressed. His shirt was unbuttoned and spread open, exposing his chest. His pants were also unbuttoned and unzipped. Both the pants and his undergarment were pushed down to mid-thigh. The dead man wore no shoes or socks, and the sheets of the bed were pushed down to the foot. Carter moved and got a better look at the man's face.

The dead man was clean-shaven save for a mustache of brown hair. His eyes were frozen open, the strain of surprise still clearly etched in his skin. The mouth, shaped in an O, showed teeth that needed brushing and never would be again. The throat was a mess. Whomever sliced this man's throat did the deed with a sharp blade. The cut appeared clean. All of the blood, ligaments, and cartilage had spilled out of the body. One conclusion Carter could definitely reach on taking in the evidence at hand was that it was a romantic encounter that went horribly wrong.

But he had no time to deal with the corpse now. He needed to slip out of this room and get down to room twelve. He turned off the lamp, telling himself that he'd report the crime later on that evening. Now, he had work to do.

In viewing the hotel from outside, Carter noted that most of the windows had light behind him. He guessed few of the residents were sleeping. Now, inside, the sounds of the hotel confirmed his suspicion. From the other side of the wall, Carter heard the steady rhythmic thump of a bed hitting the wall. From another room, came more sounds of passion, this time in the form of a woman's moans and a man's grunts. He shrugged. This was Guy Town, after all. Nothing odd here. In fact, it might prove beneficial. If everyone was in a room, Carter could slip down to room twelve without the fear of being seen.

He gripped the door knob and turned it gently. It was still prudent to keep as quiet as possible. The door squeaked a little on its hinges, but Carter pulled up on the door handle and the sound stopped. He opened it wide. The hallway was dimly lit by a lamp at both ends. Nonetheless, Carter was able to make out the number, painted in white, on the door he now held.

Twelve.

He sucked in his breath. "Shit," he whispered, and gently closed the door again. This time, he turned the lock. It thunked into the door jamb and he turned to face the room. Carter walked around the bed and turned up the lamp to full brightness and raked his detective eyes and mind over the room.

Other than the bed, the room's furniture consisted of a chest of drawers with a mirror and wash basin on top, a chair and a small writing table in the corner, and a small wardrobe in the other corner where folks could hang clothes. Other than a threadbare rug under the bed, the room was empty.

Now that he was examining the room, Carter noted the man's gun and holster was haphazardly tossed over on the chair, well out of reach for the victim. Likely planned by the killer. The more he thought about his situation, the more he called into question Colby's admission to Jackson. Jackson could be very persuasive, but Carter couldn't figure out why Colby had any reason to lie. More to the point, who was this man in the bed? A partner? The leader of the gang? One thing was for sure: this was likely no coincidence.

Carter opened the wardrobe and pulled out the single piece of clothing. It was a suit jacket. After riffling through the pockets turned up only a few paper bills and coins, Carter replaced it on the hanger. In the floor of the wardrobe was a war bag. The leather was cracked, and it showed signs of being repaired more than once. Carter opened it and looked inside. More clothes. He set the bag on the chair and pulled out everything in the bag. Other than a few personal effects and clothes, nothing was out of the ordinary or even suspicious. Carter replaced everything in the bag and put the bag back into the wardrobe.

He turned and scanned the room, then made his way over to the chest of drawers. The couple in the next room had finished their tryst and now the headboard thumping ceased. The couple down the hall still moaned and grunted. It would be a wonder if anyone could get some shut eye in here, or if this hotel was even meant for sleeping anymore.

All the drawers were empty. Carter even pulled out each drawer and examined the backs and undersides, hoping to find some clue. Nothing. He stood next to the bed, turning his gaze slowly around the room. That left only a couple of places he still had yet to check: the man's boots and the man's pockets. He opted for the boots first.

They were on the floor past the foot of the bed. He bent down and examined them, catching first the acrid odor of unwashed feet and grunting with the assault on his nose. He turned over one, then the other. When nothing but stinky air emerged, he set them both on the floor and focused on the body.

"Apologies, sir," Carter murmured to the corpse, "but I'm afraid I'll have to disturb you."

Carter did his best not to touch the dead man's flesh as he snaked his hand into the man's left pocket. Still, Carter couldn't help feeling the cold skin through the fabric of the pocket. The touch sent a chill through his arm and up the length of his body. When his fingers found only lint, he came around to the right side and repeated the investigation. His fingers clasped over something. More than one thing, in fact. He grabbed everything and pulled out his hand, the thrill of discovery superseding the touch of the man's cold flesh.

He opened his palm and examined what he had found. A stub of a pencil, teeth marks up and down the shaft. A folded piece of paper. A pocket watch, completely worn of any etching on the exterior. Reflexively, he thumbed the latch, opening the turnip of the watch. The watch face was scratch from years of wear, but the time could still be made out. On the underside of the case, etched in a thin scrawl, were the words "Elroy Brown." The corpse now had a name.

"Sorry your life had to come to this, Mr. Brown."

Carter set the pencil and watch down on the bedside table and unfolded the piece of paper. In fancy writing, with ink, were the following words: "St. Louis Hotel, Room 12, Lacy."

Carter threw a sharp glance at the corpse. Elroy Brown had been directed to this room, and to his death.

In the hallway, Carter heard the sounds of heavy footfalls. Then voices. Not the voices of passion but of conversation. "Yeah, he was here. Checked in around six." The footfalls were getting closer.

Carter froze in place, actually slowing his breathing. His mind replayed how the hotel looked from the outside and where this room was in relation to the rest of the rooms. If the footsteps were getting closer, then room twelve was at the end of the hallway and likely their destination.

Carter pocketed the paper and scooped up the pocket watch. He made to leave, then remembered the lamp. He reached over just as a knock sounded on the door. He quickly turned the knob and the lamp light died away.

"Mr. Brown?" came a man's voice from the hallway. It was probably the hotel manager. "Are you okay?"

Carter dared not move for fear the creaking floorboards would give himself away.

"Mr. Brown?" The hotel manager again.

Another voice, this one gruffer. "Open the door."

It was only three words, but Carter could have sworn he recognized the second voice.

"Mr. Brown," the manager said again. A key thunked into the lock. "The police are here and they need to speak to you."

Police? Carter's mind whirled, piecing together the familiar tone of the second voice with the word "police" and he arrived at a conclusion: the voice belonged to Bobby, the policeman who had tried to beat answers out of Hiram Colby. But how in the world was Bobby here, at the St. Louis Hotel, at the same time Carter was?

There was a moment when Carter thought that the arrival of the police was a good thing. He could flash his badge and tell them what he was doing and how he found the body of Elroy Brown. Another thought brought to mind the reception Grooms and his men had given Carter and Jackson back at the police station. Chances were good Carter would not have the ability to explain what he was doing there in any rational way.

When the key turned the lock, Carter made his decision.

CARTER TOOK two long strides to the window and sprang up onto the sill. Just as he had feared, the floorboards creaked under his weight. But he no longer cared. The only thing on his mind was escape.

"Who's in there?" said Bobby. The door slammed open. Light from the hallway splashed into the hotel room and out onto the roof.

Carter barely noticed. He was already running along the same edge he had gingerly walked a few minutes ago. His boots clomped on the wood, creating quite a racket. Down below him, on the right, the ground was bathed in darkness. He had no way of knowing what, if anything, was down there even though that would have been the fastest way to get down off the roof and away from the angry policeman. The only way he knew for sure was the route he had come, which, of course, was farther away. So Carter kept running. He wondered if Jackson was still standing guard.

"Come back here!" Bobby roared.

The gunshot proved a surprise. Carter didn't feel the

bullet pass by him, and thanked his good fortune that in his own attempt to maintain his balance on the roof's edge, Carter made himself a moving target that much more difficult to hit. But he didn't want to tempt fate again. He redoubled his speed and reached the edge of the roof and leapt into space.

The second bullet spewed chunks of stone from where Carter's foot had just been.

The detective sailed down, his arms pinwheeling to maintain balance as he descended to the ground. Carter got his answer as to where Jackson was as he sailed over his partner. In the dim light of the streetlamp, Jackson's face was wide with surprise.

Carter hit the ground hard, rolled with the impact, and came to a rest his knees. He sprang up and looked back to the hotel. The figure of a man, silhouetted by the hotel room's light, was making his way along the path Carter had just traversed.

Jackson came running up to him, gun already in his hand. "You okay?"

"I'm fine," Carter said. "That's Bobby the policeman up there. I'm not sure you should be shooting back at him."

Flame blossomed in the darkness from Bobby's position. A bullet thudded into the ground a few feet away from them, sending up a spray of gravel and dirt.

"Why's he shooting at us?" Jackson said. He didn't wait for a response. He turned, aimed, and fired. Carter noted the trajectory of his partner's shot. It was clearly wide of Bobby's form, but close enough to give the policeman pause.

Jackson's volley paid even more dividends. In his surprise, Bobby stumbled on the roof. He couldn't catch his balance and he fell down. A loud curse bellowed from his lungs.

Carter didn't hesitate. "I think we need to get out of here."

Jackson didn't holster his gun. "Where?"

The map of the area flashed in Carter's mind. He grinned. "I know just the place. This way."

They charged east across Lavaca and ducked inside an alley. Immediately the two detectives were engulfed in darkness, which was good to escape the notice of Bobby but not so good when it came to threading their way through the piles of debris and garbage. The odor was ripe, and it stung Carter's nose. The buildings and structures bordering the alley ranged from stone and brick to little more than shanty lean-tos. But Carter had his mind on one building in particular. He hoped he could recognize it from the rear, seeing as how he always approached it from the main entrance on Cedar Street, just to the north and left of them.

He needn't have worried. If feeble lamplight illuminated every room in the St. Louis Hotel with nocturnal activities, then the Dupont House positively gleamed into the night. The two-story house, built to resemble its owner's New Orleans heritage, was a wooden structure painted white to bely the business that goes on inside. Both floors were built nearly identically, with a porch that ran around three quarters of the house, the east being the only side not used. Intricate lattice work framed both the upper and lower parts of the porches. On the first floor, east side, was the great sitting room where Bernadette Dupont would welcome her customers and have them wait for a lady to be free or until their favorite was available. The rear of the house had two exits, one for the kitchen staff to receive food for the girls and to take out the trash, the other for discrete patrons who preferred not be seen from the front door on Cedar Street. This door was still fancy, and had a small vestibule to keep the patrons out of the elements.

It was up the few steps to the vestibule where Carter stopped and knocked on the door. A few moments later, the door opened. A lovely young woman, blonde and wearing an evening dress, welcomed them inside. The small entryway was lit brightly and had a cushioned couch against the wall. The aromas in the room smelled like lavender and perfume. No other clients waited in the alcove.

"Good evening, gentlemen," the blonde said, closing the door behind her. Dupont had trained her well. She could almost carry herself off as an upstanding member of society. "What is your pleasure tonight?"

Jackson shot Carter a quizzical look. "This is your hiding place?"

"It's perfect," Carter said. "And discrete. Besides, the lady of the house likes me." He hadn't seen the blonde in his previous visits so he couldn't talk to her by name. "We'd like to see Madame Dupont, please."

The blonde was taken aback. "I'm sorry, sir, but Mrs. Dupont isn't available. But there are a number of pretty girls that would be happy to entertain you."

"You don't understand," Carter said, "I need to see Madame Dupont. Just tell her Calvin Carter is here."

The blonde was momentarily hesitant, but at the insisting of Carter, she walked out of the room, her high-heeled shoes dampened by the long oriental carpet on the wooden floors.

"A whorehouse?" Jackson said. "You want us to hide in a whorehouse?"

"Relax. You know Bernadette Dupont, don't you?"

"Only by reputation. She runs one of the best and most clean whorehouses in town. But how does that help us now?" He pointed back west to where the St. Louis Hotel was a half block away. "Bobby's a cop. If he's really irritated, he'll just get all his men to search everywhere. Sooner or later, they'll get here, and when they do, they'll barge in here and find us. Besides, why the hell are we hiding from the law? We are the law."

Carter acknowledged the point, but also quickly filled in Jackson on what he saw in the room, Elroy Brown's body, and the folded piece of paper. He ended with, "I think Brown was set up by someone, and that led to him being killed. Which makes me think Colby might be in some danger."

Jackson screwed up his face. "He's in the city jail. How in the world do you think the man who killed Brown can get in there?"

"Because," came the voice of a woman who now stood in the doorway, "everyone in this town can be bought. Everyone."

Carter and Jackson turned and took in the sight of Bernadette Dupont. From conversations he had had with her in the past, Carter knew she was in her early fifties, but despite the hard life she had led, her features still showed to be a half decade younger. Her raven dark hair was pulled up in a bun behind her head, a few strands perfectly loose and dangling to her shoulders. Exquisitely applied makeup gave her face a smooth complexion, the rouge accentuated her cheeks, the red lipstick offering a tantalizing frame for her white teeth. The red dress would have made her a perfect guest for the museum event earlier that evening. It possessed a neckline that plunged far down to the tops of her bosoms. Bernadette may have retired from activity plying her trade, but she still was a beautiful woman and enjoyed the admiring glances of her customers.

"Bernadette, my dear," Carter said, coming over to her and taking her hand in both of his. He kissed the knuckles. "How good of you to see us."

Bernadette appeared charmed at Carter's greeting, but quickly arched an eyebrow when, from outside the house, the sounds of shouts and cries echoed in the night. "You didn't come for a social visit." She withdrew her hand.

Sheepishly, Carter shrugged. "A little of both, actually. Do you think you could hide us out for a bit?"

"Who are you running from? A woman's husband?"

Carter appeared shocked and offended. "Bernadette, I would never impinge in the middle of a marriage."

"Really? What about that time when you…"

"Anyway," Carter interjected. He cast a suspicious eye at Jackson, then continued. "There's been a misunderstanding."

"Isn't there always. Who are you running from?"

"The police."

Another arched eyebrow. "I thought you were the police."

"We're railroad detectives. Our badges open lots of doors and carried a good amount of authority, but not when a policeman thinks you murdered someone."

Bernadette opened her mouth at that, but Carter quickly held out his hands. "I didn't do it. I merely found the man, dead, in his bed over at the St. Louis."

At the mention of the St. Louis hotel, Bernadette sniffed in derision. "I run a high-class brothel, and old Sam thinks he can beat me at my game. Who's the cop?"

"Bobby's his name."

"Bobby Anders?"

"Not sure. Tall guy, plug ugly, looks like an ape."

"That's Bobby alright."

Someone knocked at the front door of Bernadette's house. She turned to the blonde. "Sally, won't you see who's at our door." When Sally left, Bernadette turned back to Carter. "Best way to hide you is up in the rooms." A slight curl formed on her mouth. "I can give you a discount, but I can't have my rooms occupied without any work. If you get my drift."

Despite the circumstance, Carter indeed got her drift. "I do."

Bernadette chin-nodded at Jackson. "Who's this handsome devil?"

"Thomas Jackson, ma'am," Jackson said. Carter swore that if his partner still wore a hat, he'd have tipped the brow at her. "I'm Cal's partner."

Bernadette regarded him for a few seconds. The bellow of men's voices sounded from the front foyer. "I think I'd better go see to things. Take these back stairs and go up. Rooms five and six will be your hideouts. And Calvin, you'll want room five." She winked.

"Thank you," Carter said. He made to turn, then remembered something. "Oh, and I'll need to bend your ear about something. It's connected to the murder. Maybe you might know something about it. It's a name."

"What name?"

"Lacy."

At the mention of name "Lacy" in connection with a murder, Bernadette's face went white. "Oh dear."

Carter frowned. "You know this person?"

"If it's Lacy Stanton, then I know her very well."

"Who is she?"

"You don't want to know." Without another word, Bernadette scurried out of the back alcove and into the front room. The last thing Carter heard before a door closed was Bernadette saying, "Officer Anders, how are you this evening?"

Carter indicated the stairs. "Let's get upstairs." He led the way and Jackson followed. This wasn't the first time Carter had been to Bernadette's house, but it was the first time arriving at the second floor from the back stairs. He felt vaguely conspiratorial.

On the second floor, the hallway floor was covered with a long rug, only partially worn down the middle. Carter was on familiar territory and made a beeline to the last room on the left.

"How do you know which room is five?" Jackson asked.

Carter paused with his door on the handle. "I've been here before," he said. "You should try out what Bernadette has to offer." He pointed. "That's number six." Both detectives paused, listening to the muffled conversations from the first floor. They were muffled by some of the sounds on the second. They heard the front door open then close.

Carter shrugged. "Might as well take it easy while we wait out Bobby the Beast. How about thirty minutes?" He opened the door and looked inside.

The young woman looked at Carter through the reflection of the mirror in front of which she sat. The brown trusses cascaded over her shoulders and down onto the thin straps holding up her undergarment. When she saw Carter, she broke into a huge grin.

"Calvin," she breathed. She stood and turned, revealing that the only thing she wore was a sheer nightgown, open at the center. The brunette made no move to cover herself, but walked over to Carter. The movement opened her gown even more, revealing most of her body to Carter. She reached him and threw her arms around him, planting a huge kiss on his mouth. Her tongue shot out and found his. Their two organs intertwined.

He broke the kiss and leaned back out into the hallway. The last thing he said to Jackson before he shut the door to room number five was, "Better make it an hour."

❧   6   ☙

An hour later, Carter and Jackson relaxed in Bernadette's private office. Judging by the spring in his step, Jackson had enjoyed his time hiding out. Carter had inquired as to with which girl Jackson spend his time, but the taller detective played coy. "A gentlemen never talks about his loves." Carter had smiled at his partner's more Puritan nature, but respected it nonetheless. Now, with cigars lit and glasses of whiskey from Bernadette's personal collection, the three of them sat around her desk and discussed the night's events.

Her office would have made any of the state senators proud. The room was painted a deep coat of red, almost the color of bricks. The money Bernadette made enabled her to furnish her office with the finest desk, well-upholstered chairs, and art that hung from the walls. The room had few books, however, the shelves being filled with various knick-knacks she had acquired her the years. Her desk was minimal, with only a lamp, blotter, and inkwell. A small stack of papers was the only sign this was a working office.

Bernadette had insisted Carter retell what had

happened during the evening, and he did so in great detail. He even found time to add a little nuance to his actions at the museum, making himself a bit more of the hero.

"I'm sorry," Jackson said, interrupting the monologue, "but I was there, too. And I took out the first owlhoot."

"Sure, but I talked Colby down from shooting the place up."

"I believe my bullets took out more of the goons than yours."

"Actually," Carter said, "from my position on the dais, I had the better angle to—"

"Enough!" Bernadette said, raising her voice. "Mercy me, but you two are talking like a couple of johns comparing the sizes of their peckers. Y'all each did great, so move on." She downed the last of her drink and poured herself another, muttering something under her breath.

Carter continued, relating everything up until he and Jackson knocked on Bernadette's back door. "And you know the rest." He winked. "Thanks again for keeping us out of sight."

Bernadette grunted. "Y'all paid for it." Getting serious a moment, she said, "And the name on the paper directing Colby to the St. Louis was 'Lacy'? Are you sure?"

Carter reached into his jacket and pulled out the paper. He handed it over to Bernadette who unfolded it and read the words. When Carter saw the madam shaking her head, he asked, "You know this Lacy?"

Tossing the paper on her desk, Bernadette sighed. "Only by reputation." She sighed. "You would think my business is simple. I have a product and customers come to me wanting that product. They pay for services rendered and that's that. But it's not that simple. Buying an hour with one of my girls is not like buying wood from a lumberyard or grain from a mill. Emotions gets involved. With emotions comes other things, like violence. Sometimes a customer doesn't want to pay for services rendered. It doesn't happen to me all that much, considering the clientele I attract, but others aren't so lucky."

She gestured to Carter. "Well, there was the time when you helped me, Calvin. Remember that?"

Carter did. It was soon after Carter had enough money to visit Bernadette Dupont's house. He made frequent visits and got to know Bernadette herself. Gradually, she learned his name and his profession, both as an actor and a railroad detective. When a traveling man down from Dallas came to town during one of the legislative sessions, he brought with him a certain predilection for more curious sexual escapades. Those types of things Bernadette didn't cotton to and told the man. He got violent with Erica, the girl he had purchased, beating her up pretty bad. The police had no jurisdiction since the man had returned to Dallas, but Carter had no such qualms. For a small price, Carter traveled to Dallas between cases and made sure the man didn't try anything like that again with any of Bernadette's girls.

"I do," Carter said. He knew his job involved violence and didn't shy away from it. His philosophy, however, mandated that he try to avoid violence whenever possible. Most of the criminals he hunted down thought violence was the first order of business, so they got what came to them. In the instance of the man from Dallas, Carter had tried talking at first. The man wouldn't hear of it, so violence ensued.

"What can you tell us about this Lacy?" Carter said. He blew a smoke ring up at the lamp fixture hanging from the ceiling.

"Again, it's only by reputation. You know the service you rendered for me? Well, you didn't actually kill that son of a bitch. You just taught him a lesson. That's my preferred way when there are disagreements." Bernadette pursed her lips, wetting them with the tip of her tongue. "This Lacy person does similar things like you did for me. Except for one thing: she does kill people."

"Wait," Jackson said, sitting up in his chair, "you've never seen her?"

Bernadette shook her head. "She's like a ghost. But she's also available for hire. She always signs her name by carving her initials in her victims. Did you see anything like that?"

Carter replayed the image of Elroy Brown in his mind. "Maybe at the neck, but I would have had to clean up the mess to see for sure. Can't say."

Bernadette shuddered. "Sounds like either she worked on her own and lured your victim to the St. Louis or someone else hired Lilly to meet Brown there. Either way, if she's involved, that's bad news."

AT NEARLY ONE in the morning, Carter and Jackson left Bernadette's house, again through the back door. The detectives reckoned Bobby had moved on, scouring the city for them or else losing interest. They walked along the alley a couple of blocks east until they hit Congress. The activity had wound down a bit, but a few cabs still rolled along the street. Carter signaled one. They got in and Jackson directed the cabbie to his boarding house. Carter kept his eyes peeled, even turning to swatch the rear of the cab to keep any of Bobby's men from bushwhacking them.

The boarding house in which Jackson lived was a small mansion. The exterior resembled something a man who lived out in the country would build, and indeed, Roger Dodge and his wife Margaret, had lived and worked the land for most of their lives. But as they grew old, they had wanted to work a less strenuous job, so they moved into Austin and opened a boarding house. They were quite strict as to whom the allowed to stay in their lodgings, and Jackson fit the bill perfectly. The Dodges had been especially impressed that Jackson was the son of a rancher who also happened to be a railroad detective. It was his badge they initially saw, but his integrity and honestly they had come to love.

The house was dark, and the squeaking wheel of the cabbie threatened to wake the occupants. Gas lamps glowed in a dotted line along the street. No other soul was visible.

Jackson paid the cabbie and got out. It was Carter who saw the figure emerge from the shadows of a nearby alley first.

"Tom!" Carter said. "Watch out."

Jackson whirled, fists coming up in a fighting stance. The sudden movement spooked the horse, who jumped, knocking Carter back onto the seat. He scrambled up to his feet and leapt to the ground, ready to assist his partner in a brawl.

The fight never came.

The figure who emerged held a white handkerchief in his hand. He held his other hand out, palm open. When he spoke, Carter recognized his voice.

"Carter, Jackson, it's me. Eckhardt."

On a second look, Carter realize it was Max Eckhardt, a fellow railroad detective. The man was pudgy, with permanent bags under his eyes that were accentuated at this time of night. His suit was rumpled, tie askew, and he smelled like the dried salami he gnawed on during the day. He possessed a gift for being able to conduct research and come up with information from the papers. Not typically a field agent, Carter couldn't figure out why Eckhardt would be here.

"What the devil are you doing here?" Jackson asked. "You could have gotten yourself slugged. We've got the cops after us."

"I know," Eckhardt said. "That's why I'm here. Hull's at your house, Calvin."

"What's going on?" Carter asked.

"Moore sent us. He heard about what happened and wanted to make sure y'all're safe."

"Safe from what?" Jackson asked.

"The police."

Carter and Jackson exchanged a glance. They knew Bobby had chased them but Carter saw no way that Bobby knew of Carter's identity. "Why would the police be after us?"

"Because you killed that man." Eckhardt worked hard to hide it, but a little bit of disgust leached out.

"I didn't do that," Carter insisted. "That's how I found him. Wait a minute. How do the cops think I did it?"

Eckhardt chuckled dryly. "It seems your fancy clothes are something of an identifier. When you fled from the scene, Anders recognized your suit. Now he's got his men scouring the city looking for you. I'm here to get Jackson and bring him to Moore's house. You see, there's been another development tonight."

"What's that?" Jackson asked.

"In all the hubbub down at the museum, Octavia Hendrickson has now realized she's been robbed."

❧ 7 ❧

Colonel Jameson Moore's house dominated the block of Red River Street between Mulberry and Ash Streets. Built from the money he made working with the railroad for nearly a quarter century, Moore told anyone who visited that he wanted to bring a little bit of Virginia over to Texas. The mansion would have fit right in with the other houses along the James River back in Old Dominion. The front sported four columns, all painted white. Eight windows faced the street, each room an ornate wonder. Jameson Moore himself designed the house, but he left the interior designing to Catherine. If ever the governor needed a second home to welcome guests and entertain, he could do worse than rent out the Moore mansion.

But now, Carter and Jackson found themselves in Moore's personal study. This was the one room he reserved for his own design, and it reflected the man. Oil paintings hung from the walls depicting battles from the Late Unpleasantness as well as landscapes of the west. Bookshelves filled with leather-bound volumes lined every shelf.

One cabinet Moore reserved for his military decorations and his collection of guns. Ever the military man, he had amassed a unique collection of weapons that he studied and gained proficiency. The room possessed a giant mahogany desk with a lamp, blotter, and various stacks of paper, all from his work at the detective agency. Moore sat behind the desk and puffed on a pipe.

"So you snuck into the hotel and found the body?" Even at this hour, Moore still wore his tie and formal wear. The only concession to the time was that his jacket was hung on the back of his chair.

"Yes, sir." Carter sat up straight in his chair. Some of the adrenaline had worn off and the events of the evening were beginning to wear on him. He compensated by refusing Moore's offer of whiskey, choosing water instead.

"And you saw no sign of this Lacy person?"

"No, sir. Have you ever heard of her?"

Moore regarded Carter for a moment. "Unlike you young men, I satisfy my personal needs here at my home. I don't find the need to satisfy them elsewhere. As such, no, I've never heard of her." He looked at Carter, then Jackson. "But I'm much more concerned that you ran from the police. We all badge-toters. Why not just reveal yourself?'

Carter shrugged. "It was a hunch. Either Colby set us up or Anders beat it out of him. Throw in the cold reception we got from the police and it makes for a recipe of distrust."

Moore considered Carter's words and left his verdict unspoken. "You both will stay here tonight. In the morning, I'll have a talk with Grooms and see if we can't smooth out this little issue. But there's something more." He folded his hands and leaned his elbows on the desk. "Octavia Hendrickson's collection has been robbed."

Jackson said, "When did she figure this out?"

"After the altercation tonight. After y'all left, she retired to her private office on the second floor." He shook his head. "I've seen entire houses that looked worse than that one room. It was like a museum in itself. Glass cases showing off various artifacts, drawers full of old papers and curios, I'm surprised she sifted it all out to just the stuff she has on the ground floor." He puffed on his pipe.

"Sounds like she should just sell tickets to her office as well as the ground floor," Jackson said.

"But someone already made off with something?" Carter asked. "What's missing?"

Moore looked at Carter, scrutinizing him. The younger detective did his best not to shrink under the old man's inscrutable gaze. "She didn't say," Moore said after a time. "But she specifically asked for you. Any reason why that might be?" More puffing as Moore waited.

Carter's mind whirled in concentration. "Well, sir, I've known her since my acting days. Maybe she just has some familiarity with me."

"Familiarity?" Moore repeated. Another puff. "How familiar?"

Carter shot a nervous glance at Jackson then back at Moore. "I've visited her house a few times." He grinned sheepishly. Jackson sighed.

"Dare I ask what for?"

"Um, acting lessons," Carter said. "Specifically how to project one's voice to the back row."

Moore grunted. Jackson chuckled again. He recrossed his legs and gave Carter a bemused expression. "Is there anyone you haven't been with?"

Carter arched an eyebrow and smirked with one side of his mouth. "Of course."

Abruptly, Moore stood. Carter and Jackson shot up to their feet as well. "That's enough. I don't want to hear any more. Catherine has set up a couple of rooms for y'all. Make yourselves comfortable. We start early in the morning." He walked across the room, opened the door, and paused, his hand on the knob. "And please wash up before you lay down. My dear wife just had the sheets laundered."

8

CARTER FOUND himself amazed at Octavia's upstairs office. If the downstairs part of the museum was fancy, then her office was ornate. Much more so than when he last saw it a few years ago when she had the building renovated. The walls were lined with wooden cabinets with glass doors. Inside each of the cabinets were shelves lined with all sorts of artifacts and pieces of art. Free standing cabinets, similarity constructed, occupied the floor space. He counted nine, arranged in neat rows of three. In these cabinets, all four sides were made of glass as well as the shelves. Smaller art objects and artifacts were on display in these. Octavia had devised some of the gas lamps to beam their light directly on certain sections of the cabinets, likely for nighttime viewing.

But now, bright morning sun shone directly into the large office space cum museum. All the freestanding cabinets cast long shadows on the far wall. With windows on all four sides of the room, enough light was cast in the room that the area felt like it was outside.

One of those cabinets was empty. Unlike the other cabinets, this one possessed no internal shelves. Instead, a wooden stand had been fashioned. Whatever was in this cabinet was long and tall. A piece of fishing line dangled freely from the top of the cabinet.

Octavia now wore a less formal dress than the previous evening. The simple cotton fabric may have been cheaper to construct, but the cut and tailor bill would have made up the cost. The only sign of worry on the older woman's face were the bags under her eyes. They shadowed her features, giving her expression a worried look.

"It was stolen from this one," Octavia said.

Naomi stood next to her mother, a look of curious exasperation registering on her face. Unlike her mother's old-fashioned dress, Naomi wore a modern but casual cotton dress. It gathered at the waist, but not in an overtly showy way. Carter had seen enough corsets in his time, and he realized Naomi wasn't wearing one, yet her figure inherently possessed the beautiful shape of a woman.

"What was it?" Carter asked. He still wore last night's suit, wrinkled and dirty as it was. He had wanted to sneak off back to his boarding house, but Moore advised against it. When Carter had insisted, Moore had all but ordered him not to go. "We don't need the local police messing up this investigation," the colonel had said. Carter had acquiesced. He didn't like wearing the same clothes, especially given the present company. Octavia might have understood the situation, but Naomi had thrown Carter a mild look of disdain at his clothes.

Jackson, on the other hand, seemed not to be bothered in wearing the same clothes again. His only concession was ditching the tie. He now stood apart from Carter, thumbs in his belt.

"A sword," Octavia said.

"A sword?" Moore repeated. "Like a cavalry sword?"

"Not in the least," Octavia said. She tried to hide her tone of annoyance and didn't quite succeed. "Does it look like I would showcase a cavalry sword?"

Moore harrumphed and was about to make a retort when Carter cut in. "The stand looks like it was specially built." He had opened the cabinet door and was examining the interior. He saw no signs of forced entry. "Where is the key for these cabinets?"

"In my desk."

Jackson walked over to her desk. It was large and ornate. In some ways, it resembled the kind of desk at the governor's mansion or in some fancy office back in Washington, D.C. Papers littered the top of the desk. It appeared that Octavia had made some attempt to clean it up last night then gave up.

"Cal," Jackson said. "I've got lots of gouges here. Whoever stole the sword got the key from her desk."

Carter came to stand next to Jackson. The top drawers —two on each side and one in the middle—all showed signs of having a knife or some other thin, metal object being forced in the cracks. Chunks of wood were missing, and Carter noticed them swept under the desk. He pulled opened the drawers, looking inside. Like the top of the desk, the contents of the drawers appeared to have been riffled through. What were likely neat stacks of paper and other office sundries now were scattered all throughout the drawers. The two side drawers looked like they contained files and other business-related activities. They were jumbled.

"Anything else taken besides the sword?"

Octavia sniffed at him. Naomi spoke for her mother. "I only just started making a full inventory of what's still here. The sword is the obvious prize."

"What kind of sword was it?" Carter asked. He swept

his gaze over the room, doing a trick he had been taught by his mentor, Desmond Arnett. He unfocused his eyes, trying to see everything without looking at anything. Arnett counseled Carter for long hours in Arnett's personal study, a room that was literally lined, floor to ceiling, with books and all sorts of knickknacks. Arnett would have Carter leave the room and return only after his mentor had removed something. It was up to Carter not necessarily to find the missing item but to notice where something was. He performed this action while listening to Naomi.

"It's called a mazuahuitl."

"A what?" Jackson said. "What kind of name is that?"

Naomi repeated the word. "It's an Aztec sword. It's a flat piece of hard wood, more or less resembling a sword you'd find in England. Except that instead of a single steel blade, the mazuahuitl has obsidian stones mounted along the cutting edges. Legend has it that the Spanish who conquered the Aztec noted the blade, in the hands of a trained warrior, could chop the head off a horse with a single stroke."

Jackson whistled under his breath. Moore looked astonished. Octavia merely smiled.

Carter heard what Naomi said, but his eyes and attention stopped at the far bookshelf. Without breaking eye contact, he made a beeline across the room, excusing himself around Naomi who huffed in irritation, and stopped in front of the far bookshelf. He pointed. "What was here?"

Octavia and Naomi approached. When Octavia noted some of the books had been moved to hide the fact that some other book was gone, she paled.

"My God," she breathed. "He's got Gunter's journal."

"Journal?" Carter asked. "Gunter being your husband. What journal is this?"

Octavia put a hand to her mouth, her face crestfallen.

Naomi put an arm around her mother's shoulder, patting it. "It's my father's journal. He kept one for most of his journeys across the world and for his business dealings. He thought both travel and business went hand in hand. Each endeavor had an aspect of discovery to it. If it was a business deal, it was Father's idea that the other person needed something, and it was his job to discover what it was. Most of the time, Father exploited the other person's need. Sometimes, he worked with them."

Carter nodded. He had known a little of Gunter Hendrickson's business dealings. He was a master of the deal. There wasn't a deal he couldn't make. That reputation began to precede him, causing him grief toward the end of his life. When he died, many of the obituaries naturally were flattering. Carter later came to find out that Naomi had written it herself. But the newspaper editorials weren't so flattering. They enumerated all the heartache and pain Hendrickson had inflicted on his business rivals and the people on whose back he trod to get where he got. In fact, it surprised Carter that Octavia was so well respected in social circles. It was likely that she tried to assuage all the hurt feelings from her late husband with good works.

He turned, still pointing at the spot. "What would someone need with your father's journal?"

Naomi walked over and examined the space. She ran a slender finger over the spines. Carter noted how well her nails were manicured, the red polish catching the sun's rays. "It's the one from twenty years ago, not any of the more recent ones."

Jackson raised his eyebrows. "You daddy kept a journal for over twenty years?"

"He kept a journal for most of his adult life, Mr. Jackson. He loved the idea of improving himself, and he followed the advice of other men who kept a record of their lives over the years. Each volume corresponded to a particular year. Every New Year's Day, he would start a new one. Every now and then, he would write enough to require two volumes. Gunter Hendrickson was a dedicated man who loved mother, me, and my brother."

"That's all well and good," Carter said, "but why would someone steal his journal? And why that particular year? Did it have any connection with the Aztec sword?"

Naomi and Octavia exchanged a glance, one that Carter immediately caught, but Jackson and Moore missed. "Not entirely sure," the daughter said, her words coming out slowly.

Carter noted the hesitation but decided not to confront them at that time. He took another tact. "Okay, we'll come back to that later. Here's the big question: who would do something like this? It's not like this sword is money or gold. I'm guessing there's a very small market for a mazua…" He slowed down, trying to pronounce the ancient Aztec word Naomi used.

"Mazuahuitl," Naomi interrupted.

"I was trying to pronounce it myself, thank you very much," Carter said. The second time he got it right. "Mazuahuitl."

"Better than I could have done," Jackson said.

"You didn't even try," Carter retorted. "At least I tried."

"Gentlemen," Moore interjected. He remained in his position in front of the empty display case, his head cocked, looking at the empty stand. "Y'all can discuss how best to pronounce words later. Right now, Mrs. Hendrickson, let's get back to Calvin's question: who would have need for an Aztec sword?"

Naomi deferred to her mother, who stood a little straighter. "As it happens, there is one person who knew Gunter that might have an interest in the mazuahuitl." She pronounced the Aztec word flawlessly. "Juan Esteban Molina." She waited to see if the name registered for the detectives. When neither Carter, Jackson, nor Moore made any sign of knowing who that was, she continued. "He's a rich man down in Mexico. Helped Gunter get railroad contracts and build over the past twenty years."

"So they were friends?" Moore asked.

Octavia screwed up her face. "Not necessarily friends. Business associates. They had a mutual interest in building the railroads. He and Gunter didn't often see eye to eye, even with regard to the construction of the railroad, but they needed and tolerated each other."

Carter could read behind the lines. Chances were good Molina and Gunter Hendrickson didn't get along very well.

"A few years ago, Juan came to Austin on business. The last time I had seen him was after Gunter's funeral. I invited him to my house to show him all that I had and see if he knew any of the details about some of the artifacts. He got very upset when he saw the mazuahuitl. On the spot, he offered to buy it. I refused the sale, of course. This was one of Gunter's prized possessions from his travels in Mexico. I was loathe to part with it."

"Why would he be so angry?" Carter asked.

Octavia shrugged. "At the time, I thought him merely a connoisseur of the arts. But Juan has become something of a zealot. He claims he can trace his ancestors back to the Aztecs themselves before the Spaniards conquered Mexico. He wants to reclaim as much of his heritage as he can. It was his opinion that the mazuahuitl belonged to him."

Pausing to catch her breath, Octavia turned and sat down on a divan. The sunlight beamed on her face, revealing many more wrinkles here in the harsh reality of daylight than the soft glow of lamps of the night before.

Moore cleared his throat and pursed his lips. "Well,

thank you for sharing all of this information with us. I'll be sure to send a wire back to Washington and alert them of the theft and see if they can't handle the issue from here."

Octavia gave him a sharp look. "What?"

"Mrs. Hendrickson, we work for the railroad. We have no jurisdiction outside of the country. Our authority ends at the Rio Grande."

The matron sighed theatrically and turned to face the window.

Jackson raised his hand and stroked the edge of the glass case. "Ain't there something we're forgetting?"

"What's that?" Carter asked.

"The owlhoots who shot up the place last night. What's their place in this case?"

Everyone thought about that for a moment before Carter asked a question of Octavia. "When did you notice the sword missing?"

"Last night when I came up here."

"Were you up here yesterday afternoon, leading up to the gala?"

"Yes. Everything was in order as late as dinner time yesterday."

Carter pursed his lips. He locked eyes with Jackson. "You thinking what I'm thinking?"

"Think so. Sounds like all the hubbub downstairs might've been a distraction for the theft up here."

Carter smiled. He truly enjoyed having Thomas Jackson as his partner. They complimented each other's talents, and often arrived as the same conclusion at nearly the same time. So when Carter said, "Windows," Jackson moved to the windows along the east side of the room. Carter went to the south. Moore, seeing what they were doing, went to the west wall. Naomi, not to be outdone, ventured to the north.

All the windows were newly renovated, tall, and without any support in the frame itself. The south wall had four windows, each two feet across and four tall. Carter started at the first one. He examined the edges of the window sill for any sign of forced entry. It wasn't until he reached the third one that he saw it.

Outside, on the brick ledge, he spied two black smudges. They weren't too large, maybe three inches each. They were spaced about ten inches apart. Not taking his eyes off the smudges, Carter felt for the latch to unlock the window. Not surprisingly, he found it already disengaged. He put his fingers in the small recessed area that served as a handle and lifted the window.

The sounds and odors of downtown Austin filtered in. Horses whinnied, the sounds of their hooves clomping on the hard-packed dirt street, wagon wheels squeaked, people caught in conversation. The aroma was less than pleasant. The south side of Octavia's museum faced an alley. The garbage from last night's food already stunk in the early morning heat and humidity.

Carter stuck his head out of the window and examined the smudges. Both appeared to be mud and, if he were to guess, they were smudges from the soles of shoes. He looked down past the sill. The brick wall that formed the south side led straight down to the ground. A look up and Carter found the way the robber got into the room.

* * *

CARTER WAVED Jackson over to the open window. He stepped aside as his partner turned and looked up.

"Son of a bitch," Jackson muttered. "He did this job?"

Curious, Moore came over and peered up out of the window. He sighed when he saw the object.

"Can y'all tell me what's going on?" Naomi blurted.

Without a hesitation, Carter deftly leapt up onto the sill. Inwardly he smiled at the gasp of Octavia. It felt good to still surprise her after all these years. With one hand holding onto the top of the open window, he reached up and grasped the object that was attached to the brick lip of the building. He tested it first, marveling at the firmness of the object in the brick. He released it and swung back into the room. With a flourish, he presented what he had found.

A dull metal hook.

Octavia and Naomi looked at it with surprise then curiosity and finally confusion. "I don't get it," Naomi said. "What was that doing on the outside of the building?"

"It's the trademark of a master thief," Carter began. "No one know who he is, so those of us toting a badge call him the Hook Thief."

"The Hook Thief?" Octavia said. "That's catchy."

"It would be great if we could actually catch him in the act," Jackson said. "He's responsible for a great many robberies. Usually high-end material. He's not just a thief for hire to rob a bank. He's got a specific set of skills."

"Right," Carter picked up the narration, "he can get into and out of almost anything building. Judging from the types of windows y'all have, I bet it wasn't that hard."

"But why the hook?" Naomi asked.

"You see," Carter said, "that's where the Hook Thief is a real showman. From evidence collected by us and other law enforcement agencies, we have determined that he has some sort of special rope. Not too sure what it's made of, but it's flammable. When he finishes a job, he puts a flame to the rope and it goes up. The only thing left is the hook." He smiled as he retold the story. "It's a tool as well as a calling card. Brilliant."

Naomi frowned. "It sounds like you admire him."

"I admire the theater of it," Carter replied.

"Be that as it may, Detective," Moore said, "having the Hook Thief involved only makes this case more problematic. May I remind you we are railroad detectives? This is a police matter."

"If what Octavia contends about Molina," Carter said, not caring about the looks from both Naomi and Moore about him using the matriarch's first name, "then the Austin police don't have jurisdiction either. Besides, they're borderline incompetent."

Jackson picked up on the thread. "Setting the jurisdiction aside, sir, what about the bushwhackers from last night."

Spinning on his heel, Moore bore his stare at Jackson. "What about them?" His tone was sharp.

Jackson was undeterred. Like a bulldog, he saw the first order of business. "We need to head back to the police station and question Colby again. Let him know about Brown and see if he can tell us who hired him." A thought hit him. "Hell, we may have our first clue as to the identity of the Hook Thief."

Carter narrowed his eyes as he thought about what exposing the identity of the Hook Thief would do. As it was now, the Thief possessed a certain notoriety, at least among his victims and the badge-toters who chased him. There was a certain romance in not knowing the man's real identity. He almost wished the Thief would retire, stop stealing other people's things, and pass into history as a great unknown.

"What do you say, sir?" Carter prompted after Moore remained silent a few beats. "How much would you like for the railroad's detective agency, the very agency you formed from whole cloth, to be the ones who brought in the Hook Thief? Think of the notoriety. Think of the headlines. Think of how much the heads of the railroad would like to reward you."

"Enough," Moore said, his hand chopping through the air. In the silence, he stared at his two detectives. Carter got the impression their boss didn't like to be shown up in front of civilians. Moore might punish them later, but not now.

Taking the momentary quiet as her cue, Octavia broke in. "Is there any way I could hire your men? I'd be willing to pay handsomely for the opportunity to make sure Gunter's prized possession returns to my museum." She didn't give Moore much time to think. "I could always call Otto and see what he thinks?"

If Moore didn't like being put in a bad light by his detectives, he sure as hell wouldn't stand for it from people.

"I also have someone else y'all need to talk with," Moore said. His decision was made. Behind his eyes simmered anger, but he turned his attention only to Carter and Jackson.

"Who?" Carter said.

"Peter Burlingame. He's an expert on weapons. He collects them. I think he'd provide some valuable insight as to what this Hook Thief might do or, more importantly, how he might deliver it to its intended target."

$$\maltese \quad 9 \quad \maltese$$

CARTER AND JACKSON convinced Moore that talking to Hiram Colby was the first order of business, but Carter was sure as hell not going to arrive back at the police station wearing the same clothes as the previous evening. Jackson was much less concerned, but he, too, said a change of clothes was in order. Together, the two detectives traveled to Jackson's boarding house and Carter waited while Jackson cleaned up and threw on fresh clothes. This one was more like his usual attire: thick brown pants, scuffed boots, a denim shirt, bandana around the neck, and leather jacket. Most importantly, he strapped on his well-oiled gun belt. The previous evening, Jackson had dutifully tried carrying his gun in a shoulder holster in order to blend in with the fancy people. Now, in the bright light of day, he was truly comfortable.

As the two of them approached Carter's boarding house, they kept their eyes peeled. They had encountered no one at Jackson's place, but the police were mostly after Carter. Surprisingly, they reached the door of Carter's boarding house without incident. When Carter opened the door, the aroma of that morning's breakfast greeted their senses. Carter didn't own a home, but this was as close as he got since he moved away from his parents' house years ago.

Mrs. Ellen Pendergast, a woman in her early fifties, must have heard the door for she scurried from the back of the house and into the main foyer. She wore a blue cotton dress with a white apron. She dried her hands on the apron, then smoothed it out again. Her long brown hair, pulled up in a bun, showed the signs of gray scattered throughout. Nonetheless, she was a handsome woman, and all the men who lived in the house with her did their best to look out for her.

When she saw Carter, she stopped in her tracks, eyes widening. She threw a worried glance up the flight of stairs, then made a decision. She gestured to the front study and beckoned Carter and Jackson to follow.

"There's a policeman upstairs waiting for you," she whispered. "He arrived last night. I couldn't do anything about it. He even threatened to arrest me if I interfered." She paused. "He said you killed a man, Calvin."

Carter reached out and grasped Mrs. Pendergast's hands. They were lithe but strong on account of her daily life of manual labor. "I assure you, Mrs. Pendergast, I did not kill that man. I found him like that. But now we're on a case and that dead body is part of it." He smiled reassuringly.

"I see you've got young Thomas," she said. True, Carter and Jackson were the same age, but Jackson often appeared younger looking than Carter, a fact his partner enjoyed repeating.

Jackson tipped his hat. "Good morning, Mrs. Pendergast. We're much obliged that you've warned us." To Carter, he said, "How do you want to play it?"

A mischievous grin etched on Carter's face. "Let's have some fun."

* * *

CARTER AND MRS. PENDERGAST had an arrangement. His room had its own backdoor. She didn't always approve of Carter's romantic dalliances, but after he helped her solve the case of her husband's death, she and Carter agreed not to speak of whom might or might not be in Carter's room during the evening or the next morning. Mrs. Pendergast never allowed any of her other boarders to do what Carter did. When they questioned her, she gently but firmly suggested that they could find other places to live. None ever took her up on her veiled threat, and each man agreed to live under her rules. Even Carter. He just had the added benefit of a backdoor.

He kept the hinges well oiled, so he was able to open the backdoor and slip inside with barely a sound. He drank in the comfortable feel of his own space. There was a part of him that truly longed for a house of his own, a place where he could spread out and live a comfortable life. But that kind of life wasn't in the cards for him, in either profession. The life of an actor meant he traveled constantly. The life of a railroad detective was much the same, the only difference was that people kept trying to kill him in his role as a detective.

"Someday," he whispered.

Carter opened the back door, snuck inside on tip toes, and then closed and locked it. He checked his pocket watch. He and Jackson had synchronized their watches and would simultaneously approach whichever man the police put in charge of watching and waiting for Carter. He considered drawing his gun, but he had also vowed never to bring his detective work home to Mrs. Pendergast's house if at all possible. He flexed his fists. He hoped today wouldn't be the day that pledge was violated.

He made his way across his room, still on tip toes, and to the main bedroom door. He gripped the handle, ready to make his move. When the second hand reached twelve, he flung open the door and charged into the hallway. Jackson, his boots clomping up the main stairs, came from the other side.

Frank Logan sat in a chair reading the day's paper. He had stationed himself just down the hall from the top of the stairs. In this way, he had positioned himself between Carter's door and the stair landing. The pincher movement of the two detectives caught him completely unawares. He threw down the paper and stood. He turned to face Jackson, but then Carter was there right behind him.

"Hello, Frank," Carter growled. He threw a punch as hard as he could. His knuckles landed just beside the policeman's nose. It didn't break, but Frank fell away from Carter and onto the floor. That was when Jackson stepped on Frank's hand.

"Don't be thinkin' about getting up," Jackson said. His hand rested on the butt of his Colt Peacemaker.

Frank whirled his head back at Carter. "You assaulted a police officer. I'm taking you to the station and arresting your ass."

"Good to know. We're coming with you. Mind if I change first?"

* * *

THE LOOKS of surprise on the faces of the men in the police station were priceless, Carter thought. It was almost worth the price to have a photographer capture the image.

Carter and Jackson followed close behind Frank Logan. The big police officer still held a bandana up to his nose, which hadn't stopped bleeding since Carter's punch. The detectives had relieved Frank of his gun, but Jackson now returned it to him, butt first. Into Frank's other hand, Jackson deposited the six bullets he had removed from Frank's gun.

"There you go," Jackson said. "Everything back the way it's supposed to be."

"Gentlemen," Carter said, "good morning." He now wore a dark brown suit without a vest, clean and pressed shirt, green tie, and brown boots. He had washed his face, neck, and upper body back at his room, and added a dash of cologne. The rounded crown hat he wore was exactly like the black one, but only brown. In his stomach was some of Mrs. Pendergast's excellent ham and eggs. She had fed all three men, Frank included, insisting it was the right thing to do.

Leland Grooms bolted up from his chair. "What's the meaning of this, Frank? Didn't you arrest them?"

Carter gave Frank a few moments to answer—mainly he was curious as to what the defeated man might say—but ended up speaking for the man anyway. "Not really. Tom and I are here in an official capacity. We need to talk to your prisoner, Hiram Colby."

Grooms came around his desk. His hands flexed into fists and then relaxed again. He came up to Carter and stuck an accusing finger in the detective's face. "I know what you did last night. You killed that man."

Carter slapped the hand away. "In fact, I didn't. When the sawbones y'all use determines the time of death, you'll likely see that it was when your prisoner and his buddies were holding up the museum." He waited a beat, then continued.

The upper lip on Grooms' face curled. "Then why'd you run?"

Carter looked around Grooms and found Bobby Anders in the group. "Your big ape over there didn't identify himself. For all I knew, it was the killer returning to make sure Elroy Brown was dead." He arched and eyebrow and smirked. "But it's nice to know Bobby can appreciate good clothes. I hear that's how he identified me." He waved his hand back and forth between him and Bobby. "You should come meet my tailor. He does fantastic work."

"Enough!" Grooms bellowed. He glared at Carter, anger seething behind his eyes. Sweat seeped out of his pores. He looked as if he hadn't had much if any sleep the previous night.

Carter stared back, an amused expression on his face. "Sure thing. How was your night? Did you get any messages?" When he was dealing with someone as difficult as Grooms, Carter enjoyed egging on the other man.

Grooms again put a finger in Carter's face. "I know you have pull with the mayor and the governor, but so help me God, if I ever find you in a dark alley, I'll happily resign just as long as I beat the living shit out of you."

Pursing his lips, Carter said, "Well, if we meet in a dark alley, I'll definitely know why you're there." He narrowed his eyes, unwilling to back down from the challenge. "And I'll happily stand up to you any day."

Grooms had opened his mouth to reply with a gunshot sounded. It was muffled, but it appeared to have come from back inside the office.

Every man in the room understood gunshots and how they sounded. Grooms, for all his laziness at being in his cushy position, nevertheless sprang into action. As did his men. Guns instantly were in ready fists. Eyes scoured the room, the doors, and the windows.

"Bobby, that came from the cells. Go see what happened."

The tall policeman ran out of the main office and into the back of the station. The next thing Carter heard was a curse, then Bobby returned.

"Hiram Colby is dead. Shot between the eyes."

※ 10 ※

CARTER AND JACKSON looked at each other. "I'll take the west side," was all Carter had to say. The two detectives turned and ran out the front door.

The Austin police station wasn't too large. A single story brick building, it had windows that faced the main street, and windows on the east side. The boardwalk was covered and had a couple of wooden benches where people could sit if they ever needed to talk with the police. Tacked to the exterior walls were a few wanted posters. Carter barely saw them as he raced along the front and around to the side.

The west face of the building was a complete brick wall. The jail cells were located in the rear of the buildings. Unfortunately for Carter, no alley existed between the police station and the next building, which happened to be a mercantile business. Cursing himself for picking the wrong side, he poured extra effort into running as fast as he could. Pedestrians noticed his charge and halted in their tracks, partly out of surprise but also likely out of wonderment. How often did a well-dressed man in a suit charge down the boardwalk?

Carter rounded the corner of the mercantile and slammed into a man. Both Carter and the man went sprawling to the street, the man on his back, Carter to his knees. He thanked himself for wearing a dark colored suit because some of the dirt from the street got on his pants. His cuffs were another matter. By stopping his fall with his hands, Carter dirtied his cuffs. He noted it even as he wiped his hands and looked over to the man.

He appeared a few years older than Carter, perhaps middle thirties. The man was clean-shaven save for a cut along one cheek. Carter's charge into the man must have edged open the cut, for a thin droplet of blood pooled on the man's face. The blonde hair was dark, not the lighter blonde of Jackson's hair. The cut of the man's suit was fine, and Carter could tell with a sweep of his eyes across the man's clothes that the pedestrian who had gotten in his way was well-to-do.

"I'm sorry, sir," Carter said, scrambling up to his feet. He brushed off his knees and hands. "I'm a detective and I'm chasing a murderer."

The man on the ground registered shock on his face. "A murderer? Then go. I'm alright."

But Carter was already moving. He raced down the side of the mercantile and hit the alley behind the building at full speed, positive there would be no one else in his way. He was right.

The alley, like most alleys in Austin, was a collection of trash and other discarded items like crates and piles of wood. On the far end of the alley, Carter saw Jackson running full tilt. He would arrive at the rear of the jail cell before Carter, but Carter noticed one other obvious thing.

There was no other person in the alley.

In their bid to surround the shooter from both sides, somehow Carter and Jackson had missed him.

But Carter couldn't miss the flames shooting up the backside of the jail. A long, thin line of flame licked up the jail wall. His mind whirled at what could be causing the fire. When he slowed to a halt, breathing in great gasps of air into his lungs, he realized what was on fire.

A rope.

And at the top of the building was a hook.

* * *

DESPERATE, Carter looked around for a ladder or any way to scale the side of the building.

"What are you doing?" Jackson said as he came to halt.

Carter pointed up. "The Hook Thief killed Colby and got away up on the roof. We've gotta find a way to get up there." He kept searching for anything he could build or use to get to the roof.

Jackson, on the other hand, craned his neck and spotted the hook. He followed the line of the building along the route he had come and then back along the west side. Next, he turned and scanned along the back walls of the other set of building that formed the walls of this alley. After a moment, he put a steadying hand on Carter's shoulder.

"What is it?" Carter asked. He slowed his movements, but not by much.

"We've been tricked."

That stopped Carter. "What do you mean?"

Jackson pointed to the hook. "Think about the jail and all the adjoining buildings as if you were a bird or looking down at them from the sky." He traced a line with his finger all the way to the end of alley. "They all form one long structure. Even this side"— he pointed at the other set of buildings—"forms one long structure. Sure a man might be able to leap from this side to the other side over the alley, but the streets are way too wide for anyone to jump across. It's not like New York or Boston where you can get on the rooftops and scramble over multiple blocks. If anyone goes up here, he's trapped."

Carter registered the words and logic Jackson presented. He let them sink in until he can to a conclusion. "So this was a diversion."

"Yup."

"And the real killer, whether or not he was the Hook Thief, managed to kill Colby, silence him, and get away scot free."

"Yup."

Carter thought for a moment. "Did you see anyone come out of the alley?"

"Other than folks on the side street that I had to dodge around, there was no one. You?"

Carter thought a moment. "No one in the alley. I ran into a guy when I rounded the main street. Other than a few other pedestrians, there were few people." The man with whom he had collided came back into his mind. He studied the features, committing the man's face to his memory. "I wonder..."

"Wonder what?"

Carter shook his head. "Nothing." What his mind posited contained no evidence. Besides, if the young well-to-do man really was the Hook Thief, how would Carter have known? And how would he break it to Moore and Jackson he had the Hook Thief in his grasp?

But he knew what the man looked like. Did Carter now know the Hook Thief's face?

From inside the jail cell, the two detectives heard the sound of the police officers talking. Carter walked back over to where three rear windows faced the alley. All three of them had bars cemented in the brick. The windows where high, at least seven feet off the ground. He noted a crate wedged up against the wall, and two dirty footprints on top. He got up onto the crate and looked inside the jail cell.

Hiram Colby's body was stretched out on the floor. His arms were at an odd angle. Clutched in his fist was a wad of paper that, upon closer inspection, Carter realized was money. Had the murderer just paid his victim right before killing him? Colby's eyes were open, and a third eye, right in the middle of his forehead, was now open to the air. A shadow of gunpowder across his forehead indicated how close the gunman got to Colby before pulling the trigger. The impact of the owlhoot's head on the concrete floor was the event that likely triggered the bloodstain that pooled around the corpse.

Grooms glanced up and saw Carter. A mixture of emotions crossed his face. It was like he wanted to say something but didn't at the same time. Finally, he muttered, "Did y'all find anything out there?"

The question caught Carter off guard. Where minutes before Grooms was ready to arrest Carter for murder, now the head policeman was asking professional advice from a fellow badge toter. As in deep as Grooms was with the high society crowd and the patronage of his father, even he knew the suspected corruption within the police department couldn't stay hidden forever. And the outright murder of a suspect in his own jail cell would end up in the paper the following day. Reporters would have a field day throwing out their idea of what happened and likely pin it all on Grooms. Carter didn't necessarily feel pity for the man—Grooms made his own bed and he would damn well sleep in it—but he felt a sense of professionalism from the man for the first time.

Carter pointed up out of Grooms' line of sight. "A hook up on the roof, but Tom thinks it was a diversion. There's no way for anyone to escape from up there without being seen. But I'd still like to take a look. Is there a ladder we can use?"

Grooms nodded. "Fire department has one."

"Good," Carter said. "Y'all check it out."

"Where are y'all going?" Grooms said, a little irritation seeping back into his voice.'

"Another lead Moore told us about," Carter said. "But do me a favor." The look of annoyance that crossed Grooms' face inwardly amused Carter. "When you get the hook, please send it to Colonel Moore. I want to compare it to the other one?"

"Other one?"

"Yeah. It appears the famous Hook Thief is operating in Austin. And he's now added murder to his resume."

❈ 11 ❈

Peter Blasingame's white frame mansion was a
dichotomy of architecture.

On the west side, the structure resembled a standard
mansion that any wealthy man might live in or build from
scratch. A raised set of steps effectively made the ground
floor the basement and the main living quarters the second
floor. A porch, supported by wooden columns, extended on
the front and side, black shutters framed every window of
the second floor, and gas lamps hung from the low roof of
the porch.

The east side, however, was where things got unique.
That half of the house was completely round. The second
story had a porch that connected with the other porch.
Rocking chairs were placed in the wide circular porch area
complete with small tables next to each chair. When
Burlingame hosted parties at his house, the area was large
enough to accommodate any musical ensemble he hired. It
was the room under the porch that proved most fascinating.
Encased in windows that spanned the entire area under the

porch, this was Burlingame's private room. It was the room in which Carter and Jackson now stood.

When they knocked on the large black door, an old man greeted them. The butler, dressed in a black suit and tie, asked them the nature of their visit and seemed put out that they wanted to see Mr. Burlingame without a prior appointment. From their position at the front door, neither detective took notice of Burlingame himself standing in his personal study. The owner of the house noticed them, however, and rang a bell. The tone took the butler by surprise, then irritation. He beckoned them to enter the house and follow him.

The interior was a marvel of what wealth could afford when one man possessed so much. Every painting, piece of furniture, and even the rug smacked of ostentatious wealth. Even the odor of the rooms seemed to reek money. One room they passed brought with it the odor or fresh paint. Since every room was painted white, Carter couldn't help but wonder why the new paint job.

The butler led them to two sets of stairs. One set went upstairs to a third floor not visible from the front of the house. Another set descended back to ground level. They took the second set, the only part of the house that didn't have carpet. Their boots clomped on the hard wood, echoing off the wooden walls adorned with nothing. The entire small area ended at a large set of double doors with brass fittings. The butler knocked three times and a man's voice, clear and sharp, told him to enter. A look from the butler told Carter and Jackson to remain in their spots as he slipped through the door. A moment later, he returned and opened the door wide. They went in. What Carter saw astounded him.

Fully one half of the room was taken up with the circular wall he saw from the front of the house. Thin curtains were drawn closed, so that only diffuse light entered Burlingame's personal sanctuary. The other half of the room was wood-paneled walls. Hung on just about every surface were dozens of weapons. Swords, pistols, rifles, knives, even pieces of a suit of armor occupied the bulk of the room. From their position in the doorway, the first thing Carter noted was the suit of armor, but it wasn't a typical European design. Made from thick leather and heavy fabric, the armor seemed designed not to stop bullets but something else, probably steel blades. The heavy fabric afforded the soldier maximum flexibility while still offering a great deal of protection. Leather shin guards and a draped outer coat protected the legs. The metal helmet had a flared base that would have protected the soldier's neck. Atop the helmet was a design Carter suspected might have been either the soldier's rank or whatever group he fought for.

"Recognize it, Detective Carter?" Peter Burlingame stood in the center of the room. He wore a dark blue suit, the tails of the coat extending down to mid-thigh. The vest was silk, the patterning a nice contrast to the dullness of the suit. The gold chain of his pocket watch dangled from one of the vest pockets. One of Burlingame's hands was in his pants pockets, the other hooked a thumb inside a vest pocket. Burlingame's face was stern, but his eyes were alive with curiosity. He was mostly bald, and the hair around his temples was cut short. The only facial hair was a close-cropped mustache, also seemingly trimmed to perfection.

"Japanese, I think."

No muscle on Burlingame's face moved. "I'm impressed." The man's thick Texas accent indicated he spent much of his younger days outside tending cattle, and not holed up in a room. "Would that be your experience traveling around the country as an actor that gave you that knowledge?"

Carter moved his eyes to the man of the house. "Yes. I spent time in both Los Angeles and San Francisco. Although there is a large population of Chinese in those cities, the Japanese presence is large enough that I've met a few. I saw some photographs of samurai warriors but wasn't complete sure."

Burlingame barely moved when he directed his next question to Jackson. "What about you, Detective? Did you recognize this armor?"

Jackson scrunched up half his face. "No, but I saw the Martini–Henry Mark I rifle over there on the wall."

For the first time, something in Burlingame's face twitched: the muscles that moved his mouth into a thin smile. "Don't you two make an interesting pair? I can see why Jameson put y'all together." He turned and walked in a clipped gait to his desk and sat down behind it. He folded his hands. "I know why y'all are here." He gestured to two chairs in front of the large wooden desk. "Sit."

Carter hated to be commanded, but pushed his irritation deep. He took the chair on the left, Jackson the right.

"I can tell y'all've worked together before," Burlingame continued. "The southpaw Carter and the right-handed Jackson both sitting in a manner that your primary hand is ideally accessible if an intruder barged in the room. I'm still impressed. Y'all have something of a reputation. Moore has told me you two are among his favorite detectives because y'all get results. But I can tell you right now, y'all're barking up the wrong tree."

Carter crossed his legs, putting his left ankle on his right knee. "You seem to know a lot about us, Mr. Burlingame. Why do you suppose Colonel Moore directed us to you?"

Burlingame waited a few moments before responding. "I'm guessing y'all don't know much about me."

"In passing," Jackson said.

"We know you're one of the richest men in the city," Carter said. He gestured behind him at all the weapons. "But we had no idea about all of this."

A small grunt passed from Burlingame. "When you're as rich as me, it takes a lot to assuage the boredom wealth brings. It does enable, however, the freedom to follow one's passion, and my passion is weaponry."

"Did you serve in the war?" Carter asked.

More muscles twitched in Burlingame's face. "I was abroad."

Carter waited for more, but the host offered nothing else. He made a mental note to ask Moore how Burlingame got his money and just how he spent it.

"So," Carter said, filling in the pregnant silence, "you mentioned you know why we were here. I'll just come out and ask: did you arrange to steal the Aztec sword?"

For the first time, some of Burlingame's stoic facade crumbled. "The Aztec sword? That's what was stolen?" The man seemed surprised. If it was possible for him to sit up straighter, he did. "The one in Octavia's museum?"

"You knew about it?" Jackson asked.

"Of course I knew about it," Burlingame blurted. "I offered to buy it more than once. Old Gunter refused, and then after he died, I expected Octavia to part with it. But even she refused me."

Carter got the impression Burlingame wasn't used to being rebuffed and not getting anything he wanted. "Why did you want it?"

Burlingame breathed in deep and sighed. He leaned back in his chair and spread a hand out to indicate all of his possessions. "I have weapons from every continent in the world, and from a myriad of civilizations. But I have nothing from the Aztecs. That's understandable, you see. The Spaniards did their best to destroy the Aztec civilization. They were damn effective at it, too. Only a handful of Aztec weapons are known to exist, and the Aztec sword Octavia Hendrickson owns is one of them." He paused as he recalled a past memory. "I asked Gunter once how he came to possess the sword. As open as he was with all of his ideas, that was the one thing he never answered."

"I suppose there's no way you could prove that you didn't steal the weapon?" Jackson asked.

"Didn't I already tell you I didn't?" Burlingame said.

"You did," Jackson said, "but I'm one who prefers proof."

"You mean you don't take a man of honor at his word?"

"Depends on the man."

Burlingame regarded Jackson for a few heartbeats. "Why do you think your commanding officer would arrange this meeting if you think I stole the sword?"

Jackson shrugged.

Burlingame allowed his eyes to rest on Jackson a few more moments before turning to Carter. "What about you, Detective Carter?"

Carter certainly didn't want to come across as defying Jackson's hunch. That kind of disloyalty didn't bode well for a partnership. Instead, he tried a different tact. "Mrs. Hendrickson suggested a name of a person who she suspected might've had motive. A Mexican national named Juan Esteban Molina. Do know him?"

Burlingame scoffed. "Yes, I know him. He's a minor bureaucrat down in Mexico City. He's a railroad man, worked with Gunter for a time." He grew quiet. "Why does Octavia think he did it?"

Shrugging, Carter said, "She never came out and said she suspects him. Molina is some sort of zealot. Maybe he wanted the sword for personal reasons, maybe national pride."

Burlingame pursed his lips, deep in thought. "She may have a point. Molina is a man with bigger dreams than he currently has. He would love to see Mexico become a greater power than it currently is. He certainly won't be that leader, but he tends to find others he thinks he can steer into power and be there at the right hand." An idea occurred to him and Burlingame smiled. "It could also be some sort of test."

"A test?" Jackson muttered. "What kind of test?"

"Use your imagination, Detective Jackson. If Molina doesn't have the capability to be president, then he'd need to prove his loyalty to a man who does possess presidential aspirations. What better way than to acquire the Aztec sword owned by the hated gringos from America?"

It was Carter's turn to sit up straight. "That's a good idea, sir." He ignored Jackson's grimace. "You seem to know a thing or two about Molina. If you were him and you arranged this little show last night, what would you direct them to do next?"

Abruptly, Burlingame stood. He clasped his hands at the base of his back and started pacing behind his desk. "Getting the sword out of Austin by horse would be prohibitively too slow. There are a myriad of thieves along the way and even a man who planned the attack last night couldn't avoid all of them. Rail would be the best method to get the sword out of the city and down into Mexico with any sort of speed."

"But which way?" Carter mused. "South to Laredo or east to Galveston?" He paused a moment. "What would you do?"

Burlingame didn't answer right away. His head was down, his mind sifting through the possibilities. "Even if the culprit travels by rail out of town, he'll still have to pass through customs at the border. Even the most lax official could be bribed to look the other way, but the rail path is littered with small town dictators who would be eager to get a little action on the side and wouldn't think twice about confiscating the sword out of complete ignorance. But the thief likely has enough money to bribe his way all the way down to Mexico City."

He stopped and ran his fingers across the top of this leather chair. "But there is another option. He could get the sword out via a boat."

"Boat?" Jackson murmured. "Where?"

"Galveston." Burlingame patted the back of the chair. "There's a very easy way to get something out of the country and that's to ship it on a boat. And what better way to do that than through Galveston."

"Why there?" Carter asked.

"Isaiah Grummon."

"Who's that?" Jackson said.

"Isaiah Grummon is a man who has his thumb on much of what happens in Galveston," Burlingame said. "There is little he doesn't know or can't do. On the public face, he operates much of the wharfs and pretty much has a hand in what goes in and out of that city."

"And on the private side?" Carter said.

Burlingame smiled. "Grumman is the one man whose organization could be contracted to pull a job like this. He has his fingers stretched all across the southwest and along the Gulf. His influence is pretty thick. Let's put it this way: if you wanted to disappear and sneak out of Texas unseen, then leaving through Galveston would be the way to do it. The only issue would be price."

Carter and Jackson exchanged a glance. With respective nods, they rose. "Thank you, Mr. Burlingame," Carter said. "You have been most helpful." He threw a shot glance at Jackson. "I can see why Moore directed us your way."

"He's a thorough man, your commanding officer," Burlingame said. "He sent y'all here to see if I did it. I'll have to have a word with him next time I see him."

Jackson fingered the brim of his hat. "He's just helping us do our jobs."

Burlingame regarded Jackson for a moment before nodding curtly to both detectives. "I have to ask."

"What?" Carter said.

After a few moments of silence, Burlingame shook his head. "Never mind. It was a foolish idea." He put on a forced smile. He reached over and pushed a button on a small table next to his desk. A bell rang. A few moments later, the butler opened the door and beckoned the detectives to follow him.

"Happy hunting," was the last thing Burlingame said to them as they left.

❧ 12 ☙

"GALVESTON?" Jameson Moore said. He sat behind his desk, his reading glasses on the end of his nose. He put down the papers in his hands and removed his glasses.

"Or Laredo," Carter said. He and Jackson stood behind the two chairs in front of the desk, having not been invited to sit. "It was Burlingame's opinion that the Hook Thief or whomever took the sword would want to get it out of the city as fast as possible. That means rail."

Moore mulled over the new information. "That's a large hunch on his part."

"It seems," Jackson said, "that Burlingame might've wanted the sword for his own personal collection. You ever see his place?"

"Of course I have," the colonel snapped. "Why the hell do you think I sent y'all over there? I had half a mind to think he pulled the job himself. See any sign of it?"

"None," Carter said. He gave Jackson a sidelong look before continuing. "But if you don't mind a bit of personal conjecture, I'm thinking Burlingame isn't our man."

Moore inclined his head. "Okay, Calvin. Why?"

He gestured to Jackson. "We were just in his own personal museum. Burlingame's proud of everything he has. He wants to show off everything. He's vain. He can't be the one to steal the sword because he'd never be able to show it off. If anything, he would want to acquire it above board so he can complete his little collection."

Moore nodded once. "A valid point. He mentioned Galveston because of Grummon I assume."

"You know about this dude?" Jackson asked.

"Of course. Grummon's one of those men who is never linked to half the crime that goes on down there. Most of the time he doesn't bother the railroad so we don't have to deal with him. But I've talked with some fellow lawmen down there and Grummon's knee deep in crime and corruption. But let's not forget Robert O'Rourke down in Laredo."

That was a name Carter knew. Robert O'Rourke was one of the railroad entrepreneurs who, with the help of Jay Gould, helped link rail service to Laredo from San Antonio. Gould rewarded O'Rourke with control of the region. On paper, O'Rourke was a businessman with good ties to local politicians. Under the table, however, O'Rourke was a ruthless bastard who got what he wanted and killed anyone unlucky enough to stand in the way. Unfortunately, no one had yet connected him with any criminal activity so he continued to control the area. Most politicians and civilians in Laredo either didn't know or didn't mind O'Rourke's antics as long as the railroads ran on time and the money kept flowing.

"We should follow up with Laredo, too," Jackson commented.

Moore paced behind his desk for a few more moments, then turned and pointed at his two detectives. "I'll telegraph the field offices in Laredo and Galveston, have them be on the lookout for any passage directly to Mexico. In the meantime, pack your bags. You're on the way to Galveston."

* * *

FOR CALVIN CARTER, packing was not an elaborate process. It certainly wasn't as casual as Jackson—who often threw in clothes without folding them, mingling his spare cartridges with his under garments—but it was quick and efficient. A few times in his detective days he had to leave without a moment's notice and wasn't prepared. Ever since the last time, he made a point to categorize his packing.

Into his fine leather war bag, he packed clean under garments and two extra shirts. The spare .44 cartridges for his Colt he packed in a separate leather pouch and stored them in an interior pocket. He brought his toiletries, also in their own separate leather pouch, and stored them along-side his secret weapon: his actor's make-up case. This leather bag contained just about anything he needed to conceal his features in order for him to become someone else no matter the situation. When Carter first showcased his unorthodox approach to being a detective—really just another role for Carter—Jackson had scoffed and laughed.

Until Carter got results.

Then Jackson stopped laughing and so did all the other detectives, some of whom were more senior to the young former actor. Moore turned a blind eye to what he consid-ered Carter's antics as long as the younger man produced results.

On top of all these items, Carter placed a specially folded spare suit, this one black. It hid the wrinkles better. For reading material, he selected a volume by Jules Verne:

20,000 Leagues Under the Sea. Considering this case involved an ancient artifact, Carter felt the novel particularly appropriate.

He stepped in front of the mirror in his room. He adjusted his tie, straightened his coat, and put his hat on, cantering it at a rakish angle. He had already made arrangements with Mrs. Pendergast for her to clean his room while he was away, and paying her for the next month's rent in advance. It was that kind of attention to detail that had enabled Carter to earn some extra privileges around the boarding house, including the back door, which he now opened, exited, closed, and locked. He descended the short flight of stairs with a jovial stride and was nearing the edge of the alley with a thick meaty hand slammed down on his shoulder.

"I figured a coward like you would try and sneak out the back door," a man's voice said. Carter churned through his memory banks until the name appeared in his head. Bobby Anders, police officer with wounded pride.

"Hands off the suit, Anders," Carter said, putting a little extra force in his voice. "I've got a train to catch."

The hand gripped Carter's shoulder tighter and turned him around. Anders still wore the same clothes from last night. Smelled like it, too. His face was screwed up into a grimace, like he was catching a whiff of his own stink. The hand stayed on Carter's shoulder while the policeman talked.

"We got unfinished business." A little spittle sprayed from Anders's lips and landed on Carter's face. He couldn't tell if it was intentional or not.

"I don't think so."

The fist gripped tighter. "Yeah, we do. You ran from a murder scene. I don't care what some stupid doctor says or how many strings you pulled, you were in that room and I think you done in that poor sap. What's your beef with him anyway?"

"I have no beef with him. I found him that way. But I'm gonna have a beef with you if you don't remove your hand."

Carter felt the flexing of Anders's hand a second before the bigger man's knee came up. The second's lead time allowed Carter to pivot his groin away from the massive knee, but not completely. The thick bone of the policeman's kneecap struck one of Carter's balls. Bright pain shot through the detective and he fell to his knees on the ground, coughing. His hat tumbled crown up onto the ground. His hands instinctively went to his crotch which made him defenseless when Anders kicked Carter in the stomach.

The wind whooshed out of Carter's lungs in a violent heave. His eyes opened wide with the realization he couldn't draw in a breath. Carter saw Anders draw his foot back for another blow and did the only thing he could do in the situation: fall over on his left side.

In a move that was meant for Carter's face, Anders's foot grazed the detective's shoulder. The policeman lost his balance for a moment with the momentum. He spun on his planted foot and had to reach out to grab the stair rail for support.

That brief moment of relief enabled Carter to fight back. He pulled out his Colt, aimed for the wooden railing next to the big man's hands, and pulled the trigger. The gun bucked in his hand. The lead slug chewed a hole in the wood, sending chunks spewing in the air.

Anders jerked his hand away. In doing so, he lost his balance and fell on his ass, landing on the lower step and at a bad angle. He yelped in pain, but Carter didn't care.

Carter couldn't stand just yet. His gut and his groin ached like a son of a bitch. But his gun hand was steady as a rock and it was aimed at Anders's face.

"I could have killed you," Carter rasped. His lungs were still not back to normal. "And I could do it right now. But I didn't. We're both men of the law. I don't outright kill a lawman, even one who attacks me without provocation."

Anders looked at Carter, hatred in his eyes and anger curling his lips. "You're a murderer. And now you've attacked a cop. I'll see you in jail."

Carter's thumb pulled back the hammer. "If you think I'm a murderer already, let's add another to the list." He grimaced as he got to his knees. "Actually, I could likely talk my way out of this anyway seeing as how I've got witnesses." He waited for Anders to figure out what he meant.

The policeman frowned and looked around. He saw nothing and started to smile. "You're bluffing."

"Look up."

Still laying on the steps, Anders craned his neck and looked back at the boarding house. In a window on the second floor, Mrs. Pendergast looked down. Her eyes were wide with shock and fear, her hand clasped around the base of her neck.

Anders returned his attention to Carter. "You can't hide behind old ladies all the time. I know about you and your predilections. One day, Carter, you won't even know what hit you."

"Maybe. Maybe not. But know this. Anything happens to me in that respect, my partner will pay you a visit. He's a bit rougher than me. More prone to just shoot somebody as opposed to talk. Hell, he thinks I talk too much anyway. And I'm about to board a train. I'll have hours to tell him all about you." He waited for the words to sink in. Whether or not they did, Carter didn't know. But what he did notice was a softening of Anders's features.

Carter willed his body to stand. His lungs were almost

back to normal, but his groin ached with the abuse. It was all he could do to stand up straight.

"I'd be much obliged if you'd just mosey your ass out of this alley and be on your way. I'll be moving a might slow after your kick to my nether region." He wagged the Colt toward the open end of the alley.

Making sure Carter saw his open palms, Anders stood. He backed out of the alley, a funny smile on his face. "If I find proof you done in Elroy Brown, I'm coming after you."

Carter chuckled dryly. "If you find proof of that crime, that means there are two Calvin Carters running around town. I'm not sure Austin is ready for that."

BY THE TIME Carter caught sight of the railroad passenger station down on Congress and West Cypress, most of his limp had faded away. He was still not without discomfort—his ribs ached from the force of Anders's kick and his balls would still prefer he stop moving for a while—but he certainly didn't want to tip off Jackson about the attack. Over the years, their partnership had developed a strong bond with each man defending the other to a high degree. Some partnerships inside the detective agency had dissolved, sometimes through death or retirement but other times merely from both partners just wanting to work with someone else. Not so Carter and Jackson. They remained a great team, one that Moore relied on to close even the toughest of cases.

Not that this was a particularly difficult case. In fact, the more Carter thought about it as he walked the last block to the station, the more he wondered why exactly they were doing it. Railroads interests weren't particularly involved. There were no bandits attacking civilians on the various trains and routes. Sure, there was murder involved and the police thinking Carter was involved, but mostly, this was purely a treasure hunt. Find the Aztec sword and bring it back. Straightforward.

Well, there was the little matter of the Hook Thief. If Carter could catch him—or find a lead to the crook's real identity—then Carter could gain a little notoriety himself.

He smiled at the thought. Then he winced again.

Carter had taken a cab from his boarding house to the corner of Congress and West Pine. He wanted a couple of blocks to walk to the station and work out the kinks in his body. Mrs. Pendergast had rushed out of her house as soon as Anders had left, tut-tutting over Carter like a mother hen. He had assured her he was find, hiding his gritted teeth at the time and walking down the half block to the corner. As soon as he was out of her line of sight, he had hailed a cab and leaned back and let the cabbie drive him. But the ruts and holes in the streets proved more hurtful than walking, so he had the cabbie stop a few blocks away. This would allow Carter to smooth out his gait before Jackson laid eyes on him.

Didn't matter.

"What the hell happened to you?" Jackson said. He had taken one look at Carter and knew.

"What do you mean?" Carter said. His smile was not entirely forced, but Jackson could tell.

"Cal, I can tell when you're hiding something. You may be a good actor—"

"*Great* actor."

"Great actor," Jackson said without missing a beat, "but I can tell when you've been roughed up."

Carter sighed. "Anders was at my house. Apparently he still thinks I murdered Brown. He wanted to discuss the issue with me. He got in a good couple of points, but I set him straight." He smirked, a bit of the old Carter returning. "I also told him that if anything happens to me, you'll have some more words with him."

Jackson glanced up at the clock on the wall. "We've got half an hour before the train leaves." He cracked his knuckles. "I could have words with him now."

Carter gestured with his chin at the saloon across the street. "Actually, I'm a little parched. Why don't we head over there and have a drink?"

"Sure," Jackson said.

Both detectives picked up their bags and moseyed across the street to the saloon. It was around lunchtime and the room was crowded with patrons surrounding the various tables. Carter and Jackson elbowed their way to the bar. Jackson ordered a beer. Carter ordered a beer and two shots of whiskey. He had a metal flask of his favorite brandy in his war bag but wanted to save that for later. He downed the two shots in quick succession, the warmth of the alcohol seeping into his body. He sighed in relief and picked up his beer.

"To partners who always have each other's backs," he said.

Jackson nodded.

Both men drank their beers, their backs to the bar, bags at their feet. They watched the crowd order drinks and food. The types of men that frequented a bar at noon in a city the size of Austin were different than those out in the country. Well-dressed men at some tables sat next to laborers at another. A saloon was one of the few places around that enabled all the different classes of men to mingle together without any societal influence or meddling.

With a little over ten minutes before the train was to depart, Carter and Jackson paid their tabs and hurried across the street. The alcohol coursed through Carter, giving him a warm feeling. Most of the aches were now dulled and he was able to keep up with Jackson's long gait. They bought sandwiches from a vendor outside the station, edged their way up the platform, and waited to board the passenger car.

As employees of the railroad, Carter and Jackson had the opportunity to ride in sleeper cars or first-class cars as long as paying customers weren't adversely affected. Moore, on the other hand, suggested to all his detectives that they spend some of their travel time in coach cars with the regular folks. This enabled the detectives to keep an eye out for the smaller, petty crimes that sometimes occurred on trains. He also encouraged his detectives to wear their badges in full view, to comfort those who may worry about their safety during travel.

Jackson was the type of man who preferred wearing his gun on his hip and his badge on his suit jacket. He wanted everyone to know who he was and what he represented. Carter, on the other hand, preferred the more subtle approach. His shoulder holster hid his gun and enabled him to use his mouth and his brain as a first line of defense. He also tended to carry his badge in a leather wallet. If necessary, he could produce it and his credentials, but he thought it put some folks at ease not to have a badged detective in their midst.

But on this trip to Houston and then Galveston, he relented to Moore's wishes. He pulled out the leather wallet, retrieved his badge, and pinned in on his vest.

"Do you always wear your badge for all to see?"

The voice belonged to a woman and, the moment before he turned to see who it was, Carter thought he recognized the voice. As his head swiveled to confirm it was Naomi Hendrickson, his mind wondered what she was doing on the platform.

Naomi stood a few feet away. She wore a brown traveling suit, complete with a jacket cut short to end at her waist. The dress was full length, but made of cotton. Her blouse was buttoned up to her neck, the bare glint of a gold chain necklace under the thin fabric. On her hands she wore brown leather gloves. She carried a leather bag in one hand and in the other what appeared to be a ticket.

Unlike the previous night or earlier this morning when her face betrayed both fright and irritation, Naomi's face was pure happiness. The smile lit up her features and traveled all the way from her mouth to her blue eyes. The lipstick brought out the fullness of her lips. Small gold earrings dangled from her ears, catching the sunlight. All in all, she appeared quite beautiful.

"Where are you going?" Carter asked.

"With you." Her voice was cheery.

"I'm sorry, what?" Jackson chimed in.

"Mother contacted Colonel Moore and asked about the progress of the case. He told her he was sending y'all down to Galveston. I thought it best to go along as a representative of my mother's company and verify the sword when we recover it."

Carter frowned. "I think we're quite capable of doing all of that without you. We've already had one murder."

"Two, actually," Jackson said. "Colby."

"Two," Carter continued without missing a beat. "And it appears one of the more famous thieves might be involved."

"I know," Naomi said. "It's exciting. Maybe we'll even unmask the true identity of the Hook Thief."

"Maybe we will," Carter said. "But this is a hot assignment. We can't have a civilian tagging along that we need to protect."

Some of Naomi's demeanor changed. The smile faltered a bit, and some of the lines on her face hardened. "You won't have to protect me. I'm perfectly capable of protecting myself." She unbuckled her bag and opened it. Amid the clothes and cosmetics perfectly packed inside, a revolver in a leather case sat on top of everything. "Within easy reach," she said. Then she shoved her hand inside the bag, along the side, and withdrew a gleaming hunting knife. "And then there's this."

"Where in blazes did you get that?" Carter breathed.

"It was Father's. He carried it with him on some of his travels around the world." She slipped the knife back into the bag and closed it. She leveled her eyes at both detectives. "I'm not some damsel who can't protect herself. Besides, I have one thing y'all don't have that you'll likely need."

"What's that?" Jackson asked.

"Direct knowledge of the sword. I know what it looks like. Y'all have never laid eyes on it. You've only heard it described. I'll be able to authenticate its veracity as soon as y'all locate it."

Carter gave her a condescending smirk. "I think we can recognize an ancient Aztec sword. Based on the description, it's pretty damn unique."

Naomi pursed her lips and raised her chin. "Be that as it may, I'm going to Galveston. I'm on this train. And I'm going to tag along with y'all. It's mother's wish, and isn't she paying the bill to the railroad to take back what's been stolen? Besides, Calvin, you've known me long enough to know that I get what I want in the end."

Carter and Jackson had no response.

"Good. It's settled then." She brushed past them and boarded the passenger car. The two detectives watched as she made her way to the middle of the car and took a seat.

"How long have you known her?" Jackson asked.

"Too long."

❦   13   ❦

Much to Carter's surprise, the trip from Austin to Houston went along smoothly. He and Jackson had taken up seats across the aisle from Naomi. At first, still miffed with her presence, Carter started to read his Jules Verne book. Jackson comforted himself with the newspaper and a handful of dime novels. Naomi brought with her a leather-bound copy of Mark Twain's *Roughin' It*. A curious selection, Carter thought, and ended up asking her about it.

She closed the book, a finger inside the pages to mark her place. "I love adventure. Father was always traveling to different locations. Sometimes, Mother and I would accompany him. I grew to love the experience and all that I saw. So, when I can't travel for one reason or another, I like to read about travel and adventure."

"You're traveling now," Carter commented. "And this case certainly qualifies as adventure. You've got both wrapped up into one."

That little commentary broke the ice between them. They spent the better part of the trip talking about this and that. Even though Carter knew Naomi from the times in which he visited Octavia, they had rarely spoken but a few words in each visit. The elder Hendrickson even mentioned that he wasn't there to talk with her daughter, but to her. So Carter's time was always consumed by Octavia. It turned out, Naomi revealed as the afternoon wore on, that she was jealous of her mother for Carter's attention. She had many suitors, but they were all either rich boys who thought Naomi was merely a prize to show off or poor boys looking to move up in the world by way of marriage. Carter was the exception. He was his own man—an actor no less!—who had become a detective. The thought fascinated her and, she confessed a few miles outside of Giddings, now she had him all to herself.

Carter had formed his own opinion as to why Naomi was coming with them. It matched what she just said. He told as much, but her countenance changed almost instantly.

"It's true I enjoy spending time with you Calvin,"—at this, Carter heard Jackson grunt—"but there's a real reason I'm coming with you. There's a man you need to meet." When Carter questioned her further, she demurred. "I'll tell you when we get to Houston."

Frowning, Carter said, "Our destination is Galveston."

"Maybe, but we'll not get to Houston until after seven. I suggest we stay the night and let you speak with Jacob Hobson."

Carter racked his brain but could not come up with any knowledge of that name. He turned to Jackson, whom he knew was listening in, and his partner shook his head once.

"Who is that?"

"You'll find out."

* * *

HOUSTON'S CAPITOL HOTEL was located at the corner of Main and Texas Streets. The five-story structure was so named because it was situated at the site of the provisional capital back in 1836 when Texas won its independence from Mexico. The light tan color of the facade blended well with the surrounding buildings. Every room had a window that opened to allow breeze to waft in, but they were mostly closed to keep out the odor.

Much of the first floor was occupied by businesses such as a billiard bar, laundry, bath, and barber shop. Carter knew the hotel well as the railroad offices shared space on the same block. They were the typical civilian branches of the railroad, but Moore had incorporated various sub-stations around the country where local detectives could watch their various jurisdictions without having always to contact the main office in Austin.

One dictum Moore always stressed was for pairs of detectives to get adjoining rooms, preferably ones at the corners of hotels. In this manner, the detectives would have two views of the streets below and be able to spot trouble ahead of time. It also provided two means of escape if the situation warranted.

Carter also knew the Capitol Hotel as it was across the street from the Palace Theater. It was a small venue, and Carter had performed there a few times when he was just starting out as an actor. The owner of the theater had a few rooms at the hotel permanently rented and allowed actors to sleep there after performances. It had been a long time since Carter had last stepped foot in the theater, and he now looked at it through the window of his room.

A gentle knock at the door sounded. "It's open."

Naomi opened the door. Jackson stood behind her in the hallway. "Are you ready?"

"Yeah," Carter said, unable to hide the wistfulness from his voice.

Naomi came to stand next to him and saw the theater. "Do you miss it?"

"A lot of the times, yeah. But going undercover as a detective often purges the longing for the stage. Still, I try and get a part whenever I can. There's nothing like standing on a stage, all eyes pointing at you, the lights shining on your face, the smell of makeup…" He shook his head. "It's like a drug, but it's one you can control, just like you control an audience. In those seconds before you speak, you have everyone hanging by a thread."

"Right now," Jackson said from the doorway, "our stomachs are hanging on by a thread. Come on, Cal. I'm hungry. You can wax poetically over dinner."

Carter smiled, willing his thoughts away. He winked at Naomi. "The man has spoken."

"I think the man's stomach has spoken," she replied.

The hotel dining room had closed for the evening so the three of them dined at a restaurant a block away. Over plates of steak, potatoes, green beans, and rolls, Carter, Jackson, and Naomi enjoyed each other's company in talk about the theater and books and old cases. When they had finished and the waiters had removed all the empty plates, leaving only half-filled glasses of wine, Carter brought up the elephant in the room.

"So, this Jacob Hobson, who is he and why do we need to speak with him?"

Naomi dabbed the corners of her mouth with her napkin. She folded her hands and gave the two detectives a serious look. "He is the man who was present when father found the Aztec sword."

Carter arched an eyebrow at her and threw a glance at

Jackson. His partner remained impassive. "And that helps us how?"

"He'll have special insight into who might've taken the sword."

"I thought," Jackson said, "your mother reckoned this Molina guy took it. Would there be anyone else who might've wanted it?"

Naomi smiled thinly. "Seeing as how my father and Jacob parted ways years ago, I think we can add him to the list of suspects."

"Why?" Carter asked.

"Because he helped my father steal the sword in the first place."

* * *

CARTER FELT his brows furrow and his jaw open in complete surprise. "I'm sorry, I don't believe I heard you correctly. You're saying your father stole the Aztec sword?"

Naomi smiled thinly. "You heard correctly."

Jackson leaned forward, his elbows on the table. "I think you'd better start talking." He reached inside his jacket pocket and pulled out a notepad and pencil wrapped together with a rubber band. Where the years of having to memorize lines of dialogue served Carter well as a detective in hearing and retaining information, Jackson preferred to write things down. He contended that the act helped solidify things in his head and, from time to time, helped when he had to review facts of an assignment. As each notebook was full, he'd store it at his house and buy a new one. He now opened the notebook and sat ready, pencil poised to start writing.

Naomi sighed. "Remember back in Austin when we discovered that not only was the sword stolen but one of father's journals, too?" After nods from both detectives, she continued. "Well, in that journal, Father recounted how he came in possession of the sword. For years, he would only say that his connections with the railroad down in Mexico provided him with the capitol to acquire the sword. It wasn't until one day when I was reading through his journals that I learned the truth."

"Was he upset with you?" Carter asked.

"Like you wouldn't believe. He might've also been a bit embarrassed, having perpetrated a lie for all these years."

"Just for the record," Jackson said, "what was the story he told you?"

Naomi chuckled a moment, lost in a memory. "You'd like it, Detective Jackson. It was just like one of those stories in those dime novels you like to read." She took a sip of her wine. "Father said that he and Juan Esteban Molina were monitoring the progress of the new railroad. Each day, workers would lay new tracks. Sometimes they would have to clear a path, other days they would have to dynamite a clearing. It was during one of the dynamite days that the explosion exposed a cave that had been hidden for centuries."

Carter felt his heart beating a tad faster at Naomi's story. As a child, he had made up stories of lost civilizations and the adventures he would have as an adult in looking for those lost and hidden places. He couldn't imagine what he would do were he in Gunter Hendrickson's shoes.

"You're saying this is all made up?" Carter said.

"Not all of it. But I'm telling this story in order, so please don't interrupt. You know how to tell a good story. Now sit back and listen to one." She winked at him.

Carter was momentarily surprised. It was the nicest thing Naomi had ever done to him.

"Anyway, this part, evidentially, is true. Father and

Molina went into the cave together. Jacob Hobson was there, too. He was in charge of security and keeping the workers in line. A couple of others. The workers were just happy for a break. Inside, they found the sword and a few other artifacts from the Aztec times. Some pottery, some farming tools, and other assorted things. But the sword was the true prize."

"Father had enjoyed reading history and knew about how the Spaniards had conquered the Aztec with superior weaponry. Don't forget: the Aztec swords, as deadly as they can be, are still made of wood. When they're used against animals, the beasts don't stand a chance. But when they're used against armored soldiers with steel swords, the Aztec weapons fail."

Jackson was busily writing down his notes. Without looking up, he said, "So your dad and Molina divvied up the all the stuff?"

Naomi arched an eyebrow. "It was more than just stuff, Detective. These were prized artifacts from Mexico's history. Molina knew it the instant he laid eyes on them. So did Father. From what Father told me that day he discovered I had read the truth about the sword, Molina thought that he would be famous for discovering these artifacts. He even had dreams of opening a museum or having them on display at his house. But Father reminded him that the expedition to lay the tracks for the railroad was mostly funded by his company so anything discovered was half his. Molina balked, but lawyers got involved and agreed that what Father claimed was true. Father told me the moment he saw the sword, he wanted it."

Naomi sighed. She downed the last of her wine, then picked up the bottle and poured more. "This is where the story gets more difficult to relate."

"Why?" Carter asked.

"Because it proves just what a bastard my father could be." She drank some more wine and, forgetting where she was, wiped her mouth with the back of her hand. She set the wine glass on the table and turned hardened eyes at Carter.

"In what appeared to be a good faith gesture, Father gave in. 'Of course the artifacts should stay in Mexico,' was what he told Molina. 'The only thing I would do is show it off to a bunch of gringos back in Texas.' So, Father and Molina, with a handshake, entered into a gentleman's agreement for Molina to keep all the artifacts. They were dutifully packed up and shipped down to Veracruz and Molina's estate. Father even made a point to give interviews with the Mexican newspapers. The discovery made big headlines. Do you remember it?"

Both detectives shook their heads.

Carter sat patiently, waiting for the rest of the story, but was already devising a way he thought the story would go. He almost ventured a guess, but didn't want to get chastised by Naomi again.

"But Father wasn't finished. He brought Hobson and another man, David Barron, aside and they devised a plan to steal the sword from under Molina's nose. He gave it time to settle down. Molina had told Father that he wanted a proper way to display the sword but, in the meantime, he would keep it safe and locked away. As you might expect, a few unscrupulous men tried to buy the weapon from Molina. They offered him a mountain of money, but he steadfastly refused. He wanted the sword more than he wanted the money. You see, he claimed he could trace his ancestry back to the Aztecs and, to his mind, the sword was merely coming back to a proper Aztec warrior."

"Some of those unscrupulous men attempted to steal the sword, but failed. A few were caught, but not all. For the ones who were caught, their bail was paid by Father. It turns out that all the failed attempts to steal the sword were means to learn about the interior of Molina's estate. Father and Hobson and Barron took all that information and devised a foolproof plan to enter the grounds, steal the sword, and get out without anyone knowing." She held out her hands. "And they did."

Jackson looked up from his notebook. "So why didn't Molina just report the theft?"

"And lose credibility among the Mexican people? Not likely. In the years since, he has steadfastly not spoken a word about the theft, deferring to his goal of creating a museum specifically devoted to Aztec artifacts. He keeps telling people he wants more before he will open the museum. And that has kept the truth about the theft of the Aztec sword a secret."

Carter and Jackson sat quiet for a few moments, absorbing all that Naomi had related. It certainly seemed like a good story, one that managed to weave all the known facts of this current case together.

"Did your mother know about all of this?" Carter asked.

"Not while Father was alive. After he discovered I read his journal, he swore me to secrecy. He also hid the journals away. It wasn't until he died that Mother found them. Interestingly, she never read through all of them. Instead, she just put them on the shelves for viewing."

"How do you know she never read them?" Jackson asked.

"Because if she had, she would never have put the sword on display."

Carter admitted Naomi had a point. "So what do we hope to learn from Hobson? He's the same age as your father?"

"He is," Naomi admitted. "I'd like to see if he might help us."

"Help us what?" Jackson said.

"Steal the sword back."

Carter sat up straighter. "Wait a minute. If what you just told us is true and if Molina's behind it, isn't it his anyway?"

Naomi regarded him a moment. "I'll just go back to the original agreement not by Father and Molina, but by the companies that financed the railroad in particular. The only reason that line of track is laid in the manner it was is because American money paid for it. By rights, anything found along the way belongs to that company. My father's company. And, thus, my father."

Carter scowled. "That seems awfully petty."

"Petty or not, it's the truth. And, might I add, the law." She polished off her wine and stood. She glanced at the clock on the wall. "Now, seeing as how it's getting late, I suggest we pay Mr. Hobson a visit and see what suggestions he has to reclaim my family's stolen property." She moved off to the front door, her skirts swishing behind her.

Jackson caught Carter's eye. "I don't like this."

Carter stood. "Me, either."

❧ 14 ❧

THE MONEY JACOB HOBSON received from Gunter Hendrickson's company must have been good because the house the cabbie dropped them off in front of was pretty large. Not as large as the Hendrickson mansion back in Austin or even the ostentatious manor of Peter Blasingame, but the Hobson house was clearly the largest on this block. The two-story building faced the street. Two windows on the first floor and an identical set on the second both looked out onto porches. The heavy wooden door was painted black, a stark contrast to the white paint for the rest of the house. An unlit lantern hung from the ceiling of the ground floor porch while a cast iron lamp post was situated on the second floor porch. That lamp also wasn't lit. In fact, looking at the house itself, no light came from any of the windows.

Carter pulled out his pocket watch and glanced at the time with the light from the street lamps. A little after ten. He snapped the watch closed. "I guess he goes to bed early?"

"Then we'll wake him up," Naomi said. She grabbed

handfuls of her skirt and traipsed across the street. Carter and Jackson followed in her wake.

The silence was the first thing Carter noted. Other than the sounds of hooves along the street and on other blocks, this stretch of Houston was pretty quiet. He wondered if the other residents were as rich as Hobson appeared to be and if they were somehow able to keep out the riffraff. The silence was so complete that the clomps of Naomi's shoes on the wooden steps sounded deafening. So did the knock as she rapped on the door.

And the squeaky hinges as the door opened on its own accord.

Instantly, Jackson's hand shot to his Colt and he drew it. Carter unbuttoned his jacket and snaked his hand into it and grasped his firearm. The two detectives, on tip toes, climbed the stairs. Carter leaned in close to Naomi's ear.

"We're gonna have a look around. You ought to stay here."

She gulped. In the vague light from the streetlamp, Carter noted her eyes were wide with fear.

"How do you want to play it?" Jackson asked. "Both go in or front and back?"

"Let's both go in."

Carter gripped the door handle and opened it, making sure to pull the door up. The extra force from Carter enabled the door to open without additional squeaks of the hinges.

Pale light from the streetlamps filtered into the foyer. A long run ran back into the darkness. The ambient light slowly made things appear like ghosts materializing out of nothing. A coatrack and mirror stood off to the left. To the right was an opening that led into the front reading room. Up ahead, the hallway appeared to lead to the kitchen and dining room. A staircase, also on the left, ascended up to the second floor. The steps appeared to be covered with carpet as well.

The odors of the house were exactly what Carter expected. That evening's dinner still permeated the air. Hobson evidently preferred smoking a pipe for Carter caught the stale tang of tobacco. Hobson's wife, if he had one, tried to mask the odor with some sort of floral fragrance.

But the one scent that didn't belong was the odor of gunpowder.

Carter put a finger to his nose. Jackson nodded in response. Then Jackson indicated he would move toward the back of the house on the ground floor. Carter nodded, then pointed to the second floor.

Carter took the steps on tip toe. He tried each step for squeaks before placing all his weight on it. The higher he got, the stronger the scent of gunpowder. Whatever happened must have happened up here.

Like the first floor, the second story's floor was also covered by a long carpet. Carter thanked Hobson for wanting to keep his house as quiet as possible because it gave Carter the sound camouflage he needed to investigate. The second floor consisted of a long hallway with doors opening to rooms along the way. There were five doors in total, two on each side and one at the end. All but the last door was closed. Carter moved to that room, its door slightly ajar. The gunpowder was strong here.

He had found the scene of the crime.

Being a southpaw, Carter had to open the door with his right hand and lead the way into the room with his gun hand. This room faced the street and the lamps offered vague outlines of the furniture. A desk and chair faced the one window. Sheets of paper looked ghostly in the half light. A few bookshelves lined the wall. Pictures hung on the walls. Carter waited while his eyes adjusted to the dimmer light. As they did so, he saw two things. One was a pistol on the floor. The other was an empty hand.

The hand didn't move.

Gingerly, Carter walked over to the gun and put a boot on it. The hand didn't move. He fished a Lucifer out of his jacket pocket and ignited it with a fingernail. In the sudden blazing light of the match, Carter saw a man. He laid on his side, almost as if he was sleeping. He was thick set, with jowls that hung to the floor. His mouth was open and a thin line of drool seeped out. His eyes were closed. Carter knelt to get a closer look. His eyes may have been playing tricks on him, but Carter could have sworn the man's chest rose and fell nearly imperceptibly.

He stood but kept his boot on the man's gun. The one match was nearly dead so he shook it out and stuck his hand into his jacket to retrieve another.

In the sudden darkness, the only sense Carter had was sound, and he heard the distinctive sound of a man's trousers move on the floor.

Without removing his boot from the gun on the floor, Carter slid backward, bringing the weapon with him. He felt the fingertips of the man on the floor graze his own pants. Carter took another step and ran into the edge of the carpet. The gun under his hand could move no further, but Carter didn't need it to. The man on the floor didn't move again, but the sound of the man's heavy, rasping breathing could distinctly be heard.

Carter struck the second match with his fingernail and, in the light, he saw the man staring up at him. The mouth had closed, but then fell open again with his breathing. This time, a stream of blood came out and pooled on the floor.

"Are you Jacob Hobson?" Carter asked. His commanding voice sounded loud in the quiet room.

The man nodded.

"What happened?"

"Attacked," rasped Hobson.

"Why?"

Hobson coughed, then shook his head. "You might be working for him."

With his gun hand, Carter swept his jacket aside, revealing the badge he still had pinned to his vest. "Railroad detective. We're hunting for the sword."

After hearing Carter's voice, Jackson scrambled upstairs. He appeared in the doorway just as the second match went out. Carter reached down and picked up Hobson's pistol and threw it in a corner. He then lit another match and found the oil lamp on the desk. He put fire to the wick and raised the light to full brightness. He still held his gun at the ready.

Naomi appeared behind Jackson. Her eyes went wide and she pushed her way into the room.

"Jacob," she cried. She knelt beside him and grabbed his shoulders. He groaned with pain. "What happened?"

"Attacked," he said. "Two men."

"He said they were after the sword," Carter said. He holstered his Colt and adjusted his jacket. "But I can't figure out why someone would come here."

Hobson coughed. More blood gurgled from his mouth.

"We need to get a doctor," Naomi said. Panic began to course through her voice.

"Won't do any good," Hobson croaked. He moved his other hand from his stomach. The hand was soaked in blood. "Gut shot. I don't have long for this earth." He grinned. Blood coated his teeth. "Guess this is what I get for stealing the sword back then."

Carter grabbed a wooden chair and pulled it close to Hobson. He sat on it and leaned on his knees. "Who were these men? How would they know about you and Gunter Hendrickson and what y'all did?"

Hobson's eyes flashed to Naomi. "They know the truth?"

She nodded.

Another stab of pain made Hobson grimace. "They only asked me a couple of questions. The first was how many people actually knew about the theft in the first place. I told them it was only me, Gunter, and another fellow by the name of Orson Lamay."

"Who's he?" Jackson asked.

"The third man that helped steal the sword." Hobson coughed, the pain racking his body. He shuddered. "Can I have some water? Pitcher's over there."

Jackson turned, found the pitcher, poured half a glass, and handed it to Naomi. She put the glass to Hobson's lips and he drank. Most of the liquid fell out of his mouth, but some got where he wanted it to go.

"Why would someone want to get you and then go after Lamay?" Carter asked.

Hobson's grin was weak but proud. "Because we were the only ones who successfully stole that damn sword." He turned his attention to Naomi. "Did your old man ever tell you about the curse?"

Slowly, Naomi shook her head. "He never mentioned that. We only talked once, after I found out the truth."

Nodding, Hobson said, "Just as well. Throw in a mysterious curse alongside stealing an artifact and chances are good bad stuff will meet you in the end. I never believed in that old malarkey, but I'm beginning to get a good idea about it now. Probably the reason Gunter bought it the way he did."

Carter made a note of that statement. Back when Gunter Hendrickson passed away, the obituaries in the newspapers didn't mentioned precisely the cause of death. Carter would ask Naomi later.

"Did you know the men?" Carter asked.

"No."

Carter hated to ask such a leading question, but he knew he was running out of time the more Hobson's life was ebbing away. "Were these men Mexican?"

"Actually, no. They were white men just like you and me."

Carter frowned. He and Jackson exchanged a look. If the running thesis was that Juan Esteban Molina was the man behind the theft of the sword, then having white men kill Jacob Hobson didn't factor into the equation easily.

Hobson groaned again. He clutched at his midsection. Naomi began openly weeping.

"Did you recognize them?" Carter pressed.

Hobson shook no.

"Did they take anything?" Jackson asked.

Hobson's eyes traveled up to a bookcase. In a manner eerily similar to Octavia Hendrickson's own bookshelves, there was a gap where a book used to be.

Jackson walked over and fingered the space. "What was here?"

"The plans it took to infiltrate the Molina estate." More coughing followed. Hobson, still laying on his side, doubled over. The coughing led to raspy inhales of breath. Gurgling sounds followed. The way it sounded to Carter's ears, chances were good that Hobson's lungs were filling with blood and other fluid.

"Jacob!" Naomi wailed. "Jacob. Hang on. We'll get a doctor." She turned a desperate face to Carter. "Go get a doctor! Do something."

Hobson, in a final moment of clarity, reached out and clutched her arm. He gave her a reassuring smile. "There ain't nothing to do, my dear. I don't suspect I'll be seeing you in the next life, considering what I've done. I'm sorry that you had to see this." More coughing. "Just be sure to get those sons of bitches that did this to me and your father."

Naomi's mouth opened wide with surprise at Hobson's last comment. But he never saw it. His eyes glazed over and he saw no more.

The three living people said nothing for a few moments. They all honored the dead man in their own way. For Carter, it was in the form of questions that swirled in his mind. What did Hobson mean about the men getting him the way they got Gunter Hendrickson? Which men did he mean? And who besides Juan Esteban Molina was after the Aztec sword?

Those were all good questions, but for now, he needed to contact the police and get Jacob Hobson's body taken away.

❧ 15 ☙

DESPITE THE HOUR, work needed to be done. Carter and Jackson clarified no one else was still hiding out in Hobson's house, then Jackson went off to bring the sheriff and the coroner. That left Carter and Naomi alone in the house.

Carter went to a bedroom, retrieved a blanket, and covered the corpse. Even though he had never met Hobson until that evening, he still didn't need to keep laying his eyes on the dead man while he, Carter, scoured Hobson's office for clues. He searched the bookshelves, flipping open books, and finding nothing. A quick search through the drawers of the desk revealed nothing of any consequence. He found a ledger that revealed Hobson had aged out of being an enforcer for the railroad and instead was working as some sort of detective himself in town.

An idle thought passed through Carter's mind. Was all of this violence in the house a result of some local case? He replayed the conversation with Hobson and the dead man's realization that whoever killed him also took the plans he had drawn up to steal the Aztec sword in the first place.

No, this murder was connected with everything so far. Carter just had no idea why.

"What are you doing?" Naomi asked. She stood at the door, her gaze purposefully avoiding the body under the blanket.

"Seeing if there are any other clues," Carter said. His voice was soft, almost like the figure on the floor was asleep and they were merely trying not to wake him.

"Find anything?"

"Not really. He was a detective here in Houston. Did you know about that?"

Naomi shrugged. "I hadn't seen him in years. He came to Father's funeral and that was the last I saw of him. But I saw him quite a bit growing up." Her tone grew wistful as the memories wafted through her mind.

Carter closed one of the desk drawers. "Why don't you go downstairs and wait for Tom and the sheriff to return. This is liable to take a little while."

She looked at him, her eyes large and still wet from her tears. "Come to the next room. I want to show you something I found." She turned and walked down the hall.

Carter came around the desk and followed her. She went into the bedroom from which Carter had retrieved the blanket. The lamp in this room was on, its bright light filling the room. Naomi stood next to a bedside table, the drawer open. He came up beside her.

"What is it?"

She turned and looked up at him. "Hold me, please." Without waiting for his response, her arms snaked along his sides and she hugged him tightly. She placed her cheek on his chest. Carter's arms naturally embraced her and he brought him to her. He stroked the back of her head, his fingers running through her hair.

They stood there, unmoving, for a few moments.

Despite the situation that compelled her to need the closeness of another person, Carter's body couldn't help but feel the contours of Naomi's body. In the years since he had known Octavia, Carter had rarely given any notice to Naomi. She was just Octavia's daughter. Most of the time, Naomi wasn't present when Carter went to the house, and when she was, the two of them were courteous but cold. Now, Naomi was far from cold. In fact, there was a distinctive heat emanating from her.

She pulled back slightly and looked at him. "How often do you see dead men?" she whispered.

"Too often." He realized her face was nearly touching his. He felt the softness of her breath on his chin.

"Does it ever get to you?"

"It always gets to me. It's just how I cope with it that constantly changes. Sometimes, the dead man is someone close to me. Other times, it's a victim of a crime I either couldn't stop or that I have to investigate. In every time, I give the dead their due, then I bring the murderer to justice, one way or another." He smiled down at her. "And I'll do the same here."

Naomi brought her hand around and ran it along Carter's jaw line. Her thumb gently pressed on his chin. "I know you will." With little effort, she brought her lips to his. What started out as a gentle reminder of humanity and the living soon became something more primal and intense. She moaned under his mouth. A small sigh escaped him as well. He drew her even closer, drawing her up to him, pressing their bodies together. In his experience, two people who had braved death and lived wanted nothing more than to celebrate life. That wasn't quite the situation here, but he still felt the onset of a celebration.

The sound of the front door downstairs opening

changed everything. Jackson's voice was telling something —presumably the sheriff—that the body was upstairs.

Quickly, Carter and Naomi separated. No sense in having anyone else draw conclusions. Theirs had been a private, intimate moment, brought on by circumstance. She wiped her mouth and adjusted her hair. With fingertips, he also wiped his mouth and straightened his jacket and tie. When he heard Jackson start to ascend the stairs, Carter leaned in close and whispered in her ear. "Until later." He pecked her on the cheek and went to the hallway to greet Jackson.

* * *

LATER TURNED out to be much later. Not only did the sheriff—a wiry man named Deacon Lawson who honed his considerable gunfighter skills as a scout during the Indian Wars out west before settling into a more routine life in Houston—question Carter, Jackson, and Naomi for over an hour, but he called in some of his deputies to scour the Hobson house for any additional sign of the intruders. No matter what the two detectives said, Lawson was bound and determined to cross those bridges on his own. It wasn't that he didn't trust and respect the badges Carter and Jackson wore, it was just that he considered a police force bought and paid for by a corporation wasn't always on the up and up.

It was near midnight when the weary trio left the Hobson house and traveled by cab back up to the Capitol Hotel. At this time of night, few people were out and about. The sounds of saloons and dance halls could be heard wafting in the air, but on this stretch of road, it was only the sounds of the wheels traipsing over the rutted road.

Naomi sat next to Carter. Their shoulders touched. He resisted the urge to put an arm around her for fear of Jackson's reaction. The pair had an understanding when it came to the ladies they met. Each man gave the other space to pursue romance and nightly pleasures with little in the way of remonstration. Sure, there might be a little playful banter between the two, but it was basically each to their own.

And this wasn't the first time that a woman involved in one of their cases had found the allure of Calvin Carter too strong to deny. In this case, however, Jackson knew of Carter's history with Octavia, and his partner's raised eyebrows, as seen in the veil of the street lamps, said more than anything.

Carter shrugged with one shoulder and grinned.

Jackson rolled his eyes.

Before they retired to their rooms, however, the detectives needed to relay a message to their Galveston office. The nearest telegraph was a block north of the hotel. Carter talked to the cabbie and got him to go the extra distance.

"That's okay," Jackson said, hiding his smile. "I can take care of the message. Cal, why don't you see Miss Hendrickson up to her room."

Naomi smiled demurely, then noticed something up ahead. "Is the telegraph office next to the saloon?" she asked the driver.

"It is, ma'am," the cabbie said.

"Then I'll go with y'all. I could use a drink."

Jackson cantered his head at an angle. Carter replied in kind.

"What? I can't be the only one who could use a stiff drink to help ease the things I've seen tonight. And unless you boys have some liquor stashed away in your bags, I'd just as soon have my choice of drink." When neither detective said anything, Naomi nodded and settled back next to Carter.

They conducted their business first. Through the window at the telegraph office, Carter saw the night watchman sound asleep. Hard banging on the door awoke him with a start and he shuffled to the door, scratching his head and trying to tuck in his shirt before opening the door.

"We need to send a message immediately," Carter said. He stepped inside the office and flashed his badge. "I'll stay and make sure you type what I need."

After delivering the message and ensuring the night man he wouldn't say a thing, Carter accompanied Jackson and Naomi to the saloon next door. A part of Carter wondered how the night man could sleep with such a raucous room was just next door, but he realized he had been bone tired before and next to nothing could awaken him.

The saloon was of a higher class than those found along the boomtowns in the west. The San Jacinto Saloon was a solid building, two stories, with brick masonry on the first floor and a wooden structure on the second. A few lights burned in the upstairs windows and Carter needed no guesses to know what was transpiring in those rooms. The main saloon was large. Wood paneled all the walls. Paintings and sketches, all in frames, adorned most of the walls. Upon closer inspection, Carter realized they depicted scenes from the Texas Revolution a half century ago.

The bar itself was massive and occupied fully one wall on the west side. Bottles lined two shelves behind the bar, and three bartenders scurried about, filling orders and taking money. The rest of the saloon sported tables where various games of chance were being played. Most of the tables looked like poker was the game at hand, but Carter noted faro as well.

He led Naomi to the bar and sidled up next to her.

Jackson took a space on her other side. She smiled up at both of them. "It's nice to have two detectives protecting me tonight."

Jackson merely smiled. Carter tipped his hat back farther on his head. "What'll it be?"

"Tequila. Two shots." She paused a moment. "Better make it three."

Carter's eyebrows shot up. "Ain't that quite a bit to drink?"

"I need to forget what I've seen tonight," Naomi said. "Besides, you don't know how well I can hold my liquor."

When the bartender arrived, Carter ordered Naomi's three shots of tequila. The liquor wasn't normally his drink of choice, but with Naomi partaking, he relented. He ordered the same amount. Jackson settled on whiskey. Only two shots.

The bartender filled the order and took Carter's money for all of it. He hefted one of the glasses, taking in the destructive aroma of the tequila. Its golden color was a tad paler than the brandy he favored, but only a shade. "To Jacob Hobson," he intoned.

Naomi and Jackson raised their glasses and they all downed their drinks. Carter felt the warmth of the alcohol flood down his throat and into his gut. It was a pleasant sensation, one that he immediately chased with his second glass. With two inside him, he paused on the third. He turned and swept his eyes over the patrons and their activities.

Carter never envied the lives of men who were paid to enforce the rules in a place like this. He was nowhere close to the burly type needed to instill fear by the mere sight of him. Carter was a more nuanced lawman, quick with his brain to compensate for the slightly slower draw. Jackson was a far better gunsmith than he was, a fact that his partner reminded Carter of often.

Across the bar, a lady, clad in the seductive dress meant to inspire men to part with their money, let out a small shout. The sound got Naomi's attention as well as Carter's. A man, scraggly beard and a beat-up hat with a dent in the crown, was tugging on the lady's arm. The appearance of irritation gradually morphed into outright pain. No one else seemed to notice the woman's distress. Or, if they did, no one cared.

Naomi leaned off the bar and started straight to the woman in distress. She grabbed handfuls of her skirt fabric to make the progress easier. Carter, surprised by Naomi's sudden flight, made a move to follow her. Jackson shot out a hand and stopped him.

"Let's see what she does," he said. "We're right here if she needs us. Remember: she didn't ask for our help."

Carter nodded slowly. "This should be good."

They couldn't hear what Naomi said to the prostitute when she neared the man and the lady, but the woman's face brightened at the prospect of a distraction. She took the opportunity of Naomi's arrival to yank her arm free from the man's grip. With a huff, the whore scurried away, rubbing her arm.

The man, however, was more than irritated. He raised his voice, but what he said was unintelligible over the din. He made to stand, but Naomi forced him back into his seat. One of her hands moved to the man's side while the other was placed on the table in front of the man. This enabled Naomi to lean in close to him. It might have been his imagination but Carter could have sworn he saw the glint of something metal in the hand that was situated on the man's side.

Naomi kept talking to the man. Carter didn't see her

move her hand at the man's side, but he definitely noticed the man wince in pain.

"I think she's got a knife on him," Carter said.

"Yup." Jackson continued to stare at Naomi. "And it appears she knows how to handle it. I don't think she's as naive as she makes herself out to be." He turned and looked at Carter. "You best be careful."

Carter said nothing. He took the warning for what it was, but there was a part of him that grew more excited at the prospect of a woman like Naomi in his bed.

In a few moments, she returned. Her face was still screwed up with anger. She made a beeline for the bar and her two unfinished drinks. In quick succession, she downed both.

"I saw your father's knife in your bag," Carter said. "I didn't realize you had another."

She smiled dismissively. "It never hurts a woman to carry around a weapon." Her hand disappeared into the folds of her dress. When she withdrew it, a small knife, about four inches long with a smooth wooden handle that appeared to be ebony. Engraved along the side of the blade were the initials "NLH."

"That's a fine looking blade," Jackson commented. "May I?"

Naomi handed it to him. Jackson hefted the blade in his hand, moving it around. "Nice. Light." He scrapped his thumb crossways along the blade. "And sharp as all get out." He handed it back to her. "That'll do some damage."

"All it needs it to do is make a man think twice about either attacking me or chasing me. If he's dumb enough to go after me after I've cut him, well, it's his neck on the line."

Carter arched an eyebrow at the comment. "What's the 'L' stand for?"

"My middle name." She sighed heavily. "I'm ready for bed. Let's go."

Quickly, Carter and Jackson finished their drinks and escorted Naomi back to the Capitol Hotel. They climbed the stairs to the fourth floor and gingerly walked down the hallway to their rooms. Naomi's room was the farthest away. Carter's was the first. When he stopped at his room, Jackson kept moving to his. Naomi stopped as well. She turned to Jackson.

"I'm sure you'll be discrete in your report, Detective Jackson, when it comes to writing about tonight. But after all that I've seen tonight, there's a little more that I want than just alcohol." She grabbed Carter's arm. "And Calvin here is going to give it to me."

Carter was a romantic man. He enjoyed the pursuit almost as much as the conquests he had over the years. But few women were as direct as Naomi. And it excited him.

He caught sight of Jackson in the dim light of the hallway. He smirked.

"Be sure to get some rest," Jackson said. He slipped the key into the lock of his room and stepped inside.

Carter fumbled for the key to his room.

"You'd better hurry, Detective," Naomi said. She stood on her tiptoes and took his ear into her mouth. She ran her tongue up and down the lobe. "When I want something, I want it right now."

Carter shoved the key into the lock, turned it, and opened the door. They nearly spilled into the room and onto the floor. He reached out a hand and caught the door frame. His other arm wrapped around her, steadying them both. Naomi ended up under him, almost as if they were dancing and he dipped her. She pivoted in his embrace to face him. She reached up and kissed him, hard and with much more passion than before. Where their first kiss in the Hobson home might have been borne out of mourning, this kiss was wholly formed by passion.

"Close that damn door," she commanded after she pulled away and stood upright. She turned and walked to the bed. "And then help me out of this dress. I want to show you something."

Carter did as he was commanded.

✎ 16 ✎

THE NEXT MORNING, Carter woke surprisingly rested. Sure, he hadn't gotten as much sleep as he might've wanted, but the deep sleep that he experienced after being with Naomi made up for it. Their lovemaking had been passionate and direct. Carter had realized he didn't have to seduce her. In fact, she was seducing him. But even at that, there was little in the way of seducing. The sex was rather matter-of-fact. Not bad by any stretch of the imagination, but he didn't get any deep emotion out of the saturation.

Jackson appeared well rested over breakfast in the hotel dining room. He proceeded Carter and Naomi by a few minutes and secured a table in the far corner. The room was nice and formal, with white tablecloths and white plates and cups. He brought the steaming cup of coffee to his lips as Carter and Naomi arrived.

In another of their pre-arranged agreements, Jackson said nothing about the romantic assignation from the previous evening. He greeted Naomi as he did the first time he met her. To Carter, Jackson merely nodded. No jokes other than a raised eyebrow.

"Good morning, Tom," Carter said. "Have you ordered yet?"

"Waiting on y'all, but I heard the bacon is the best in the city."

A waiter arrived and brought coffee for Carter and Naomi. "Well, then, bacon and eggs it is."

They dined and made small talk. Truth be told, the conversation was a tad awkward. Carter never relayed the details of his romantic trysts with Jackson, but there was something about Naomi that nagged at him. Perhaps it was the urgency of the lovemaking from last night, perhaps it was something else. He wasn't going to give details to Jackson, but Carter wanted a few minutes alone with his partner to talk shop.

He got that wish after breakfast when they went upstairs to grab their bags for the cab ride back to the station. Carter, after years of practice, was ready at a moment's notice. Jackson was, too, so they stood in the foyer of the hotel, looking out onto Main Street. The traffic was already busy, with wagons, horses, and pedestrians scurrying back and forth, ready to tackle a new day.

"Something bothering you?" Jackson asked.

Carter screwed up his face. "A little."

"What, did she not satisfy you," Jackson said, a little jokiness in his voice.

"No, not that. But it was rather direct. Impersonal almost. She knew what she wanted and pretty much drove the entire night."

Jackson grunted. "I heard part of the driving. So, what's wrong?"

Carter shook his head. "I'm not sure I can put a finger on it yet."

"Put a finger on what?" Naomi said. She had walked up to the detectives. She held her bag in her hand.

Carter reached out and plucked it from her. "On what this case hinges on. There's always a focal point. We just haven't found it yet."

"It's the sword," she said. "That's all that matters. Everything that's happened, including Hobson's death, is because some bastard stole my father's sword. It's pretty straightforward, don't you think?"

"Yeah, I get that," Carter said, "but who?"

"Molina," Naomi said, matter-of-factly. "Your boss sent some men down to Laredo to catch the killer if he went that way. We're going to Galveston and see if we can stop it here." She brushed passed both men and stepped out of the hotel. She raised her hand to signal a cab, then turned back to them. "With all of your wishy-washy nature, Calvin, I might as well have come here myself."

Few things wounded Carter's pride more than questioning his talent, either as an actor or as a detective. As soon as her words hit him, a fire lit inside his gut. He moved toward her, stopping only a few feet from her. "Now listen here, Naomi. I never understood why you needed to tag along. I don't get it, but there it is. But we're the detectives, and we know how to pursue this case. Colonel Moore assigned this case to us and we're going to see it through. Now, I'll have no more of you questioning our capabilities or our drive to see it through to the end."

The cab arrived, slowed, and came to a halt. Without ceremony, Carter dropped Naomi's bag to the ground. "Get your own damn bag." He reached up, opened the door of the cab, and climbed inside.

Jackson stepped forward and picked up her bag. With a twinkle in his eye, he said, "Perhaps he should have gotten more sleep."

* * *

UNION STATION in Galveston was on the north side of the island, facing Galveston Bay. The island mirrored the coast-line of Texas, angling from the southwest to the northeast. The Gulf of Mexico lapped gently on the island's southern side while the business district was across the island on the north side.

The salt air carried with it a freshness rarely received from land. The humidity was heavier, but Carter was used to it. The aromas of dirt, oil, and the steam that heated everything were strong in the station, which turned out to be quite the busy hub of activity. Travelers to and from the island were sitting and waiting for the next train. Newcomers like Carter, Jackson, and Naomi flooded into the depot, many looking up at the high ceiling and windows letting in the morning light. Some of the passengers from the Houston train meandered, not knowing which way to go for their next destination. Carter knew, having been to Galveston many times, and he led his trio out the door and onto the street.

He gave serious thought to directing Naomi to take their bags and check into either the New Orleans or Buffalo Hotel, but he assumed she would rebuff him. Besides, the railroad offices were situated between the depot and the hotels so it didn't matter.

The trip down to Galveston had been somewhat tense, with Jackson taking up the talking duties with Naomi. Carter buried himself in his Jules Verne novel, but rarely read any of the words. He kept mulling over what was bothering him. The point, whatever it was, remained elusive.

The offices of the railroad were located on Avenue B, sometimes called the Strand. The depot sat on Avenue A, or Water Street on account of its proximity to the bay. Carter swept his gaze over the bustle of Water Street. A busy thoroughfare, Water Street was thick with businessmen and travelers. Being one of the largest cities in Texas, Galveston rarely slept at night and was constantly busy in the day. The street teemed with people and animals and wagons and cabs. Irritated that he didn't see an empty cab right out in front of the doorway, Carter noted a cabbie on the other side of the street and down half a block.

He started moving and only barely threw "I'll be right back with a cab" over his shoulder at Jackson. He never heard his partner's response.

Carter knew he could have merely whistled for the cabbie, but the noise around the depot proved quite loud. The departing train had already signaled it was ready to go with a loud shriek of its horn. Men and boys hawked various goods for sale. Carter passed a paperboy and exchanged a coin for a paper. He tucked it under his arm as he kept walking along the street.

Truth was he wanted to get away from Naomi for a little while. It wasn't as if she was going to be content sitting in a hotel room waiting for Carter and Jackson to do their jobs. No, she wanted to be in the middle of everything, and in the middle she was.

He was so deep in thought, eyes down, staring at the ground, that he never saw the men who reached out and grabbed his shoulders and yanked him into a small alley. He lost his balance and had to flail his arms and spread his legs so as not to fall to the muddy ground. His bag was ripped from his fingers and thrown out of reach. The man who still gripped Carter's jacket pulled harder, slamming Carter's back against a brick wall.

"Coming to Galveston was a bad idea, you lousy detective," were the words one man uttered. "Now it's gonna cost you." The next moment, another man appeared in front of the detective, his shadow darkening Carter's sight. He never saw the fist that punched him in the gut nor the second one that struck him on the jaw.

The man holding Carter's jacket let go at that instant and the detective fell alongside the wall. One knee was on the ground, but his hands stopped him from hitting the ground completely. He knew from past experience—even yesterday with Bobby Anders—that to get on the ground was to lose the battle. He blinked rapidly, trying to clear the stars from his vision. He couldn't catch his breath, and whatever breath creeped in his lungs seemed to do so at a snail's pace. He wondered if Jackson had seen the attack, but quickly dismissed the idea. No matter what, the next few seconds would be Carter alone against these assailants. He had to deal with it now.

Both men crowded around him. Carter, still staring down, now on all fours, counted the legs. Four legs became six as a third man entered the picture. They were on Carter's right, and to his left was the wall. Carter saw one of the men bring his boot back to kick him in the face. As the boot came forward, Carter dropped face first to the ground. The boot sailed over his head, catching the owlhoot off guard and off balance. Carter shot out his right hand, clutched the boot of the man who tried to kick him, and pulled hard. The man further lost his balance and fell on his ass in a muddy puddle.

With his back to the wall, Carter couldn't roll away from the men, but he could do the unexpected and roll toward them. He did, ending up on his back. The move caught them unawares and they backed up a few paces to avoid Carter knocking them over, their hands, still balled into fists, at their sides.

With a pivot and without losing eye contact with the men, Carter got to his knees. The looks on the men's faces no longer conveyed angered confidence. Now, it was pure terror, for Carter's Colt was now in his grip.

It was a good thing, too. The full complement of oxygen hadn't returned to Carter's lungs. The smack on the jaw must have been harder than he realized for stars wavered in his vision. He tried to blink them away, but darkness now settled on the edges of his sight. He wobbled at the suddenness of being upright. The owlhoots who jumped him took that opportunity not to further attack an armed man, but to flee. They scurried down the alley and disappeared around a corner.

From the closer end of the alley, Jackson rounded a corner. He assessed Carter's situation and ran straight for him.

"You okay?"

Carter nodded. He reached out for the steadying arm of Jackson as his partner helped him to his feet. He stood for a moment, gasping, willing his lungs to fill faster. He had just started breathing steadily when Naomi arrived. She sat in an open air cab. The look of fear on her face was a nice thing to see.

"Oh, Calvin. What happened?"

A couple more gulps of fresh air and Carter said, "They knew I was coming. Said I shouldn't have."

Under the brim of his hat, Jackson's brows furrowed. "How?"

Carter shook his head. "Don't know. But we're gonna have to move faster now."

* * *

A FEW MINUTES LATER, carrying their bags, Carter, Jackson, and Naomi entered the railroad offices. A clerk behind a desk took one look at Carter and squinted his small eyes, presumably for having someone who looked like he had been roughed up sully the office. Not wanting to delay any further, Carter flashed his badge at him. The clerk, who had greeted them as strangers, now nodded sagely and directed them to a room off to the left. Carter opened that door, walked the short hallway, and went into another, larger room.

This was the Galveston branch of the railroad detective agency. It nearly surpassed the opulence of the main Austin office, not unimaginable considering Galveston's size and importance. One might be lured into thinking a posting at the Galveston branch a cushy job. It was on the off hours, but the men who manned this office had their hands full not only with the rails but also the shipping traffic.

Four desks, arranged in a grid pattern, all facing each other, occupied most of the floor space. On each desk were stacks of papers. On the far wall, under the window, were stacks of yellow telegraph paper. On one wall was a map of Galveston, enlarged so as to encompass the busiest parts of the island.

A young man, blonde like Jackson, looked up as the trio entered the room. The agent had removed his jacket and hung it on the back of a chair. His long sleeves were rolled up to the elbow, the tie loosened enough to allow his neck to get some air. The jawline was severe, and a small scar, about two inches long, traced a line across the man's cheek. When the agent spoke, his voice came across as educated but direct.

"Calvin Carter?" the agent said.

Carter, the memory of his thrashing still vivid in his memory, momentarily hesitated. "You're an agent, right?"

The man frowned. The more Carter studied him, the more he realized the agent was a few years his senior. "Why of course I am. Why else would I be here." He extended his hand. "Victor Olmsted."

The name registered in Carter's memory as the station head of the Galveston field office. He came around a desk and clasped Olmsted's hand. It was dry and the muscles underneath taut.

Olmsted took note of the bruise on Carter's cheek. "What happened?"

"The Galveston welcoming committee got to me first." He worked his jaw back and forth. "I don't particularly care for the way they say hello." He laughed dryly, letting Olmsted know it was joke.

"You must be Thomas Jackson," Olmsted said. He shook Jackson's hand, but his eyes were already focused on Naomi. "And who might you be?"

"Naomi Hendrickson." She let Olmsted take her hand in his and bring it to his mouth. It annoyed Carter that she now seemed to play the dazzled young heiress.

"Ah, yes. The daughter of one Octavia Hendrickson. It's her sword we're to be on the lookout for, yes?"

"Yes," Carter said. He dropped his bag on the floor and took a seat on the desk next to Olmsted's. "Moore should have wired you. Any news on that front?"

The mere whiff of irritation passed over Olmsted's face at the prospect of being ordered around in his own office, but professionalism triumphed and he got to business. As if quoting the orders, he intoned, "Be on the lookout for any passenger or manifest directly to Mexico from Galveston. Particularly note any shipment of crates longer than three feet or bags of roughly the same size." He shuffled through the piles of paper on his desk until he brought out a telegram and put it on top of everything else. "There it is." He sighed and ran his fingers through his hair. "I've already got men out in the field and the docks keeping a sharp eye out. But the request is nearly impossible. Even with the locals we employ as extra sets of eyes, we can't see every-thing. And we can't go around to the local customs officials asking either."

"Why?" Naomi asked. She had taken a seat behind the far desk. Jackson merely leaned against the wall, his arms folded over his chest.

"Because as much as we'd like to think customs officials are officers of the law, they are human and susceptible to bribes. Plus, we don't always know which ones are on Grummon's payroll. Then there's the other disadvantage."

"What's that?" Jackson asked. His face conveyed an attitude that nothing better get in his way.

Olmstead ran his hands across his body. "We all look like detectives. Admit it: there's a certain look that a lawman has that's hard to disguise."

A smile formed on Carter's face.

Jackson uncrossed his arms. "Cal, what are you thinking?"

Carter pointed to Naomi. "Take her either to the hotel and leave her there or have her show you where our third mystery man lives and get him to talk."

"And in the meantime?" Jackson proved.

"In the meantime, I'll have a look at the latest manifests the customs agents have."

Olmstead looked at Carter in surprise. "How do you propose to do that?"

"By becoming one of them."

❧ 17 ❧

IN ALL OF Carter's time as an actor, he learned that the barest minimum makeup could be used to alter a person's appearance, and if accompanied by some sort of physical characteristic, an actor could fully become someone else. So when he emerged from the next room, still dressed in his regular suit, but sporting both a goatee on his face as well as a scar that closely resembled Olmstead's, he made a grand entrance.

"Who are you supposed to be?" Jackson asked. He had finally taken a seat and was reading through some reports. Naomi had excused herself and gone to the ladies room. Olmstead sat at his desk and shuffled through his papers.

"Ah am Randall Daley, customs agent from Georgia, in town for an inspection." Carter spoke with an exaggerated Southern accent typical of Georgia, pronouncing the 'I' as 'ah.' "Ah came all the way from Washington to supervise and see how well the good folks in Galveston are doing their jobs."

Carter walked over to Jackson, throwing in a particular

gait in his step. He kept his body fully erect, which gave off an air of aristocracy.

Olmstead stared in disbelief. "I've heard tales of your tendency toward the theatric, but I had never seen it in person." He squinted. "That's really you, Carter?"

"No, suh," Carter replied, staying character. "I am Randall Daley. Now tell me, which building might I go to in order to learn about ship manifests?"

* * *

GALVESTON SPORTED MORE than one customs house. The more permanent structure was located up on 20th Street and Avenue E, or Post Office Street. That building was standalone, and built specifically for its purpose. Closer to the waterfront, however, was a customs office that shared a building with a bank and a cotton sampler. Across the street from this smaller office was a cigar shop. Carter ducked inside and purchased a couple of different types of cigars, ones specially made in Cuba. If he was going to play the part of Randall Daley, then he wanted an extra prop. He also bought a small notepad and pencil.

As he did for any job that involved sneaking into a building, Carter performed reconnaissance. In his erect stance and peculiar walk—just in case he were seen by someone inside the customs office and be remembered— Carter walked the perimeter of the building. It was a three-story structure, with a smaller fourth floor housing the water tank. The structure was brick for all three stories. A boardwalk extended on two sides of the building, the sides that faced 22nd Street and the Strand. An alley was on the third side and a fenced-in area faced the fourth. Inside the fenced area was a pile of coal, ready to be delivered into the building when needed.

In previous cases when he had sneaked inside a building, being direct often proved the best course of action. He was prepared, however, for the possibility of stealth and had purchased a length of rope and a metal hook from a hardware store along the way. The rope was now coiled in a small loop and tucked inside his jacket and hung around his shoulder holster. The likelihood of having to draw his weapon was small, even considering the beating he had received. Whomever knew he was here in town had no clue of his next move, so he felt confident that he could still draw his weapon if necessary, despite the rope covering his gun. The hook was fastened on the back of his belt and he felt it move as he walked.

The Strand was busy with people, many of them congregating around the front door and the covered boardwalk. Carter smiled at the people, tipping his hat to the ladies, and nodding to the gentlemen. All sorts of people were present, some giving him odd looks as he pushed through the throng and entered the office. It turned out that many of those people were waiting to get into the bank, for the foyer of the office was not as crowded. Making a quick survey of the entryway, Carter spied the stairs with a sign that led to the customs office. Still with his gait, he strolled across the floor and ascended the stairs. The din of people talking grew steadily quieter. The sliding of his shoes on each step sounded louder to his ears and a line of sweat formed on his brow. With fewer people around, the chances of him being successful grew more difficult.

Not that he wasn't up to the challenge. It had been a few months since last he performed on stage, and the previous few cases hadn't required any disguises. So he considered this something of a one-man performance.

At the top of the stairs was a short hallway. One side led to a long counter, much like a bank. Four men, seated behind the counter, were dealing with four different lines of people, all needing to claim something or whatever one did with a customs official. The other side had a door that evidently led to the offices. He took a look at the lines of people and figured someone of "Randall Daley's" stature wouldn't stand in line for an inspection. Carter raised his chin and boldly strode to the office door.

Carter put one of the cigars in his mouth, lit it, threw the match on the floor, and barged into the inner office.

A clerk looked up, his eyes wide, Carter clearly having startled him. The wide eyes gradually narrowed and his brow furrowed. He have stood. "I'm sorry, sir, but this office is off limits…"

"It is off limits to the general public," Carter intoned, dragging out his Southern accent," but I am far from the general public." He stopped, clipped his heels together, and bowed at the neck and shoulders. "My name is Randall Daley and I am here to inspect your operation and see how efficiently—or inefficiently as the case may be—your operation is run." He puffed on the cigar, letting the plumes of smoke waft in front of his face. Despite the situation, the cigar tasted quite good. He would have to buy more before he left the city.

The clerk completely stood now behind his desk. "I'm afraid you are mistaken, sir. We are not due for another inspection for three more months."

"Quite right, which is why I'm here. The boys back in Washington thought it a good idea to pop in at irregular intervals, between the normal inspections, to check in on how all of its agents are doing." He smiled around the cigar. "Today is y'all's lucky day."

Clearly flustered, the clerk nonetheless had the wherewithal to ask for supporting documentation. Carter was prepared. Not only did he carry about his make-up kit full of tools of the actor's trade, but he carried a few standard types of documents, blank except for the name Carter planned on using. A year or so ago, he had consistently used the same alias in different towns. Unfortunately for him, word got around that one Sylvester McBride wasn't who he said he was and Carter barely got out from under a rabid throng of townsfolk with only a few bruises.

Carter handed over the forged documents. To distract the clerk, Carter asked his name.

"Brady."

"Brady what? Is that your family name or your birth name?"

Brady looked up, shifting his gaze from Carter to the paper. "That's my last name. Ike is my given name."

Carter stretched out his hand and snatched his forged documents from Roberts's hands. "Well, Mister Ike Brady, first I need to see the manifests for all ships that left port bound for Mexico, say, in the last two weeks." Carter didn't want to tip his hand on his true search. Had he asked for just the last day, Brady might've started asking why the search was so narrow.

Instead of complying with Carter's request, Brady made no move to comply.

To speed up the process, Carter pulled out his pocket watch, flipped open the turnip, and made tick-tock sounds with his mouth. "I know your normal day-to-day routine doesn't involve requests like this, but if Mister Mallory were to come down here and inspect his shipping lines, woe be the man who doesn't step lively." Carter specifically namedropped Charles H. Mallory, the owner of C. H. Mallory and Company out of New York. He was one of the top shippers in Galveston, even possessing his own wharves.

Brady gulped and his eyes went wide again. "The manifests are this way, sir. Please follow me." The clerk came around his desk and made his way to another interior door.

Carter snapped his watch closed, pocketed it in his vest, and followed.

The moment before Brady opened the door, a small breeze wafted into the office from the open window. Along with the sea air and the odor of the coal stacked outside, another distinctive aroma met his nose.

The smell of something burning.

WITH A LITTLE WHIMPER OF CONCERN, Brady threw open the door. He, as well as Carter, feared the worst.

"What the hell?" Brady said under his breath.

Carter craned his neck to see the interior room. Papers were scattered everywhere, over the desk, on the taller cabinets up against the wall, and on the floor. Many of the sheets of paper blew in the breeze from the open window. Nothing, however, appeared to be burning.

That was a good thing.

But Carter's eyes moved to the open window. What he saw surprised him.

A thin rope dangled from an unseen perch on the roof. And the rope was burning.

"What the hell?" Brady said again as Carter roughly shoved him aside and charged to the window. He stuck his head out and looked up to the roof. There, secured over the lip of the roof, was a gleaming iron hook. Carter turned and looked to the ground. A figure, wearing black pants and a black jacket under an inverness coat, sprinted across the fenced in area and toward the back alley. The face was covered by a large hood and short-brimmed hat.

Carter took one look at the burning rope and knew he

couldn't use it to scale down the side of the building. Being on the second floor, however, wasn't too far off the ground. Without a second thought, Carter swung his legs over the window sill.

"What are you doing?" Brady gasped.

"Following your thief," Carter muttered, still maintaining the Georgia accent. He hooked a thumb over his shoulder. "See if you can tell what's missing."

"Sir?"

Carter swirled around and gave Brady a last, furious look. "You've just been robbed. Find out what he took." With that, Carter slid off the sill and plummeted to the ground.

He hit the ground and rolled with the impact. Without hardly breaking his momentum, Carter sprang to his feet and dashed after the Hook Thief. As his arms pumped like a steam engine's pistons, he realized he had just seen the Hook Thief in person. Was Carter the first lawman to stake that claim? He hadn't caught a glimpse of the face, but he was damn sure going to catch the guy.

The Hook Thief had run south along the back alley. Carter passed into the alley just as he saw the Thief turn right, heading to the railroad depot and the wharves. Carter's mind flashed an image of him disembarking from the train and walking through the depot an hour ago. If the streets of Galveston were crowded, the depots and wharves were even more so. If the Thief managed to get to the wharves before Carter could catch him, he would likely vanish.

Remembering how he plowed into a pedestrian back in Austin, Carter slowed only slightly as he burst out of the alley. He didn't take as sharp a turn as he did before, instead rushing out into the street.

And in front of an oncoming cab.

The horse was startled. It stopped nearly dead in its tracks. The poor cabbie fell forward, but he was able to catch himself before he toppled head over heels to the ground and under his horse's hooves. He blasted a curse at Carter, but the detective was almost out of earshot and gave it no extra thoughts.

The Hook Thief may have worn the inverness to conceal his identity when sneaking into the customs house, but the caped outer garment, flapping in the wind, was like a beacon for Carter. The Thief had crossed Avenue A and into the wharf area beyond the tracks. Luck was against Carter. The howling whistle of a train and the screeching of metal on metal told Carter a train was slowly lumbering away from the depot. The next instant, he saw the front of the engine emerge from the depot and creep along the tracks. Beyond the train, the Hook Thief kept running.

Carter looked at the distance between himself and the rails and knew instinctively he couldn't make it ahead of the train. There was no way. No matter how fast he ran or how slow the train moved, it would soon block his path. And the Thief would escape again.

So Carter devised a scheme he had heard about from the other detectives when they were all shooting the bull together in saloons back in Austin. Carter had never tried it, but a particularly lean detective by the name of Luke Selby had bragged that he was able to time the movements of a train and leap through the gap between the tinder and the first car. Most of the men had thought him a fool, but Carter had been fascinated.

Later that night, Carter had taken Selby aside and asked specifics. Selby had told Carter that the trick to the entire stunt was to leap through the gap with a little forward motion so as not to be clipped by the passenger car. "Oh, and have a mighty good reason for doing this," Selby had said, "because if you miss, you'll get sliced by the wheels." Carter had asked about Selby's reason and the other detective told him about nabbing a particularly nasty owlhoot that had enjoyed killing. "So you got him?" Carter had asked. "Damn straight I did," Selby had responded.

Carter saw the speed of the train and started to mimic the forward motion, angling himself as he ran to match the speed. Damn, but the gap between the tinder and the passenger car looked small. But if he had any chance of catching the Hook Thief, extraordinary measures would have to be deployed.

Thankfully, most of the pedestrians didn't particularly enjoy getting hissing steam blasted in their faces and his path to the tracks was clear. The closer he got in the next two seconds, he started to have second thoughts. What if he missed? No, he told himself, he wouldn't miss.

Carter planted his right leg and sprang up into the air. He vaulted the link between the tinder and the first passenger car. He passed by the car so close that he could see the wide eyes of the first passengers, a young girl and boy. Then they were behind him. His landing was less than perfect. He stumbled, flailed his arms, couldn't catch his balance, then, with forward momentum continuing, righted himself. He grinned. He couldn't wait to tell Jackson about this one.

The last time Carter saw the Hook Thief, the bandit was heading out onto the wharf behind the tracks thirty yards ahead, the waves of Galveston Bay lapped against the sturdy piers. If the Thief went to Carter's right, it was mostly open area before the next set of wharves and ware-houses offered him shelter. So Carter turned left.

Only a narrow walkway separated the larger wharf from the land where the train depot was located. Beyond that were the warehouses of the Mallory shipping line. The structures and loading docks there were numerous enough that in the time it took Carter to search the area or call for a sweep from the police, the Hook Thief could merely slip away. This time, luck was with Carter. He caught a glimpse of a flapping black cloak darting behind a pile of lumber. The detectives changed course and made a beeline straight for the lumber pile.

When he got there, he didn't slow. He charged out and readied for a fight. What he saw chagrined him. In front of him were the tall warehouses, three of them, with all their doors open. Men scurried about, unloading and loading. They kept their heads down and their eyes to their work. None of them, however, seemed to have seen anything untoward.

Carter rushed up to a group of men carrying a large, heavy crate. They didn't even turn and look his way.

"Hey, did y'all see a man run through here? Wearing black." When he got no response, Carter did something he rarely did. He swept his jacket aside, fished out his badge wallet, and flashed the tin at the workers. "Railroad detective. I'm hunting for that man. Where did he go?"

All of the men were burly, but one was larger than the rest. "The man you want is down that way." He head nodded to the end of the wharf near where crates were stacked three high waiting to be unloaded.

Carter put his wallet back in his pocket. "Thanks," he said, over his shoulder as he started to run. He rushed pass other men working the docks, some holding the bridle of horses, leading them to the loading area. Few of the men gave Carter much more than a passing glance. It was as if a couple of men running along the pier and wharves were an everyday occurrence.

Slowing when he got to the edge of the one warehouse, Carter pushed past the corner. Immediately, three gunshots rang out. The wood next to Carter's face exploded into thin shards, some of them slicing into his face. He sprang backwards, putting the warehouse in between him and the shooter. Carter didn't get a chance to see from where the shots came, but he turned around and spied a door that led into the warehouse. Perhaps he could circle around the Thief and catch him unawares.

Carter pulled out his gun and held it up by his ear. He needed to convince the Thief he, Carter, was still at this location. He thrust his arm around the corner of the warehouse and triggered once. Withdrawing his arm, Carter turned and raced to the door. He opened it and plunged himself into the dim murkiness of the warehouse interior.

Despite many of the doors being opened, the windows high above were coated with grime. The shafts of sunlight only penetrated so far. Beyond that, the interior was in twilight.

Carter scurried between two stacks of crates. The wood smelled new, as did the paint used to stencil the final destination. He saw New Orleans, New York, and Vera Cruz. An idea trickled into his mind, but he pushed it aside for the time being.

The soles of his shoes scuffed along the cement floor. The sound almost died considering the closeness of the crates. He brought his gun up to his ear, pressed his back against the side of a crate, and readied himself to turn and face what he expected to be a window with a clear view of the Hook Thief's position.

He turned and discovered something highly unexpected.

A line of five men, all holding pistols or rifles, stood between Carter and the window. They all appeared rough characters, all taking nothing from nobody. Beyond them,

Carter saw a flash of black and realized the Hook Thief was escaping.

Carter held his hands up, barrel of his Colt pointed up at the ceiling. "My mistake, gentlemen," Carter said. "Railroad detective. I'm chasing a thief."

"Detective or not," the man in the middle said, "nobody fires any weapons on my docks without me knowing about it."

Carter frowned. "I'm on official business and the thief just got away." He pointed out the window.

The man in the middle raised the pistol and thumbed back the hammer. "Drop your gun or I drop you."

Carter realized he was too far away from the edge of the crate to duck for cover. He was incensed that the Hook Thief was getting away, but he also realized he had no choice.

Slowly, he bent down, kept eye contact with the middle man, and placed his gun on the ground. He stood up again, hands at his sides. "And who might you be?"

The man scowled, screwing up his face and emphasizing his nose which had been broken sometime in the past. The bowler hat sat atop his head and a thatch of dark hair laced with gray showed underneath. A collarless striped shirt was under a red vest, buttoned and displaying a gold watch chain. The dark pants were nice but worn at the knees. Thick work boots completed the ensemble. On his hip, the man wore a black gun belt and holster.

"If you're a railroad dick, how is it you don't know the name Isaiah Grummon.

﷼ 18 ﷼

THE LONGER CARTER stood in the warehouse floor, surrounded on one side by unmoving crates and on the other by Grummon and his men, the more he wondered when some other party might come investigate the gunshots that sounded a few minutes before. But Carter heard no whistles or shouts of other lawmen coming to the wharf and warehouse and resolved himself to figure a way out of this mess on his own.

With his hands still open-palmed to Grummon, Carter said, "You do realize I'm a badge toter, right?"

A muscle in Grummon's cheek twitched. He followed that up with, "You realize I can lock you in a crate, put that crate on a boat, drop you into the Gulf, and no one would be the wiser, right." He smiled, yellowed teeth under dry gums.

Carter shrugged that he understood. "So, now what? My partner and my detective agency know I'm here. Sooner or later, they'll come looking for me."

Grummon raised his eyebrows. "Will they now?" He lowered his pistol and holstered it. He cracked the knuckles of his gun hand, one at a time, then proceeded to do the same thing to the other hand. "Kick yer gun this way."

"I can't do that," Carter replied. "It belonged to my father. How do I know one of your goons won't confiscate it or toss it into the bay?"

Grummon regarded Carter for a moment before speaking. At a signal, his men lowered their guns. They didn't return their weapons to holsters, but at least the deadly barrels weren't pointed at Carter's face.

"Fair enough," Grummon said. "But if you go for it, we'll have no recourse other than to shoot you."

"Fair enough," Carter replied. "What now?"

Walking over to where Carter's gun lay on the floor, Grummon picked up the pistol and inspected it. He ejected the cylinder, spinning it. He pulled back the hammer and worked the action. "Nice feel. Not too much pressure to fire a bullet."

"I find it's a good idea to shoot at someone who's shooting at you in as efficient a way as possible."

The wharf boss ran thick fingers over the worn cherry wood of the butt. "Nice finish." He found the insignia Carter's father had specially commissioned. It was a silver seal, about the size of a dime. On the seal was the image of a drama mask. This mask was smiling. Another seal, on the other side of the handle, also in silver, depicted the Greek mask of tragedy. "What are these?"

Carter inhaled, happy for the moment to talk about something other than his predicament. "Those are the Greek masks representing tragedy and comedy in drama. The comedy mask is historically associated with Thalia, the Greek muse of comedy. Melpomene, the muse of tragedy, is the sad face. Back in the Greek days, the actors would often wear masks as props. They would assume a role often associated with the masks. There used to be more, but over time, only comedy and tragedy survived."

Grummon pursed his lips, clearly impressed with Carter's little recitation. "That's a bit odd for a detective to have on his gun."

Sighing, Carter nodded. "I agree. My father gave them to me before he was killed. They used to be cufflinks, but after I brought my father's killer to justice and became a railroad detective, I had them refashioned for the gun handles."

"But why the masks?" Grummon persisted.

"Because I used to be an actor."

A few of Grummon's men chuckled. Their boss didn't. "An actor? How the hell does a man go from being an actor to being a detective who kills people?"

"I only kill when there's no choice." Carter shifted his feet, the movement bringing twitches from the gang. "As I said, I brought my father's killer to justice. After that, I tried my hand at detecting. It seemed I had multiple talents." Carter grinned.

Grummon's brows were still furrowed. "What's your name?"

"Calvin Carter."

Slowly, Grummon's mouth opened. "Calvin Carter? The actor who solved the Christmas Carol murder?"

Carter thought back to one of the cases he had solved that wasn't under the jurisdiction of the railroad's detective agency. "One and the same. I hope there's not another Calvin Carter running around." He stopped and it was Carter's turn to frown. "Wait, you know about that?"

Now, it was Grummon's turn to smile. "Mister Carter, there are few things in this town I don't know about."

Inspiration struck and Carter pressed his momentary yet incredulous goodwill. "How much do you know about what is shipped down to Mexico? It's part of my case and why I was, um, shooting in your warehouse."

Grummon's eyes flinched with the memory. "If I know most of what goes on in this town, I know everything about the wharves. I keep things running smoothly."

Carter's mind flashed to some of the things he had read about Grummon's tactics. If it was sweat and blood that helped the railroads run on time, then he would have to add murder and extortion to the list of things used to ensure the boats shipped on time.

"Smuggling," Carter blurted. "What I'm talking about it smuggling."

A slow smile formed on Grummon's face. "Again, Mister Carter, you're talking about things I already know about. I'm not sure how much I should say to a man in a badge…" He stopped. "Say, how do I know you're not just acting a part?"

Carter pointed to his jacket. "My bona fides are in my jacket pocket. I can get them or you can?" When Grummon gave him the stink eye, Carter said, "You're boys'll make quick work of me if I do anything odd." At a nod from Grummon, Carter reached inside his pocket, withdrew his wallet badge, and handed it over to the wharf boss.

Grummon inspected the badge and the papers. "Nice badge. Almost looks like a prop." He handed it back to Carter. "So what's going on that you're shooting on my wharves?"

Carter slipped the wallet back into his pocket. "Speaking of that, why didn't lawmen come running when they heard the shots?"

"What shots?" Grummon was deadly serious.

Frowning, Carter gestured outside the window. "The shots I fired at the thief, and he back at me?"

Grummon slowly shook his head. "I didn't hear

anything. Boys, y'all hear anything?" He turned and caught them shaking their heads. "Must have been hearing things, Mister Carter. There were no shots fired here."

Confusion melted into realization for Carter. Grummon controlled the docks to such an extent that men could open fire on them and the law would stay away. That was power.

"Of course, my mistake. Never mind who I was chasing…actually, I wasn't chasing, was I?" At the nod from Grummon, Carter continued. "But I'm looking for some stolen property that was likely smuggled out of here to Mexico."

Again, Grummon's smile broadened. "Mister Carter, between you, me, and these crates, there's a lot of stuff shipped out of this town. What cargo?"

"An Aztec sword."

The warehouse grew strangely quiet at Carter's revelation. Grummon's men shifted uncomfortably. Grummon stared at Carter for so long that the detective started to feel uncomfortable, especially since the wharf boss still held Carter's gun.

Grummon wet his lips. "An Aztec sword. That's not something you hear about every day. Care to elaborate?"

Carter went through the broad strokes of the case, up to and including the theft from the customs house. When he finished, Grummon regarded the detective for a moment.

"What?" Carter said.

Grummon tapped his temple with a finger. "I see you got a head for learning and knowing things. Probably why you were able to learn all those words for your plays." He regarded Carter. "Tell you what, Mister Carter. You caught me on a happy day. Things are working smoothly today. The boats are all leaving on time and we're ahead of schedule. Plus, I like to go to the theater. If you were a regular railroad dick, you might have to be taught a lesson. Oh, who am I kidding?" With that, he plunged his fist into Carter's midsection.

The air gushed out of Carter's lungs. He fell around Grummon's arm, grabbing the other man's forearm with his hands. As he started to fall, Carter gripped Grummon's arm with more urgency. Carter went down on his right knee, which was on purpose, for it gave him leverage over the bigger man who was most likely not expecting a counterattack. Sure enough, Carter, still barely breathing, had enough wherewithal to pivot, taking Grummon's arm over his shoulder, and yanking the wharf boss over Carter's back and down to the ground.

Grummon's men stood motionless for a moment. Then they scrambled forward. Some of the men rushed around Carter to attend to their boss, two grabbed Carter, one holding each arm, and pulled the detective to his feet. Carter was still gasping for his breath and stood on wobbly legs, desperately gulping in air.

With the help of his men, Grummon stood, turned, and, to the surprise of his men, smiled at the detective. He still held Carter's gun down at his side. With his other hand, he wagged his finger.

"Did you learn that move as an actor or a detective?"

"Detective," Carter rasped.

Grummon walked over to Carter. "You impress me, Mister Carter." To his men, he said, "Let him go." He waited for his goons to release Carter's arms before continuing. "Few men get a chance to impress me with me being on the butt side. So, let's make sure you understand that I don't like to lose." With that, he swung a fist and smacked Carter in the jaw.

The fist was big and covered almost half of Carter's face. His head jerked back and he nearly lost his balance again, but he ran into one of Grummon's goons and righted himself. He stared at the floor, stars swirling in his vision. He tried to keep a smile from creasing his face. Grummon needed to do that. Carter understood and went with it. He stood, rubbing the knuckles of one hand over the bruise that was likely already forming.

"You've got a punch on you," Carter said.

"And you've got guts," the wharf boss said. "You get what happened here?"

Carter nodded.

"Good." Grummon handed Carter his gun. He waited while the detective holstered the pistol. "Okay, so you earned this. We loaded a steamer, the Poseidon, bound for Vera Cruz earlier today. There were a few crates and large bags loaded, but most of it was mail. What did this sword look like?"

Carter described it. "But I actually haven't laid eyes on it yet." His breath was coming back to him now. "That's why we're after it."

Grummon nodded. He fought back some inner struggle and laid a hand on Carter's shoulder. Not surprisingly, it felt like an anchor. "Tell you what I'm gonna do. And if word ever gets out that I did this for a lawman, I'll have to hunt you down. I'll have a little chat with the good folks over at the passenger pier. See if they saw anything. Where can I reach you?"

For a moment, Carter thought to question the wharf boss why he was aiding Carter, but he forced the thought out of his head. Evidently, among all the other things Grummon did or had done in his name, he enjoyed theater. Carter made a note to tell Jackson and rub a little salt in their lighthearted rivalry.

"We actually haven't checked in to a hotel yet."

"We?"

Carter nodded. "My partner's with me, and the

daughter of Octavia Hendrickson."

Grummon scowled. "You brought a woman into this mess? What kind of man does that?"

Carter scratched the back of his neck. "She was rather persuasive."

"You couldn't say no?"

"I couldn't say no." The pair stood silent, momentarily contemplating how difficult it was to say no to women. "Okay," Grummon finally said, "I'll send one of my representatives to the Dangiers Restaurant down on 22nd. Be there around noon."

Carter extended his hand. "Thank you."

Grummon grasped Carter's hand and held it tight. He pulled Carter close and got in his face. "This is a one-time deal, Mister Carter. I don't usually take kindly to badge-toters in my wharves. Don't think we have a relationship. We don't. I liked what you did last year and I liked your performance. Maybe I'll see another if you ever come back to Galveston and act. But I'd strongly advise you not to return to the wharves with your badge without permission. Do you understand?"

With graveness in his voice, Carter said, "I do." He nodded once and tried to withdraw his hand.

Grummon's grip tightened even more. "Are we clear?"

"We're clear."

Grummon released Carter's hand and started to walk away. He stopped, turned, and stared at Carter. "One more thing: You'll also owe me a favor. Who knows when it'll be called in, but you'll fulfill your end of the deal when the time comes. No questions asked."

Carter swallowed, his mouth suddenly dry. "And if I refuse?"

Grummon snapped his fingers. All his men raised their guns and aimed them at Carter. "I kill you."

❧ 19 ❧

CARTER HAD LEFT word with Olmstead to have Jackson and Naomi meet him at the Dangiers Restaurant. When Olmstead had expressed surprise, Carter asked why.

"Because the Dangiers is run by Walter Thorne, a man with ties to smuggling. The restaurant is the front he uses to make the money he receives from smuggling appear legal. I can recommend a dozen other places better than that."

But Carter had insisted. He surely wasn't going to reveal the deal he had struck with Grummon. To be honest, he wasn't entirely sure he'd even tell his partner.

Jackson hovered over Carter. "Enjoying your lunch?"

Carter surveyed the plate of sautéed shrimp, freshly caught that very morning. The dirty rice and sweep potatoes made for a filling and rewarding lunch. "I am. Please, have a seat and fill me in before I tell what happened to me."

"I already know," Jackson said. He sat in the chair to Carter's left. Naomi took the seat across from Carter. Victor Olmstead himself appeared and sat to Carter's right. "Olmstead told us. So this Hook Thief was here? Blast it! How does he always precede us?"

Carter shrugged. "Not sure." He eyed Olmstead out of the corner of his eye. He wondered what, if anything, Olmstead may have told Jackson about the Dangiers or what Carter's insistence on eating here actually proved. "What's the story with Barron?"

Jackson took a look at Naomi. It was only then that Carter noted the girl had experienced something that made her nearly shake in her shoes. "Want to tell him or should I?"

"I will," Naomi said. She folded her hands on the table. "David Barron, along with Father and Jacob Hobson, all worked together to steal the sword from Molina's house. Father was already dead. Hobson is now dead as well. That only leaves Mr. Barron as the sole witness to the theft. And he's missing"

Carter was about to ask for more details, but a waiter arrived and brought glasses of iced tea and gave the three newcomers menus. They quickly surveyed the offerings, placed their orders, and kept silent until the waiter was out of earshot.

Before Naomi continued, the head waiter, dressed in a black suit and tie despite the lunchtime attire of the guests, approached Carter. "Sir, there is a message for you."

Carter grabbed his napkin and wiped his mouth. "Okay, let's have it."

"No, sir. The message is to be delivered directly and only to you. The messenger is back in the kitchen."

Carter stood, pointedly avoiding the gaze of the three people at his table, especially Olmstead. At a gesture, Carter bade the head waiter to lead the way. Carter followed.

The kitchen was cramped and hot. The interior of the

restaurant was cool by comparison. Carter broke out into a sweat almost instantly and he reckoned it wasn't only on account of the temperature. He was stepping on thin ice with this deal with a known criminal. He would have to do his best to ensure Jackson or the railroad wouldn't suffer because of it.

A man stood near the rear door. The head waiter indicated he was Carter's messenger. Carter threaded his way around the scurrying cooks and other waiters and came to stand in front of the man. He was about Carter's height, maybe a few years older, with a thin line of whiskers along his cheeks. Dirty blond hair was combed to the side. The man's suit looked like it was tailored but had seen better days. He wore a gun on his right thigh and Carter noted the latch had been permanently removed. The man kept his hand near his gun.

"You Grummon's man?" Carter asked.

"Yeah."

"You got a name?"

"Yeah, but I ain't gonna tell you." He sniffed at the aromas wafting in the air. "I'm here to deliver a message. You Carter?"

"Yeah," Carter said, mimicking the tone and delivery of the man.

The man squinted. "You making fun of me?"

"Nope. What's the message?"

The man reached inside his pants pocket and pulled out a slip of paper. He handed it to Carter. "There's another steamer bound for Vera Cruz that leaves later tonight. It's an overnight trip. The *Cassiopeia*. If you miss that one, you'll have to wait a couple of days."

Carter opened the slip of paper. A single name was written on it. Salvador Musgrave. "Who is this?"

"The man who boarded the earlier steamer that set sail

this morning. Mr. Grummon's contacts said Thorne boarded the steamer with an oddly shaped bag. Oblong. About this big." The messenger extended his hands about five feet. "The porters said he was very particular about the package. He didn't allow anyone to touch it."

That was a slim lead and one that could prove completely false, but it was all Carter had. "That's it?"

"That's it. Only that Mr. Grummon wanted to remind you of the terms of y'all's deal. Do you?"

Carter sighed. He slipped the paper into his pocket. "Yeah, I do."

The man slipped out the back door and disappeared.

Carter spun on his heels and walked back into the main room of the restaurant. By the time he returned to his seat, the others all had their food.

Olmstead gave Carter a pitying look. Naomi gazed at him, eyebrows raised in expectation. Jackson merely sat and waited for Carter to speak. The New Yorker knew his partner well enough to know Carter would eventually tell him everything.

When Carter finally spoke, it was with command in his voice. "We're going to Vera Cruz."

WITH LITTLE TO DO IN their investigations, Carter, Jackson, and Naomi spent the rest of the day preparing to cross the Gulf of Mexico on a steamship. Carter went to a telegraph office and sent a report back to Jameson Moore in Austin with the update and what they expected to do. He half wondered if Moore would consider the Aztec sword lost and order them back home, but late in the afternoon, the word came from him to proceed as normal. The only caveat was jurisdiction. Basically, Carter and Jackson had none.

When Jackson heard Carter's pronouncement at lunch, he immediately protested for the very reason—jurisdiction—that Moore overruled. Jackson was concerned that they were overreaching, that this case, when you boiled it down, was a private citizen hiring the railroad detective agency to fetch stolen property. It was like the agency was at Octavia Hendrickson's beck and call. Carter had agreed, and thus he had sent the message. Now, he had their response.

Naomi had excused herself just after lunch. She didn't offer any reason or indicate where she was going, but Carter was too busy listening to Jackson fume about the possibility of being ordered across the gulf to care. Jackson had only been on a steamship once, when his family moved from New York to Texas, but at the time, he was too young to care. Now, the thought of some accident befalling the Cassiopeia was proving to worry the big detective. Carter, on the other hand, had been on a steamship a few times in his acting days. Until the railroads had connected Texas to the rest of the country, steamship travel was the fastest way to get to New Orleans, where Carter had performed a few times. To be honest, he was looking forward to the passage.

Victor Olmstead had stayed relatively silent for the rest of lunch. He knew what Carter had done and Carter sensed a veil that had come down between them. Olmstead seemed to be a man of remarkable character and held himself to the highest standards. Based on what Carter assumed how things ran down here, Olmstead's standards were what kept him on the good side of the law.

It were these thoughts that sent Carter to the shoreline. The brown waters of the Gulf lapped on the beach. Their gentle sounds soothed Carter's conscience as he gazed out at the broad horizon. Somewhere, out there, was the Aztec sword, the thing he needed to recover. Jackson's concerns were not unfounded. Nothing about this case was normal, including the deal he had made with Grummon. He didn't allow himself to have second thoughts, but they gnawed at his gut nonetheless. He began to question his motives. The way he saw it, the only way to get out of Grummon's clutches alive was to make the deal. What else was he supposed to do? That went a long way to assuage his conscience, but not all the way. There was still doubt, doubt that he might compromise his ideals again, and the next time, it would merely be easier.

By late afternoon, Carter and Jackson met at the docks for the steamships. The passengers were in a line waiting to board the Cassiopeia. Carter's eyes passed over all the various workers, his mind whirling and wondering which one of the men were bought and paid for by Grummon. To some extent, he assumed they all were. He chewed his inner cheek with frustration. What surprised him was the arrival of Naomi. She carried her travel bag with her.

"Where are you going?" Carter asked.

"With you."

Carter and Jackson exchanged a glance. Jackson merely rolled his eyes. "I don't think so."

"Actually, you need me."

"How do you figure?"

"For starters," Naomi said, sidling up next to Carter, "you'll need help in figuring out how to get the sword." At Carter's frown, she shook her head. "Don't you get it? By the time we get there, this Salvador Musgrave person will likely have already delivered the sword to Juan Esteban Molina."

"We still don't know Molina's the one who took it," Carter replied.

"He did. And you'll need help in getting it."

Jackson, unable to leave himself out of the conversation, blurted "How are you able to help?"

A twinkle formed in Naomi's eye. It matched the confident smirk on her face. "Seeing as the three men who did it once before are either dead or missing, I'm the only one who knows how they did it."

The pieces fell into place in Carter's mind. "Because you read the journal."

Naomi nodded. "If you considered me just a tagalong so far, now, we're partners." With that, she turned and walked across the gangway and boarded the ship. "See you on board."

Jackson, muttering to himself, followed her.

Carter merely wore a grin. However he had reached this point, this was actually going to be fun.

* * *

THE SOUNDS of retching came from behind the door to the lavatory. Carter winced at the pain Jackson must have been going through.

"Tom, how are you doing?"

"Go away!"

"If you come outside, the sea air might help. And you can throw up over the side of the ship."

"Go away." This time, the words came out more as a moan than with anger.

"Tom, there's a steward here. He's…"

"Go away!" Back to anger.

Carter looked at the steward and offering a lopsided grin. "If you don't mind, could you stay here a few minutes and give him that when he's sane?" He indicated the glass of seltzer water the steward was holding.

"Yes, sir."

"And please let me know if I can help with anything." He slipped the man a coin.

"Where will you be, sir?"

Carter's eyes drifted down the long central hallway and out onto the foredeck. Naomi Hendrickson stood on the railing, enjoying the night air. "I'll be checking on my other traveling companion." He winked and slipped away to the sounds of Jackson's next dry heave.

The Cassiopeia was a sturdy liner, long from stem to stern, but even the most stable boat was no match for the waves of the Gulf of Mexico. Most of the cabin doors were closed by now, well into the voyage. The captain and his crew were making good progress. The sounds of the engines were a constant hum to Carter's ears.

As he exited the main covered area, the blanket of stars appeared overhead. They were countless. With the ship's lights at his back, the only light came from the heavens. A thin crescent moon was the largest object in the sky. A few brighter stars shown. Carter noted both Venus and Mars as well as the Scorpio constellation. His mind drifted for a moment, wondering how the ancient Greeks came to see certain patterns in the skies.

At the railing, Naomi stood with her hands firmly clasped around the iron bars. She still wore her traveling dress, but had unfastened the top button. Her head was raised to the sky, her eyes closed. The breeze lifted her hair and swirled it around her face. The mist from the waves splashing against the hull moistened her face and, coupled with the starlight, gave her an allure Carter had never noticed before.

He sidled up beside her and grabbed the railing himself. He closed his eyes and mimicked her. After a few moments, he said, "It feels good, doesn't it?"

She jumped, then gasped. "You startled me."

Carter opened one eye. "With the engines and the waves, little sounds can easily get drowned out."

"How's Detective Jackson?"

"Empty. Now his stomach's just going through the motions. He'll probably be in there most of the night. And even if he gets back to our room, he'll likely groan all night."

"Too bad. I love sea travel. There's nothing quite like it. When the waters are smooth and the boat you're on is gliding, it's almost like you're a bird flying through the air." She held out one hand.

Again, Carter mimicked her. "I see what you mean, although this bird is flying through a squall."

"You know," Carter said after a few moments, "we're likely to run into some stiff opposition when we get to Mexico. Have you had any experience handing yourself in situations like that?"

Naomi considered him for a few moments. "Calvin, are you trying to save me before we get into trouble?"

"Not really. Just wondering what kind of resources I need to allocate. You know, like a third eye or another detective that can tag along."

"You know anyone in Mexico?"

"A few."

"Any you can contact?"

Carter stifled a laugh at the thoughts of the people he knew in Mexico. Of the half dozen Mexican nationals he had met in his time as an actor, four were women. And based on what happened at the end of each of those rendezvouses, contacting them wouldn't be a good idea.

"Not really." He smiled. "I know you carry that knife around. Can you handle a gun?"

Naomi inclined her head. "I can."

"Of course you can. Your father train you?"

"No. It was"—she said, pausing to select the right word, a grin forming on her face at the thought—"someone else."

"Good. We'll find you a gun when we land." Carter swept his eyes along the dark horizon. He ended up turning to face her, an elbow on the railing. "You know, back in Houston, you caught me off guard. I'm usually the one pursuing the ladies."

Naomi turned and faced Carter, angling her elbow on the railing as well. "Like my mother?"

Carter nodded. "Touché. But you never gave me the chance to show you how I woo women."

"I didn't want to wait. I wanted what I wanted, when I wanted it, and how I wanted it."

"Very direct."

"With money comes privilege. With privilege comes getting pretty much whatever I want. And, with your history with my mother, I wasn't sure you wanted me." Her voice trailed off, drowned by the crashing waves and the hum of the engines.

Carter reached out and put a finger under her chin. "Are you kidding? A beautiful woman like you? Any man would sell a year's wages to be with you."

She pulled her chin away from his finger. "You never did."

Carter shrugged. "You mother came on to me first. I couldn't very well abandon her and walk down to your room. Besides, the last time was nearly two years ago."

Naomi angled her head. "How?"

Raising his eyebrows, Carter said, "How what?"

"How would you woo me? Say we're here on this ship and we just met. I came out here for air, and you came to join me."

The grin that creased Carter's face was broad. He lowered only one eyebrow. "I've already started."

The short gasp from Naomi followed by the playful slap on his arm told Carter things were progressing nicely. But he didn't want to take things for granted. He leaned in closer.

"But after telling you how lovely you look, we'd engage in some conversation. We've already done that, so that just leaves the next step." The nearness of her skin enabled some of her perfume to mingle with the sea breeze and formed an intoxicating aroma.

"What is the next step?"

"I'd ask you to join me for a drink."

"The dining room is closed."

"But my room isn't. Or, it normally would be if I didn't have a sick partner accompanying me."

Naomi's tongue peeked out and ran along her lower lip. "My room is unoccupied. Perhaps we can pretend it's your room."

"We can do that." He tapped his jacket pocket. A feeble metal clink sounded. "I have my favorite cognac with me. It's French."

Naomi ran her tongue over her upper lip. "I like things from France."

Carter leaned in ever closer. His lips brushed her gently, then he brought his mouth to her ear. "I like French things, too." He brought his mouth back to hers and pressed his lips down. The warmth of her mouth revealed itself when she opened it and allowed her tongue to meet his. The two organs intermingled, twisting and turning over each other. Carter brought his free arm around Naomi and drew her to him. He had certainly enjoyed their night in Houston, but there was something different, something more exhilarating about this kiss that the others didn't possess.

Naomi broke the kiss. She looked up at him, her eyelids half closed. She bit her lower lip. "I'd like that drink now."

"Lead the way."

She grabbed his lapel and brought his mouth back down to hers. This kiss contained more urgent passion, but Carter pushed away.

"Remember, we're doing things my way tonight."

Impatience flashed across her face, but Carter assuaged her with his words. "Good things come to those who wait. And believe me: you'll be amply rewarded."

He stood up straighter and crooked his arm. "Shall we?"

With a lascivious grin, Naomi snaked her arm through his and guided him to her room. Their pace was not slow.

❀ 2O ❀

WHITE CLOUDS FLECKED the bright blue sky over Vera Cruz, Mexico. The waters of the Gulf of Mexico were a nice blue as opposed to the brown, silty water around Galveston. The air was crisp and clean, at least as the Cassiopeia sailed into port.

The port of Vera Cruz and the city that surrounded it appeared as mostly white buildings built in the Spanish colonial style. The main building and customs house bordered a wide plaza. Vendors cooked various foods, the smells mixing in with the sea air. For Carter, the aroma was wonderful. For Jackson, it wasn't. He was happy to again be walking on dry ground, but his pallid face and sunken eyes betrayed the evening he had experienced.

Many people flocked here and there, most taking no notice of the three Americans. Carter was a trained detective, however, and he spied a few young men who seemed to have nowhere to go. When he looked their way, they casually turned their attention elsewhere. After a few moments, Carter, too, turned his attention to the four-story tower that overlooked the port itself, from which flew the national flag of Mexico. The breeze wafted the fabric and Carter had no problem making out the green, white, and red of the Mexican flag.

Jackson stood on wobbly legs. Carter was convinced his partner would kneel down and kiss the ground. "I don't kiss any land other than Texas. I may not have been born there, but it runs in my blood. Still, it's mighty good to be on a surface that isn't moving."

"Well," Carter said, "at least you know what to expect on the return trip."

Jackson's jaw muscles flinched at the thought. "Maybe I'll catch the train."

Carter turned to Naomi. The memories of the previous night still fresh in his mind, he smiled at her. They agreed that they wouldn't openly hold hands or anything like that. Officially, they were still on an assignment with the most dangerous part of the case in front of them, so they needed to focus on their present task. After they had acquired the sword and were traveling back to America, then they could think about being more open.

"We're here because of what you know," Carter said. He spread his arm out. "Lead the way."

The trip through customs was surprisingly short. On Naomi's recommendation, Carter and Jackson kept their badges out of sight. Moreover, Jackson didn't wear his gun belt, but stored it in his bag. Carter, with his hidden shoulder holster, got through the official questions as he was. It didn't surprise him in the least when Naomi began speaking Spanish to the customs official, a man with round spectacles that enlarged his eyes when he faced the two detectives. Carter got the distinct impression that the shorter man was wary of the two American men, but Naomi, with smooth talk, assuaged his concerns. Carter knew a decent amount of Spanish, but Naomi's abilities surpassed his. When the official nodded and bade them enter his country, Carter tipped his hat to him.

"*Muchas gracias*," Carter said.

Various open carriages awaited passengers from the arrived ship. Naomi flagged one and directed the cabbie to the Hotel Hidalgo off the main plaza. The cabbie nodded, gratefully accepted the American dollar she gave him, and urged the horse to move along nicely.

Riding in the open air cab, Carter got his first look at the city in over five years. Most of the main buildings hadn't changed too much. The port and customs house certainly hadn't, and neither had the streets. They were still lined with pedestrians and merchants, all trying to get somewhere or sell something. From out of a few restaurant windows came the sounds of music. Carter had always appreciated Mexican music, particularly the guitar. He had tried his hand at learning to play it. While he was able to strum chords and perform a few pieces, he had never mastered it like he had acting or detective work.

The Hotel Hidalgo was a glorious three-story building that seemed to consume an entire block. It was one of the fanciest hotels in town and had been built since Carter last left Veracruz. The sumptuousness of the entry way made him smile. Carter enjoyed the good things in life and, even though his salary from the railroad wasn't exorbitant, he tried to maintain a certain standard. The Hidalgo was clearly above that standard.

The color in Jackson's face had returned. He scowled at all the ornate features inside the hotel. "Why are we staying here?"

"Because this is where I want to stay," Naomi said. "Since y'all are basically working for me, you get the benefits."

Carter and Jackson exchanged looks. There it was, out

in the open. Jameson Moore may have assigned the case to Carter and Jackson, in reality, this was a private affair and always had been. Carter shrugged. Jackson kept his thoughts to himself.

Naomi booked two rooms. For the sake of camaraderie, Carter and Jackson dropped off their bags in the same second story room. Naomi had remembered Carter's admonition about staying in a corner room. Their window looked down upon a plaza teeming with people.

Carter unpacked his bag long enough to retrieve one of his folded shirts. He removed the one he had worn since Galveston. He poured some water in the bowl on the dresser and splashed water on his face and under his armpits. A bar of soap sat next to the bowl, so he lathered up and cleaned his face and upper body. The soap contained a gentle fragrance and it calmed him. He donned the new shirt and buttoned it to the top. It felt good to have clean clothes. He took out a different tie, a blue striped one, and lassoed it around his neck. He ran a comb through his dark hair and looked at himself in the full-length mirror with satisfaction.

"Happy with what you see?" Jackson said. Shirtless, he moseyed over to the bowl and cleaned himself up as well.

"At present, yes. How're you feeling?"

"I've been better, but I'm on the mend," Jackson said through his hands and the water. "I haven't been that sick ever."

"We'll get you something for the return trip."

Jackson paused, looking at Carter through the smaller mirror on the dresser, water dripping from his face. "Do you trust her?"

Carter spun and met Jackson's look. "Sure. Why do you ask?"

"Cal, come on," Jackson said, "I know you. Whenever

you bed a woman, some of your heart goes with her. I just don't want any feelings you might have for her to cloud your judgement. We're down here on a private mission. This isn't technically legal. What are we gonna do? Just ask Molina for the sword? What happens when—not if—he refuses?"

Carter gave the matter some thought. A few options presented themselves, most of them not what he'd consider good. "I don't know. Let's see what our next step is."

A gentle knock sounded at the door. Carter walked over and opened it. Naomi stood there. She had changed her clothes. Gone was the dress and frilly attire she had worn back in Texas. Now she wore what appeared to be a man's suit, but tailored to her figure. Brown trousers were tucked into calf-high boots. A white shirt, open at the collar, was under a cotton jacket, a lighter shade of brown than the pants. On her head was a leather hat, sitting at a rakish angle. Across her chest was a strap that held a leather satchel. Pointedly, on her right hip was a holster and pistol.

Carter raised his eyebrows at the gun.

"You asked if I could handle myself, Calvin," Naomi said. In a swift motion, she cleared the leather of the holster and aimed it at his stomach. Involuntarily, he flinched, which brought a chuckle to her mouth. "What do you think?"

"I think you'd best be pointing that thing somewhere else," Carter said. His hands had instinctively moved to his shoulder holster, only a last-minute thought stopping his hand from grasping the butt of his Colt.

Naomi shrugged. She holstered her gun and waltzed inside the room. She gave Jackson's broad chest, with its healthy tuft of blonde hair across it, a nice appraisal. "Good to see you looking better, Thomas." At the use of his first name, Jackson frowned. Naomi shrugged again. "We're no longer in Texas. Out-dated rules of decorum don't apply down here. Besides, if we're going to get my father's sword back, we'll need a lot more familiarity." She snapped her fingers. "Hurry and clean up. We have somewhere to go and someone to meet."

Carter held up a finger. "Wait a minute. You asked me if I knew anybody here in Veracruz."

The grin etched on Naomi's face would have been right at home on the Cheshire cat. "Right, but you never asked me if I knew anyone."

* * *

THE SOMEWHERE TURNED out to be a large mansion built in a stucco style. The two-story building spotted a porch extending all the way around the house. On the covered porch were chairs, benches, tables, and a hanging swing. Oil lamps dangled from the ceiling, and round columns supported the weight of the second floor. A broad, winding sidewalk connected the house to the street, with freshly cut grass and neat gardens on both sides. The house sat off by itself at the end of a cul-de-sac. The cab in which they rode made the circle and ventured out back into the throng of the main street.

The someone was the owner of the house, who met Naomi at the front door with an exclamation of excitement and surprise. The man was dressed in a suit, tie loosened, and shiny black shoes. He wore a thick, bushy mustache under a broad, flat nose. Dark eyebrows and dark, well-groomed hair matched the color of his mustache. When he faced Carter and Jackson, the man offered a toothy grin.

"This is Orlando Escovedo," Naomi said in presenting him to the two detectives. "Orlando, this is Calvin Carter and Thomas Jackson."

Escovedo moved down the stone steps to grip the hands of both Carter and Jackson. "So nice to meet you, friends of Naomi," the man said. He shook hands with both of his. "Friends of Naomi are friends of mine." Escovedo noted Jackson's gun, which he now wore openly on his leg. "A *vaquero*?"

"Something like that," Jackson agreed.

In a lower voice, Naomi said, "They're railroad detectives." At a surprised expression from Escovedo, she continued. "They're here to help me take back the Aztec sword."

Most of the joviality that flooded Escovedo's face vanished in an instant. He shook his head. "That damned *espada*. I swear it will be the death of me. Come, let's talk inside."

He led the way through the airy interior of his home to a second-floor room that appeared to be his personal study or office. Books lined shelves that dominated one wall. A large bay window overlooked the backyard which was nearly twice the size as the front. On the other walls hung various photographs and pictures, all featuring a railroad motif. Carter strolled over and studied the photos. In each one, Escovedo, at various ages, stood with other people. In the backdrop of nearly every one of them, something associated with railroads was featured: locomotives, passenger cars, freight cars, stacks of timber, or gleaming steel rails.

One photograph in particular caught Carter's attention. He called Jackson who came to stand beside him and looked at the image Carter discovered. Escovedo stood in the middle of four other men. Judging by the way Escovedo looked now, the photograph was likely taken two decades ago. Carter had known what Gunter Hendrickson looked like from meeting him once and from the photographs in the Hendrickson household. He also knew what Jacob Hobson looked like for he had met the man right before his death. Carter indicated the other white man.

"Think that's David Barron?" he asked Jackson.

"Not sure. Never saw him."

The last man in the photograph also appeared Mexican. He was taller than Escovedo but shorter than Hobson. He was standing in the center, next to Gunter Hendrickson.

What stood out to Carter was the object that all four men held in front of them. The sword was probably about four feet long including the handle. At the end of the handle was a hole carved into the wood, perhaps to secure a leather thong. The business part of the sword was flat, maybe four inches across. Various engravings marked the flat surface of the sword. Along the edge, small black pieces protruded from the wood. Carter counted eight in all, four on each side.

He turned, still pointing to the photograph. "This is it, right?"

Escovedo nodded gravely. "*Si*. That is the mazuahuitl. It is on the day we found it."

Carter thought back to the story Naomi told about how her father had stolen the sword out from under Molina's grasp. The truth of those events belied the happiness the five men in the photograph displayed on the day of their find. Too bad jealousy got in the way.

"You know the tale of the stolen mazuahuitl?" Escovedo asked Carter.

He nodded. "Naomi told us. But what you don't know are the current events."

Escovedo sighed. He gestured to thick leather armchairs. They all sat and Carter conveyed the facts of the current case. Not knowing Naomi's history with Escovedo, he purposefully left out the more romantic details.

When Carter had finished, Escovedo turned to Naomi and looked at her gravely. "I know why you have come."

Carter perked up at Escovedo's comment. He was pretty sure he knew the answer, but wanted to hear it from her own lips.

Naomi reached out and grasped one of Escovedo's hands. "I need your help to steal back the mazuahuitl."

Escovedo shot a look in Carter's and Jackson's direction. "And you only brought two men?"

Naomi grinned. "You and Father did it years ago with only four men. Now, we're going to do it again. And yes, before you say anything, I am the fourth person." She let go of his hand and put it out, palm facing Escovedo. "Please spare me whatever gentlemanly virtue you have stored up. I can take care of myself and I've made up my mind."

"She's pretty determined when she's got her mind set on something," Carter quipped.

Jackson grunted.

Escovedo sighed. He stood. "Then allow me time to change clothes and I'll take and show you what stands between us and that mazuahuitl."

* * *

"You have got to be kidding me," Calvin Carter muttered under his breath.

"I am not, Señor Carter," Escovedo replied. "That is where Juan Xavier Molina lives."

The four of them crouched in a small thicket of trees on a hillside. The terrain was rocky and dry, and pebbles rolled down the hill with nearly every foot fall. The trees lined a driveway that meandered from the lower part of the main street up the hill to the house where Molina lived.

And what a house.

Near the top of the hill, the terrain grew rockier. What Molina had done—likely to a considerable expense—was fashion the upper part of the hill to resemble an Aztec temple. Large stone piers, each one smaller than the previous, were carved into the stone ground. In the middle of each side were carved smaller steps for people to climb to the top. There was another expanse of trees and foliage near the top, but half of it was already cleared. It appeared Molina's house was still under construction.

The house itself sat on top of the hill. The masonry was a dark adobe with white roofs. A wall ringed what Carter could see of the house, likely forming a perimeter. A tower occupied one corner of the wall, behind which the house loomed. A central dome rose above all structures save the tower. Various terraces and porches dotted the exterior.

"He doesn't lack for money," Jackson muttered.

"When your American railroad companies came down to my country, they were supposed to bring wealth and jobs for my people," Escovedo said. "For the most part, that hasn't happened. A few, like Molina, latched on like leaches, sucking as much money as possible from the American gringos. But most of the workers live like slaves, too poor to find other work, too trapped otherwise." He spat on the ground at the thought of it.

Naomi, her father a part of the problem Escovedo just mentioned, stayed silent.

"Well," Carter said, "we can't do much about that. Besides, that's not why we're here." He pointed up the hill. "Where does the driveway lead?"

Escovedo pointed and used his finger to draw in the air. "At the top of the hill, just beyond that stand of trees, the driveway makes a loop in front of the main door. I've seen guards stationed at that door during the evenings."

"You've been here before?" Carter asked.

"*Sí.* As part of the national railroad company, I have many meetings with Señor Molina. Even a few fiestas. That is why I know what I know."

Carter pursed his lips. The gathering twilight obscured his face and his furrowed brows. "Two guards. What else?"

"Just inside the wall…"

"How tall?" Jackson asked.

"About eight feet. Just tall enough that a man cannot scale it on his own. He needs either a ladder or a rope." He rubbed his palms on his khaki pants. "As I was saying, just inside the wall is an open area, like a mini plaza. It has a fountain and a small garden. It is about forty feet from the gate to the house."

"What about the tower?" Carter said.

"The tower is the lookout spot. There is a man up there at all times. He is a marksman."

At this, Jackson perked up. "Can he hit us from here?"

"Most likely."

"Then we'll have to get in there unseen," Jackson said. Carter recognized the firmness in his partner's voice. When Thomas Jackson set his mind to a task, few things could stand in his way.

"Forgive me, Señor Carter," Escovedo said, "but how do you plan on getting in there?"

"I dunno," Carter murmured, his eyes fixed on the Molina mansion. "I'm making this up as we go along."

Finally, Naomi spoke up. "What about me?"

The heads of her three companions turned to her. "What about you?" Carter asked.

"I can get in there. Molina knows me. He knew Father. I can be visiting from Texas and come to say hello to him."

"That's an awfully long way to go just to say hello," Jackson said. He scratched his neck. "I don't buy it."

"You don't have to buy it, Thomas," Naomi said. "All

you have to do is acknowledge that it is a feasible idea." She pointed up the hill. "How the hell else do you plan on scaling that wall unseen by the guards and shot? You forget that Molina has the government, as corrupt as it may be, behind him. Those are likely official army soldiers or else paid by Molina himself. Either way, they are likely not the kind of men to take a prisoner. They are probably the ones who shoot first and report back later."

"You sound like you know an awfully lot about this Molina character," Jackson said. He shot a glance at Carter.

"I've met the man a few times," Naomi blurted. "I've seen him up close and know the way he used to talk to Father and how he tried to bully Mother into giving or selling the sword. The retinue he brought with him last time were army men. That's why I know how he operates."

Sighing heavily, Naomi leaned against one of the trees. "There's a reason I insisted on coming with y'all. Yes, Father, Escovedo, and the others successfully infiltrated the compound and took back the mazuahuitl. But that was before Molina had all of that." She threw her arm up toward the top of the hill. "Things have changed now. What Father did is now impossible. We have to improvise." She grinned at Carter. "Something an actor is very good at."

Carter looked at Naomi as the growing bright orange of sunset glowed on her face. "What are you thinking about?"

"I'm wondering how good your Mexican accent is."

❦ 21 ❦

ONE OF THE more fun aspects for Carter going undercover in makeup was crafting the name of the character and the backstory. Based on Naomi's idea of simply riding up to the gates of Molina's house and waltzing inside for an impromptu visit on her way to Mexico City to meet with some of her father's old business associates, Carter created Cristobal Cotilla, a businessman with ties back to Galveston, New Orleans, New York, and Spain. He worked in shipping and had a fondness for ancient artifacts. Naomi and "Cotilla" were scheduled to depart by train the next day, but she wanted to stop by and see Molina again and allow him to show "Cotilla" the Aztec pieces in Molina's collection. Escovedo was a simple addition to the cadre for he and Naomi had history.

Jackson, on the other hand, was the issue. While he had allowed Carter to apply makeup and teach him some acting traits to pass himself off as someone else, those times were all back in Texas and other parts in America. Jackson's command of Spanish wasn't great, but he could get by with talking to Mexicans on his father's ranch. But there was no way he would pass muster as anything other than a Texan. So Jackson stayed as himself, a gunslinger hired by "Cotilla" to protect him on his travels. The only concession was that Jackson needed to spruce up his appearance, which he did with the purchased tie and vest from a local tailor.

"The colonel won't let the company pay me back for this, you know," Jackson had said as he handed over American money to the tailor whose eyes bulged with his payday.

"It'll boost your meager amount of good clothes for future parties," was Carter's flippant response.

Carter wore his dark blue suit with silk gray vest and tie. The watch chain he wore daily was replaced with the fancier one, made with shiny silver, and it now dangled from his pocket. He affixed a mustache and goatee to his face and used a makeup pencil to darken his brown eyebrows. He could do nothing about his skin color. Were it winter, he could don gloves and coat his face with a foundation of makeup to darken his complexion. If asked, he would pass it off by stating his job was mostly indoors and, as such, didn't see the sun much. He made sure his belt held enough cartridges for reloading for he knew, no matter how much planning went into a scheme, chances were high bullets would start to fly. He made sure the derringer was strapped to his right forearm and that the mechanism meant to launch it into his palm worked without error.

He regarded himself in the full-length mirror in his hotel room. Jackson sat at the small writing table and played solitaire. At a knock on the door, he rose and opened it. Naomi had changed into a red dress that ran all the way to the floor. The neckline plunged down as well, just to the upper scoop of her breasts. When Carter turned and appraised her, she smiled demurely.

"We're in Mexico now. Standards are different." She pecked him on the cheek. "And who are you?"

In accented English, Carter told her of his alias and backstory. "I would be much pleased to see the artifacts of your friend, Juan Esteban Molina."

Naomi chuckled. "You could fool anyone, couldn't you?"

"That's the idea," Carter said.

She looked at his open leather makeup bag he carried with him on all cases. "Well, you've got an assortment in there. Lipstick, rouge, powder, eyeliner, mascara. It's almost enough to make a woman jealous." She poked her fingers around a few small balls in one of the open compartments. "What are these?"

"Be careful," Carter said. "They might explode in your face." At her look of confusion, he continued. "The blue ones are smoke balls. The red are flash bombs. I have a friend who goes by the stage name of Solomon Abercrombie. Ever heard of him? No? Doesn't surprise me. He carries on usually west of Texas in the territories. He's a magician. Anyway, we met one day after I became a detective, I told him about a particularly tough predicament I had been in. He put a few of these in my hand. I had seen his show. I knew what they could do. Now, I carry them around as part of my standard tools."

Naomi pursed her lips. "You come prepared."

"Always."

"You ask me," Jackson said, coming over to stand next to the pair, "I prefer the straightforwardness of bullets."

"But sometimes, Tom," Carter said, "circumstances call for more nuance."

He held up his fists. "That's why I got these." He looked skeptical. "Are we sure this is the best idea? I mean, we're literally going to walk into a house that looks like an Aztec temple and try to steal this sword. And how are we going to do this again?"

"Simple," Naomi said. She reached inside of the small purse she carried and withdrew a small, glass vial. A cork was stuck inside the open end. The liquid inside was clear. "As soon as Molina shows us where the mazuahuitl is, I'll suggest we have drinks. I'll slip this inside his drink and he'll be fast asleep."

"What about the others?" Jackson asked. "His wife, his associates?"

"There's enough in here to knock anyone else out."

"You've though of everything," Carter said. "Maybe you should be a detective, too. We've already got one woman," he said, his voice growing ever so wistful at the memory of Evelyn Paige, his former lover—"I'm sure Colonel Moore wouldn't mind another."

Naomi appeared to give it some thought. "Y'all certainly lead interesting lives. Maybe I'll give it some thought." She slipped the vial back into her purse. She turned and stuck out her hands, meaning for both of them to crook their arms and escort her out of the room. Carter complied. Jackson walked ahead of them.

"I'm the paid gunslinger," Jackson muttered. "I might as well start playing the part."

❦ 22 ❦

THE SOUNDS OF THE HORSES' hooves and squeaky cab wheels echoed off the stone wall and heavy wooden door at the entrance to Juan Esteban Molina's house. The climb up here was gradual, but Carter still felt himself pressed down into the seat, unlike riding in a cab on the level surface. The driveway was paved with large, flat rocks hewed from the hillside and, while they certainly wouldn't wash away when the rains came, Carter wondered how a cab could make it up here with wet.

Twilight had settled on the region. The Gulf of Mexico, visible from the front gate, was already cast in darkness. So, too, was Veracruz down below. The lamps of the city already winked on, the visage a wonderful sight. Two lamps that flanked both sides of the main gate had already been lit as well as the lamps on each corner of the wall. If nothing else, Carter expected Molina's compound to be as impressive at night as it was during the day.

Two men guarded the front gate. They were dressed in a simple uniform of crisp white shirt, khaki pants, with a matching vest. Their collars were open. Each man wore a gun belt and pistol, but also had a rifle slung over their shoulders with a canvas strap. When the cab rolled to a stop, one of the two guards approached the vehicle.

"*Qué deseas?*" he asked the cabbie.

Carter thought it a good sign he understood the question: What do you want?

By the arrangement she had made with the cabbie, Naomi answered. In Spanish, she said, "I am an old friend of Señor Molina. I am in town for a visit. I would like to see if he is available, please. My name is Naomi Hendrickson."

The guard looked at Naomi impassively, but gave Carter and Jackson a wary eye. Carter, in costume as "Cristobal Cotilla," had the protection of his makeup. Jackson was the most exposed. He compensated by remaining still, offering the guard a laconic appearance.

Escovedo leaned forward and spoke to the guard. "Pray, inform Señor Molina that Orlando Escovedo is accompanying Señorita Hendrickson as well."

At the mention of Escovedo's name, the guard stood a bit straighter. "*Si, señor. Un momento.*" He spun on his heel and disappeared inside the gate. The other guard didn't take his eyes off the cab until his partner had returned, all smiles. "*Por favor, entra.*"

Carter needed no translation for that either. They were in.

It was Jackson's suggestion that he depart the cab last. That way, the first thing the guards would not be an American gunslinger. As such, Molina exited first, followed by Naomi. Carter came next, with Jackson bringing up the rear. As he predicted, the guards appeared shocked that an armed man was in the cab. They brought their rifles off their shoulders and gripped them, ready to bring them to bear.

"*A gusto*," said a powerful male voice from just inside the gate.

At the order, both guards, however warily, reluctantly relaxed and slung their rifles back up over their shoulder.

It didn't take any deduction on Carter's part to know who issued the order. The main gate—a double wooden door that swung outward—was open. Some of the lamps from the interior garden were already lit, so Carter got a good look at the man who gave the order and now approached his front door.

Juan Esteban Molina was a middle-aged man, probably in his early fifties. His jet black hair showed only a few strands of gray. It was perfectly styled and swept back over his forehead. A thick bushy mustache dominated his face. The nose was thin, as were his cheekbones. He wore a black formal suit, complete with tails that extended down to mid-thigh. Instead of a vest, he wore a red sash across his belt. Carter got the impression that Molina's get up was ceremonial, like he was dressed to attend a formal government function.

Molina took a look at Naomi and extended both hands. The smile on his face was huge and genuine. "Naomi, Naomi! How so very nice to see you again." He took her hands in his and pecked her on both cheeks. He stood back at arm's length, looking at her up and down. "You have grown into a fine and beautiful señorita." He shook his head at her. "Your father would be so proud."

"Thank you, Juan," Naomi said. "It has really been too long." She brought his hands to her, and then gave him a big hug. Stepping back, she moved aside to present Escovedo.

"Orlando," Molina said. He extended his hand.

Escovedo clasped it. "Hello again, sir." His smile was warm.

Molina's attention now turned to Carter. Before any performance—be it on stage or on a case—Carter's stomach was aflutter. It wasn't stage fright, per se, but often, especially when he was undercover, he had to nail a character from the first words he uttered. He had to come across as exactly who he portrayed himself to be. In the hubbub of Molina greeting Naomi and Escovedo, Carter had quietly cleared his throat so that when Molina spoke to him, Carter delivered his lines perfectly.

"And who are you?" Molina said.

"My name is Cristobal Cotilla" Carter said in Spanish. He extended his hand. "I work in shipping back in America and Cuba. I am traveling with Señorita Hendrickson for business. She told me about your collection of artifacts and she suggested we visit you to see them."

Molina took Carter's hand and shook it. The grip was firm edging on too firm. On the spur of the moment, Carter decided that "Cotilla" was a weaker man and he flinched. "Señor Molina, your grip is too much for me."

"My apologies," Molina said, releasing Carter's hand. "I like to judge a man by his handshake." Finally, he took in Jackson. He looked the detective up and down, fixating on the gun on Jackson's thigh. "Are who are you?"

"Juan," Naomi said, this time in English, "this is Thomas Jackson. He's a concession to my mother who thought I shouldn't be traipsing around Mexico without protection. He's a hired gunslinger she sent with me for protection. He understands Spanish mostly, but isn't very fluent when it comes to speaking your language." She let out a little chuckle. "He has to go where I go. That's his only stipulation."

Molina regarded Jackson again. "A man of the gun?" he said in English.

"I am," Jackson said. He tipped his hat to Molina.

Carter smiled inwardly. Jackson may already have been more gunslinger than Carter ever would be, but even Carter could tell Jackson was putting on a show. Jackson even laid on a thicker Texas accent. "Miss Hendrickson said she wanted to visit you, seeing as how you and her old man knew each other. I wanted to get some shuteye, but I gotta go where she goes."

Molina extended his hand. Jackson took it. Carter noted the whites of Jackson's knuckles and knew he and Molina were gauging each other through the handshake.

Withdrawing his hand first, Molina said, "You are a strong man, Mister Jackson."

"I have to be," Jackson replied. "You never know who might be looking at Miss Hendrickson and think they could get a little money off her."

"Indeed," Molina said. He turned and walked to Naomi. He offered her his arm. She took it. "Please, gentlemen, follow me."

$\maltese$ 23 $\maltese$

THE INTERIOR of the Molina house was just as elegant as the exterior gardens. Lamps, built into the walls, were lit and cast bright light all throughout the rooms. Every floor was tiled with thick, red stones. Rugs covered much of the floor, but when they all walked on the tile, the heels of their shoes echoed off the walls. Candles were lit on some of the tables, their gentle fragrance wafting in the breeze that came in through open windows. They passed the dining room that featured a long table with place settings for ten laid out.

"Are you expecting guests tonight?" Naomi asked.

"I am," Molina said. "It's a small affair, mostly business."

"Then we won't keep you."

"Nonsense. You shall join us."

Naomi glanced over her shoulder at Carter. He remained impassive.

A servant, dressed in a black suit, approached Molina. "Diego, please serve drinks in the display room. Tequila." Diego bowed at the neck and disappeared around a corner.

"You said you wanted to see my collection, Señor Cotilla," Molina said. He still led the small party through his house.

"*Sí*, Señor Molina," Carter said.

"What types of artifacts catch your fancy?"

Carter had prepared for this. "Being a citizen of Mexico, I enjoy learning as much as possible about our ancient ancestors, both the Aztecs and the Maya. I have traveled down to South America as well, so I enjoy learning about the Incan culture as well."

"Indeed," Molina said. He stopped at an entrance to a room that had no door. He gave Carter a broad grin. "Then you will certainly appreciate what I have." He gestured into the room. Naomi walked in first, followed by Escovedo, Carter, with Jackson bringing up the rear. Carter slightly frowned at Jackson. His partner's only response was the slight raise of his eyebrows.

The display room, as Molina described it, was exactly what he said it was. It was round with the ceiling high above. The only windows were two floors up, just under the domed room. This was the central part of the house Carter had spied from the outside. Not much light filtered into the display room now, at night, but Carter expected it was quite a sight with the sunlight streaming inside. To compensate, lamps, mounted all around the room, were brightly lit.

Various display cases sat around the room. Most of them had no glass protection, leaving the artifacts exposed. Despite himself and the situation, Carter felt himself amazed at all the history on display in front of him. Pottery, tools, and carved stone artwork filled the wooden cabinets. Carter could feel the weight of history as he stared at the pieces. Even Jackson, who normally didn't convey any type of reverence for art, stood and mutely stared at the pieces.

"Over here," Molina said, "is my most recent acquisition." He stood next to a long display case. Carter moved over to it and studied the object hanging from a leather thong in the center of the case.

The Aztec sword. The mazuahuitl.

Having only seen a drawing and heard it described by Naomi, Carter's heart beat faster at the sight of the ancient weapon. The metal embedded in the wooden handle and flat edge caught the lamp light and glittered. The obsidian stone blades, eight in total, looked as if they sucked in the light. But even after hundreds of years, Carter could tell the stones could still do damage to a person.

"What do you think of it?" Molina asked.

"It's a beautiful specimen," Carter breathed. They had a plan on getting the mazuahuitl out of Molina's house, but, despite himself, Carter was fixated on the sword. Up until now, he had only considered it the object of this assignment, a thing to find and return to Austin. But being in its presence, knowing the history of the mazuahuitl, he felt awe.

"It is," Molina agreed.

"If I may ask," Carter said, "how did you acquire it?"

Molina sniffed at the question. But he didn't have a chance to answer. Diego strode into the room carrying a tray. On the tray were six short glasses and a matching bottle. Inside the bottle, light yellow tequila sloshed. He placed the tray and glasses on a small table.

"Oh, tequila," Naomi purred. "It's been so long since I had good tequila." She moved over to table, brushing Diego aside. She uncorked the bottle, poured a little of the liquor into the glass, and drank it down in one gulp. She closed her eyes in satisfaction, a smile forming on her face. "So good." She opened her eyes and refilled her glass. "Don't mind me, Diego. I'll take care of it." She busied herself with filling all six glasses.

A part of Carter's mind was curious. Why were there six glasses?

Molina returned to Carter's question. "Senor Cotilla, you asked where I acquired the sword. I used to have it, long ago, but it was stolen me. For the longest time, I never knew where it was. Gunter Hendrickson hid it well. It wasn't until his death that his wife discovered it and put it on display. As soon as I saw it, I knew I had to reclaim what was rightfully mine."

An alarm inside of Carter started to sound. Did Molina just admit to stealing the mazuahuitl? Perhaps this case might end differently. His eyes shot to Naomi to see if she picked up on Molina's confession. All she did was busy herself with pouring the tequila.

Naomi picked up two of the glasses and brought them to Jackson and Escovedo. She returned and brought two more glasses to Carter and Molina. She returned and picked up her glass. Interestingly, the sixth glass was still on the tray. It was full.

Carter shot a glance at Jackson. Ever so subtly, Jackson shook his head once, then directed his eyes to his glass of tequila. Carter got the message.

Don't drink the tequila.

To Molina, Carter asked, "On behalf of the Mexican people, I'm so glad you reclaimed our heritage, Señor Molina. *Por favor*, regale us with you discovered the mazuahuitl." He spoke the true name of the Aztec sword having practiced it over and over while dressing for the evening.

Molina didn't answer. He merely smiled. Another man's voice broke the silence.

"Detective Carter, I think you know the answer to that."

It was a man's voice from the hallway. It was a voice Carter recognized but didn't expect here in Mexico. The sounds of the man's clipped gait echoed off the walls.

Peter Burlingame strode into the display room. He was

dressed in a formal black suit complete with matching vest and tie. The only white garment he wore was the shirt. In another context, he might come across as a priest.

Escovedo frowned at Burlingame's arrival. Jackson's betrayed his surprise as well. His jaw muscles flexed. Naomi merely stood there, mute.

Carter buried the shock at seeing Burlingame under a pretense of not understanding what the man said. In his accented English, Carter said, "Who is this Detective Carter you mention?"

Burlingame picked up the sixth glass of tequila. "I know you're a gifted actor, Detective, but you can stop it now. Your ruse is exposed, and you are quite literally trapped." He sipped the tequila, grinning around the rim of the glass. "I've won."

In playing the part of Cristobal Cotilla, Carter had stooped himself ever so slightly so as to appear shorter than he truly was. At Burlingame's words, Carter shed Cotilla's skin and stood to his full height. He gave Burlingame a lopsided grin. "Actually, Mr. Burlingame, you've made three mistakes."

❊ 24 ❊

Peter Burlingame chuckled at Carter's comment. "I've heard about this thing you do. Moore told me it is one of the things that makes you so unique. Pray tell, Detective Carter, what do you think I've done wrong?"

With his tequila glass in his hand, Carter's mind swirled about how to break the news long enough to get in a better position to escape with the Aztec sword.

"First, Mr. Burlingame, you offered to bribe my partner and me." At Burlingame's attempt to scoff, Carter pressed on. "I wouldn't dismiss that. It was the first clue I had that there was something more to you. I'm guessing your money can buy you anything, right? Few things are beyond your reach, and to see something you want but can't have probably drives you crazy. Crazy enough to bribe a lawman. Or try to. You never uttered any words in that direction, but we both knew what you were going to ask." He indicated Jackson then pointed back at himself. "Speaking for Detective Jackson, it wouldn't have worked, but I can't help but wonder what you thought our price would be. Care to share?"

Burlingame said nothing.

"Too bad. I would have liked to have known what I'm worth. Maybe if it was a large enough amount, I could have retired from the detective business and gone back to acting. Most of the time, even if you have a bad performance, nobody shoots at you."

Escovedo looked confused. "I'm sorry, but what is going on?"

"Señor Escovedo," Carter said, jumping in before anyone else could tarnish the man's opinion, "you have been dragged into the middle of a play that has no happy ending. My partner and I are detectives for the railroad. We were tasked to track down a piece of stolen property and return it to its rightful owner."

At the mention of his true role, Molina barely flinched. At the comment about the rightful owner of the Aztec sword, he blurted, "I am its rightful owner. I claim ancestry rights to this artifact. It was the damned gringo business-men, including your father"—he pointed an accusing finger at Naomi—"who took it in the first place." He turned to her. "Besides, that was part of the deal, no?"

All eyes turned to Naomi. She grew defiant, raising her chin and looking down her nose at everybody.

"And that would be the second mistake," Carter contin-ued. He smirked and tried to keep the sarcasm out of his voice. "You made it, Naomi dear. Your insistence on accom-panying us. True, it made the case easier, what with you leading us to Hobson's house in Houston and then to Barron's house in Galveston. One point of view certainly shows that. But from another point of view, say, from Señor Molina's point of view, your trips to those houses could be the proof you needed that the arrangement y'all made was completed successfully. If part of the plan all along was to kill off those who knew about the sword, then what better way than to see for yourself?"

Escovedo's jaw dropped open. "Señorita Naomi, is what this man said is true?"

"Of course it is," Carter answered for her. His voice now rose, filling the room as if he were on stage. Which, for Carter, was entirely the truth. This was the one moment, in every case, in which his detective life and his acting life merged seamlessly.

"It's the only explanation for how the entire case got started. Bandits raid your mother's museum on the day of its opening. As bad as that is, it's all part of a distraction for the real crime: the theft of the sword by the legendary Hook Thief. By the way, I assume you hired him. What's his name?"

Naomi merely sneered. "Wouldn't you like to know?"

"I would, in fact," Carter said. "But there's also a part of me that appreciates his anonymity. Sometimes, when we learn the truth about a person, it can change the way we think of them. We can't help but regard them with new eyes, kind of like how I think about you now and Tom from the moment he met you."

He placed his tequila glass on top of a nearby cabinet. "Won't be needing that," he murmured. Besides, he wanted to have his hands free for what he knew was approaching.

Carter returned his attention to Burlingame. "Your third mistake was hiring those owlhoots to rob Octavia's museum that night. I didn't think anything of it at the time, but the killing of the one man back in the St. Louis Hotel, especially the accompanying note about meeting there, that was the initial clue."

"I don't know what you're talking about," Naomi said. Her voice had a sing-song quality to it, almost playful.

"I'll let you know it wasn't one thing, but numerous things along the way that added up," Carter said. He moved closer to the cabinet that housed the Aztec sword. In this position, the cabinet was now between him and Molina, who stood to Carter's right. "Elroy Brown, the dead man in the hotel, was killed by having his throat slit. The rendezvous was arranged by a killer who goes by the moniker "Lacy." You are quite adept with a knife. You demonstrated it perfectly well back in the saloon in Houston. It was a marvel to see. Then, when we asked to see your knife, you showed it to us. The engraving on the blade is your initials. NLH. I'm guessing the "L" stands for Lacy, your middle name. Am I right?"

Jackson, a few feet away on Carter's left, had subtly shifted his feet during Carter's diatribe. At one point in their relationship, Jackson had lamented Carter's penchant to giving a monologue to the bad guys right before they took them in. He thought it pretentious. But he also recognized its significance. It distracted the owlhoots in the moments they usually think they had won.

Escovedo's jaw was still open in astonishment. He stood to Carter's immediate left, Naomi to his left, and then Jackson. Burlingame's position was nearer the one exit from the room.

Naomi turned and smiled at Escovedo the way an older sibling would smile at a younger sibling who was just too stupid to do anything correctly. "Of course it is, Orlando. And do you know what? You're also one of the last two people that know the truth about the mazuahuitl and, even though standards down in Mexico are different, I just can't have you talking."

Her arms flashed out in an arc. Something gleaming was in her hand, and Carter knew what it was even as the razor-sharp blade connected with Escovedo's throat and sliced through the skin.

The movement was so fast that Escovedo didn't react for a second or two. He dropped his glass. It shattered on the floor, the sound being the only sound filling the room. Then the gurgling started. Escovedo's hands went to his neck in a vain attempt to staunch the flow of blood. Instead, the crimson liquid, dark in the lamp light, cascaded through and over his fingers. He dropped to his knees, staring up at Naomi with disbelieving eyes. His lips moved, but no words emerged. With a last sigh, he keeled over and landed on his side, then slumped to the floor. His arms relaxed, yet his heart kept pumping for a few more spasmodic seconds before it realized it was no longer necessary.

As shocking as the act was, Carter pushed his disgust down deep into the pit of his stomach. This was no time to lose his cool. He took the opportunity to slip his hand into his pocket and retrieve what he had put in there back at the hotel.

Jackson appeared none the worse for Naomi's murder, but Carter noted Jackson's holster was empty and his hand behind his thigh.

Molina, on the other hand, was in complete shock. "What the hell have you done?" he burst out in Spanish. "This is sacred ground. You cannot have murder in my house." He made to move closer to Escovedo, but stopped.

Burlingame casually swept back his jacket and revealed the holster high on his hip. With casual movements, he gripped the butt of his gun and cleared leather.

Molina's brows furrowed. "What is this?"

"The third mistake," Carter chimed in. "Actually, it's the fourth, but who the hell's counting?" He caught Burlingame's eyes and wagged his index finger between

Burlingame and Naomi. "You and she were in it together, right?"

Burlingame shook his head in wonder. "Jameson did well when he recruited you, Detective Carter. You are one observant son of a bitch. You'll be dead soon, but I just wanted to let you know that I admire your abilities. Too bad I never saw you act. I hear that's where your true forte lies."

Without being asked, Carter raised his hands. "Is it just money?"

"I just want the sword. That was my deal with Naomi here."

Naomi, still holding the knife, shrugged. "And I just wanted money. Mister Burlingame offered an incredible sum to my mother, but she refused." The anger practically dripped from Naomi's lips. "I didn't refuse. I couldn't care less about Father's pieces of junk. As soon as Mother dies, I'll be selling all of it anyway."

"Admirable," Carter deadpanned.

"And as for you," Burlingame said, focusing on Molina, "if this is sacred Aztec ground, as you claim, didn't they practice blood sacrifice? Then what Naomi did is entirely appropriate. And it's why I'll add you to the funeral pyre." Without another second's hesitation, he pulled the trigger. The gun bucked in his hand, the blossom of flame erupting from out of the barrel.

The bullet slammed into Molina, spinning him around and crashing his falling body into a case.

No more time for talk, Carter concluded. With the kind of marksman Burlingame was, Carter knew that all the businessman had to do was move his gun a few inches and bring Carter into his sights.

Carter, his hands still raised, threw the things he held in the crook of his palm at Burlingame. Two balls flew through the air, one purple and one red. Surprisingly,

Carter's aim wasn't exactly true. Both balls landed at Burlingame's feet. The purple one—the smoke bomb—with a soft thuft, started to billow. The red one—the flash bomb—thunked on ground. The flash was bright and the bang was loud, but Burlingame merely chuckled as he swiveled his body and brought Carter into line with his gun.

He never got the chance to fire.

Jackson brought his Colt from behind his leg and fired. His bullet found a new home in Burlingame. The businessman yelped a moment but didn't fall. Jackson's second bullet made sure that Burlingame was felled.

Carter shot a quick glance at Molina. The Mexican was not moving. He shook his head. Too bad. Carter had hoped to avoid as much killing as possible. It wasn't Molina's fault. He was just a patsy.

Carter opened the display cabinet and, gingerly, withdrew the Aztec sword. The weight was surprisingly hefty. He couldn't tell from which wood the sword was made, but it would certainly have made a vicious swipe. He gripped it in both of his hands and realized something. The gunshots would likely bring Molina's guards. The mazuahuitl would certainly be unwieldy, especially when running. Footsteps sounded from outside the room and Carter realized he now had little choice.

Jackson let out a yell of pain. Carter whirred to see his partner clutching his arm. His gun clattered to the floor. Naomi kicked it away then turned to Carter. The knife she held in her hand dripped with blood.

"Dammit," Carter muttered. "Why the hell'd you have to do that?"

Her lips were pulled back in a maniacal grin. "I'm getting out of here, Calvin. And there's nothing you can do to stop me. Those guards coming? All I have to do is tell them you killed Molina. They won't hesitate to gun you down."

Carter grunted. "Isn't that murder?"

"Things are different down here, remember? They know who I am. I was down here just last year, planning this whole thing. Burlingame was just the extra profit. I got paid twice."

"Too bad you won't be able to spend any of it," Carter muttered. The footsteps were getting louder.

"Like hell I won't. I'm going to walk out of here, and you'll be carried out by a coroner." She shifted the blade from one hand to the next. She approached him. "If you know the legend of Lacy, then you'll know I know how to kill."

Carter cocked his head. "Thanks for clarifying that." He took a step backward. His heel struck a cabinet. He shifted his boot and kept moving backward and around. "Why did you start?"

"Boredom. Plus I hated seeing the way women were treated. The law in Texas is man's law. Women don't have protection. So I gave them retribution. It's not the same thing, but it makes me feel good." Again, she shifted the blade in her hands.

"There are other things to do other than murder men."

"They were men that deserved it! But you, Calvin, you're different. I don't suppose I could convince you to drop that sword and come with me. We can sell the mazuahuitl for a third time, live off the riches."

The idea flashed in Carter's mind. The dinners, seeing the world because they would always be on the run, a knife stuck in his chest because that's what would happen at Naomi's earliest convenience. He saw Jackson, holding his arm, forgotten by Naomi, scooting across the floor to where his pistol ended up, a line of blood trailing him the entire way. All he had to do was keep her occupied until Jackson got his gun.

Naomi shifted the knife again and plunged her hand into the leather satchel she carried around her shoulder. She pulled out a gun—her father's gun if Carter remembered correctly—and hefted it in her hand. She judged the distance between her and Carter to be too great for him to attack. In the next instant, she started to turn, bringing the gun up to bear on Jackson.

Naomi judged the distance between her and Carter wrong. She forgot to account for the mazuahuitl.

Carter lunged forward. In the same motion, he brought the Aztec sword over his head and down on her arm. The ancient obsidian stones were not as sharp as they used to be, but they were sharp enough to penetrate the fabric and most of Naomi's arm. The pistol clattered to the floor. The arm, with a spray of blood, fell limply to Naomi's side. The angle on which is dangled was unnatural.

The screech of pain that erupted from her mouth pierced Carter's ears like pins. It was sharp and guttural. Her eyes wide, she dropped her knife and grasped the stump just above her elbow. If Jackson's fingers were no match for the flow of blood from his knife wound, Naomi's hand was woefully unprepared for the torrent of blood that gushed from her arm.

To be honest, the sight sickened Carter. He certainly didn't have a problem killing in the line of duty and his actions just saved Jackson from certain death, but most of the time, it was with a gun and a bullet. The proximity to a knife wound was always personal and visceral.

"What have you done?" Naomi screamed. Her mouth formed an O of surprise. Her pallor turned white at the sight of her own arm hanging limply by the remaining skin and tissue.

"My job," Carter muttered. Nevertheless, he came to kneel next to her. He took one look at the arm and knew it was a goner. But she didn't have to be. He yanked the satchel off of her body, then pulled the strap off the case. He wrapped it twice around her upper arm, cinching it as tight as he could. Despite the situation, she winced at his ministrations.

From over his head, Jackson fired at the doorway. Molina's guards had finally arrived. Most of the purple smoke had dissipated, so Carter got a clear view of them. The man Jackson hit fell backward, his torso out of the field of vision, only his legs and feet exposed beyond the door. The others hunkered down behind chairs or other pieces of furniture. Bullets started to fly.

"Now what?" Jackson yelled.

Carter still focused his attention on Naomi. Despite her clear intension on killing him and Jackson, Carter still didn't want her to leave. The forefront of his mind told him he wanted to bring her back to America for jail. Other parts of his mind reminded him of their nights together. The jail part of his mind beat down the other part with swift fury.

Reaching into his pocket, Carter pulled out another couple of magic balls. He threw the purple one near the doorway. It landed and rolled around, the plumes of smoke camouflaging the interior of the display room. Next he threw the flash bomb. It exploded just outside the room, giving Molina's men even more to think twice about storming the room.

"We're still without an escape route," Jackson reminded Carter. "And can you stop fiddling with her. We have a situation here."

From his kneeling position, Carter looked up at Jackson to respond. But his eyes drifted past his partner to the wall beyond.

Where a rope had been lowered from the ceiling.

Carter's gaze swept up to where the rope stopped. An iron hook was affixed to the cornice of one of the windows high above. Another figure, silhouetted against the night, gestured that they climb and escape.

The Hook Thief?

"I think we found our solution."

❀ 25 ❀

Carter stood and crossed the display room to the rope and grabbed it. It was thick, easy to get his hand around. He tugged. No sign of movement from where the hook was affixed. Curious, however, was the odor of the rope. Carter couldn't place the scent, but he chalked it up to the substance the Hook Thief used to ignite the rope and get away scot free.

Jackson had seen what Carter was doing and came to the rope. He tugged the rope, then looked up to the ceiling. He sighed.

"Can you do it?" Carter asked.

Shots rang out from the guards. Carter noted that the purple smoke was dissipating.

Jackson stuck out his gun and fired three times. He holstered his gun. "I'll manage." He pointed to the guards. "You manage them. When I get up there, you come up. We can pull you and you'll get out faster." He angled his eyes upward. "Whoever the hell he is."

Despite their situation, Carter grinned. "It's the Hook Thief. Maybe we'll get to see his face."

Jackson grunted. "I'll be sure to ask nicely." He nodded to the guards. "They're coming."

Carter snaked his hand into his jacket and withdrew his gun. He fired off a shot. "Get going." He scurried over to a heavy display case and covered his partner while Jackson, not without a fair amount of painful grunting, put his feet to the wall and started the process of walking up the wall.

That left Carter alone on the floor. He reached his hand into his pocket and pulled out the remaining magic balls. Two purple and two red. He threw one of the purples at the doorway and chased it with two shots from his gun. With practiced precision, he reached around to the back of his belt and retrieved spare cartridges. He placed them on the floor in front of him, ready to reload when the time came.

He looked around the room, trying to find anything with which he could use. He dragged the Aztec sword to him and his efforts were rewarded by a bullet that panged off the tile floor. Shards of stone bit into the skin on his hand and he withdrew the sword the rest of the way behind him. Naomi's eyes fluttered open and closed. She coughed as some of the purple smoke wafted back inside the display room. Carter marveled that she was still among the living, but gave her no other thought.

Using the sword, he reached out and snagged Naomi's dropped pistol. He scooted it towards him and was able to snatch it from the floor before one of the guards fired off another slug. Most of the guards now were shooting indiscriminately inside the display room. Bullets were breaking glass, wood, and the artifacts. Carter knew when the police arrived as well as the government officials, heads might roll when they took a look at the priceless yet damaged Aztec artifacts.

Knowing he would need his hands free, Carter reached out and grabbed Escovedo's corpse. Poor man never knew what he had gotten himself into. Carter quickly unbuckled the man's belt and slipped it out from the loops. Next, he snaked the belt through the loop at the end of the Aztec sword. Lastly, Carter put that belt around his own body. The sword would dangle as he made his escape, but it would still be with him.

He looked up to the ceiling. Jackson was nearly to the top. The Hook Thief had grabbed a hold of one of the stone pillars that formed the window and was leaning down. He grabbed the back of Jackson's shirt then helped the detective up and through the window.

Now it was Carter's turn.

But he needed a distraction.

He threw the remaining smoke bomb then emptied Naomi's pistol. He was rewarded with a yelp. The shooting stopped for a minute while the guards reassessed their situation. That was when Carter spied the tequila. He reached up and grasped the bottle. Readying one of the flash bombs, Carter threw the open tequila bottle to the front entrance of the display room. It smashed into a thousand pieces. The next instant, Carter threw a flash bomb in the middle of the puddle. It exploded and ignited the alcohol. The flames wouldn't hold off the guards long, but it would give him precious seconds to make his way up the rope.

He fired twice more from his gun then holstered it. He grabbed the bullets from the floor and shoved them in his pocket. Then, gripping the rope with both hands, he launched himself up to a standing position on the wall. Carter started walking and pulling himself up, his boots slick against the adobe walls.

He was not yet halfway when Jackson and the Hook Thief began pulling the rope. The action caused Carter to lose his balance. His feet fell into open space and he hung onto the rope for dear life. He now swung twelve or more feet from the floor and about six more feet to the top.

Carter looked up. Jackson. His face was screwed up in pain, the blood coating his coat sleeve. The Hook Thief wore a hat and, from what Carter could tell in the semi-darkness, some sort of mask over his face. At that moment, Carter didn't care what the man looked like. All he cared about was getting to the top.

Below him, the guards had decided to make a charge. Carter heard them getting ready and two figures emerged out of the dissipating purple smoke. They stood in the room, frozen in shock at the sight of the dead and dying people on the floor. Naomi's eyes were open, and she stared at Carter.

He ignored her. Carter hung onto the rope with one hand. In the other, his Colt was already in his palm. He steadied himself with a boot to the wall, aimed at the first of the two guards, and fired twice. Before he was even on the ground, Carter moved his sights to the second man. That man was able to see Carter's gun as it fired two bullets into the man's chest and face.

"Okay!" Carter yelled. He held onto the rope tighter as the two men above him pulled him up. Strong hands gripped the shoulders of his jacket and, in another moment, Carter was deposited on a small ledge that circumnavigated the domed display room. The Aztec sword came to rest on his leg.

Breathing hard, Carter first looked to Jackson. "You okay?"

"I'll live."

Carter put a hand to Jackson's shoulder. "Thanks." He turned to the Hook Thief and got as good a look as he could.

The man wore a black hat with a short brim and a

round crown. The black mask he wore covered nearly his entire face. The only part exposed was his chin and mouth. He wore a black suit, including a black shirt, which was buttoned to the top but without a tie. On his hands were black gloves. The only clue to the man's identity was the skin on his chin. He was a white man with good teeth.

"Thank you," Carter breathed.

The Thief stood. "Thank me later." The tone was educated. We still have to get off this tower."

"You have a plan for that?" Carter asked.

The Thief smiled behind his mask. "Oh yeah."

THE TOWER ON WHICH CARTER, Jackson, and the Hook Thief stood was not as tall as the guard tower, but an expanse of fifty feet stood between the two structures. Below them lay the rest of Molina's house consisting of traditional arched roofs. As long as they could scurry down the side of the domed tower, the fugitives could run across the rooftops, away from the guard tower, and get over the wall which, if Carter's eyes weren't deceiving him, was connected to the main body of the house on the east side.

But to get down to the other rooftops, they would have to descend an approximately twelve foot drop. Not a particularly difficult challenge, if it weren't for the sharpshooter who had spotted them from his position in the guard tower. The first indication was the explosion of mortar and adobe clay that sprayed Carter's face, the bullet having missed him by mere inches.

Jackson and the Thief had the main part of the display room tower to block their bodies from the sharpshooter. Carter wasn't that fortunate. He was exposed. He needed to something fast.

"Need a little help," he called.

Jackson, his gun in his uninjured left hand, stuck his body around the domed roof and fired into the open window of the guard tower. The sharpshooter, his body illuminated by the lantern fires from below, ducked back to avoid Jackson's bullets.

The precious few seconds Carter now had he spent standing back up and leaning back into the window from which he had just escaped. With frantic movements, he hauled the rope from inside the display room. They could use it to descend on the outside of the domed tower and escape.

The guards down below had realized no one was shooting back at them and they now milled around, looking for Carter. One of them looked up, saw Carter, and began firing up at him. More bullets punctured holes in the walls, but none made direct contact with Carter. To make sure, he ducked down from the window sill, avoiding getting shot, and brought in the last of the rope.

The Hook Thief casually took the hook and rearranged its position to allow them better access to climb down the rope on the outside of the domed roof. His movements were almost casual, like it was everyday he was in the middle of a shootout while trying to escape.

"I'll go first," the Thief announced. He didn't wait for any sort of confirmation. With his gloved hands, he snaked the rope around his body, one hand at his rear, the other in front of him. He leaned out, far, so that he was perpendicular with the side of the tower. Then, he jumped. At the same time, he loosened his grip. The result was that he slid down the length of the wall in two leaps.

"I'm gonna have to try that," Carter muttered.

"He has gloves," Jackson said. He fired twice more,

then holstered his gun. He gripped the rope. "I'm going down the old-fashioned way. Cover me."

Carter pulled his Colt out of its holster. He cracked open the cylinder, reached into his pocket, and pulled out the spare cartridges. He emptied the one with the used up shells and thumbed in a fresh six bullets. With a flick of his wrist, he locked the cylinder back into place. He nodded once at Jackson. "Meet you down below." With that, he stood and fired once at the guard tower.

Jackson clambered over the side of the small ledge and worked his way down as fast as possible. They were fortunate in that the open garden areas down below and to the south were at such an angle so as to make direct aim at the domed roof difficult. The only true angle was from the guard tower, and the way they had positioned the rope, the entire structure of the tower blocked the sharpshooter's field of vision. Carter felt himself relatively safe.

Until a heretofore unseen door banged open off to the north side.

Three guards charged out from inside the house, their rifles up and ready to fire. Jackson wasn't quite to the end of the rope, so Carter changed his aim. He fired four times into the oncoming cadre of men. His bullets were accompanied by those from the Hook Thief. Between the two of them, the fuselage of bullets took out the guards who crumpled onto the roof.

No more time. Carter holstered his gun, gripped the rope, allowed the mazuahuitl to dangle below him, and scrambled over the side of the ledge. Hand over hand, he descended as fast as he dared. He slipped once, his hand sliding over the rough rope, cutting his palm, but he managed to get to the end of the rope in only a few seconds. He checked on Jackson. His partner was clearly in pain but adrenaline coursed through his body and he was putting all pain aside during their escape.

"Now what?" Carter asked.

"Now it's easy," the Hook Thief said. "Follow me." He dashed across the rooftops to the east side of the house. The sharpshooter now had a clear field of range on them and he began sending bullets their direction. But they were moving too fast for him to adjust. In a few seconds, they had reached the edge of the house and the perimeter wall. What lay below them was shrouded in darkness, but Carter saw the dim glint of a metal hook, affixed to the top of the wall.

"More rope?" Jackson lamented.

The Hook Thief bent down and picked up three bent metal bars roughly in the shape of the horns of a longhorn steer. In the center of each was a smooth groove. He handed one each to Carter and Jackson. "You don't have to climb this time."

The Thief got on his hands and knees and twanged a rope that Carter had previously not seemed. It was taut and angled down the hill into the deeper darkness. The Thief positioned the iron bar with the groove on the rope. He held onto either end of the bar, then launched himself down. A high-pitched whine sounded as the Thief glided down the rope to safety.

"Neat trick," Jackson muttered. He didn't wait another second. He got himself into a position like the Thief had just shown and disappeared into the darkness.

Carter smiled at the theatricality of it all. He would have to compare notes with the Hook Thief, maybe learn some new tricks.

More footsteps sounded over the rooftop from behind him. Quickly, Carter scrambled into position. There was nothing he could do about the whine of the iron bar on the rope. As soon as he launched himself, they would know his position. Oh well. Might as well enjoy the ride.

Pushing himself off the wall, Carter glided down the rope, the mazuahuitl dangling behind and below him. The trip was surprisingly fast and about halfway down, he hoped there was not a large bang at the end. The trees whipped past him, but none of the branches slapped him in the face. The mazuahuitl hit a few, but it made the trip in one piece. As if materializing out of thin air, Carter saw a light shape. He didn't know what it was, but he was moving to it rapidly. Then he was on it. He landed on a large blanket. It wasn't necessarily soft, but it cushioned the halt. Jackson and the Thief both reached out and grabbed Carter to slow his descent.

"Wow," Carter said, "that was fun." He scrambled to his feet. He loosened the belt holding onto the mazuahuitl, then turned to the Hook Thief. "May I? I've always loved your theatricality."

The Thief nodded once.

Carter reached into his jacket pocket and pulled out a Lucifer. He struck it with his thumb, then placed the flame onto the rope. In a few seconds, the rope had ignited. The line of fire moved slowly up the rope, then with increasing speed. In a few seconds, there was a line of fire extending from their position all the way up to the house.

"Wow," Carter said again.

Jackson grabbed his shoulder. "Think about it later. Let's move."

The Hook Thief was already making his way down the hill. The ambient light from the city made the descent easier. Jackson had no difficulties scurrying down the hill. Carter, with more than once glance back up to the see the burning rope, followed close behind.

At the bottom of the hill, a covered cab waited. The

driver was already seated and ready to go. With efficient movements, the Hook Thief opened the door, issued a command to the driver, and then climbed inside. Jackson and Carter followed. The Thief knocked on the roof twice. The driver called to his team of two. The horses moved with swift motion, and they left the house of Juan Esteban Molina behind.

* * *

CARTER SAT BACK in the seat, finally able to rest. He and Jackson sat in the front seat, their backs to the driver. The Hook Thief sat opposite them. The shades were drawn inside the carriage, so little light filtered in. The Thief, nonetheless, didn't remove any of his disguise.

Despite what he told himself about the legend of the Hook Thief being more important than the actual identity, Carter couldn't help himself. "Who are you?"

"I have many names," the Thief said. "I imagine you would appreciate that, Detective Carter, seeing as you are a former actor. You could even say I am many different characters, depending on the situation."

Carter couldn't argue with that. "You were the one who stole the mazuahuitl." He felt proud to be able to say the Aztec word better each time.

"I was."

"And Naomi Hendrickson hired you."

"She did." His voice grew somewhat wistful at some thought of her. "I saw her on the floor in the display room. Dead?"

"Not when the last time I saw her."

The Thief nodded.

Jackson chimed in. "So this entire thing was arranged by Naomi to get Molina to buy the sword, have it returned here, only to have Burlingame show up and take it back? She got paid twice."

"Apparently so."

"How'd Naomi contact you?" Carter said.

"I think you know the answer to that one, Detective. In her guise as Lacy, Naomi worked inside the underbelly of society. It was in one of her little adventures that she discovered me." He chuckled. "It's really a good story. Perhaps I'll tell you someday."

Carter grew silent for a few moments. Various thoughts swirled in his mind. He wanted answers to so many questions, but at the same time, he enjoyed the mystery. He bit his lip, fighting with himself, asking himself if he should ask the questions or not.

"I think it's best if you live your life without the full knowledge of who I am, Detective Carter. It's best for me, and it's certainly best for you."

Frowning, Carter said, "Why?"

The Hook Thief sighed. "Because I have stolen things from some very powerful people. If they find out that you have met me, well, let's just say the questioning process isn't very pleasant. I've lost some good partners in that manner. I have dealt with some of the perpetrators, but not all."

"Wait a minute," Jackson said. "You steal from people, they find out it was you, they find your friends, torture them for information?"

The Thief nodded. "My work is very peculiar. It requires a certain set of skills. Most of the time, I'm anonymous. Other times, not so much. What I do needs to be done to rectify an injustice. It's unfortunate when an associate is hurt, but then I get my revenge upon their killer. It all evens out."

Jackson grunted and sat back in his chair.

The Thief pulled the curtains back and glanced outside. The carriage slowed to a halt. "We are here."

"Where?" Carter asked.

"The local doctor. His name is Anselmo. Detective Jackson needs medical attention. I need to vanish into the night." He reached over and opened the door. "Good evening, gentlemen."

Jackson mumbled a thanks as he clambered out of the carriage.

Carter extended his hand out to the Hook Thief. The other man took it. They shook. "To the mystery."

"To the mystery," the Hook Thief replied. He grinned.

Carter climbed out of the carriage. The Hook Thief reached out to grab the door, but stopped. "Oh, and Detective Jackson?" He waited until Jackson turned to face him. "I'd suggest you take something for the trip back to Texas. Ask the doctor inside. He's got a special medicine that calms the stomach."

Realization dawned on Carter. The Hook Thief had traveled on the *Cassiopeia* with them!

"Hey, wait," Carter started to say, but the Hook Thief had already closed the carriage door. A knock sounded and the driver called his team to move. The carriage trundled down the street and turned around a corner.

Calvin Carter stood with his mouth open, a broad grin forming on his face.

Thomas Jackson clapped him on the back. "C'mon Cal. Let's see this sawbones. Then you owe me the biggest glass of tequila we can find."

❈ 26 ❈

THE DOOR to the doctor's office burst open and light flooded into the streets. Anselmo, the local doctor, was a tall, strapping man who looked like he belonged more in some archeological excavation rather than a sedate office. He wore thick brown boots, crisp khaki pants, and a silk red shirt, open at the collar revealing his thick black chest hair. His swarthy complexion and well-trimmed mustache was offset by his gleaming straight white teeth as he smiled at the two Americans who stood on his doorstep. Despite the hour, it appeared Anselmo was open for business.

Carter, still in disguise Cristobal Cotilla, nodded at the doctor and hoped his Spanish would be good enough. He made mention that Jackson needed medical attention, but Anselmo waved him off.

"Please come in, *mi amigos*," the doctor said in English, gesturing for the detectives to enter his office. "Our mutual friend already told me there might be casualties." He winked conspiratorially.

Jackson and Carter exchanged a glance. Jackson's raised eyebrows asked if they could trust Anselmo. Carter merely smiled. Of course the Hook Thief had arranged everything. As a strategist, Carter again marveled at the planning by their mysterious benefactor.

Inside, Anselmo's office was decorated in a military fashion. A Spartan exam table dominated the room, with cabinet hung on the walls with various medical equipment inside. One counter top showed the main tools of his trade. All of the furniture appeared to be high quality. Photos of him in various locales hung on the walls. Nearly all of the men in the photographs were soldiers. One wall was reserved for the various medals and commendations Anselmo received over the years.

Curiously, Carter sidled up to one photo. Anselmo stood next to a man Carter didn't recognize, but he instantly identified the uniform. He hooked a thumb at the framed picture.

"You fought for the Confederacy?"

Anselmo, now standing next to Jackson who sat on an examination table, grinned broadly. "I go where I am needed. The men of the South needed me at the time, and I happily complied." He gestured to the well-appointed room. "I was well paid, of course, but sometimes cause and money go hand in hand." To Jackson, he beckoned the detective to remove his shirt to get a good look at the damage.

"Which one was it for the Rebels?" Jackson asked. He slid his bloody shirt off his shoulders. It landed in a wet heap on the floor.

"Both," Anselmo replied enigmatically.

Carter returned his gaze to the framed pictures. All the men smiled, as if they had just conquered the world. Idly, Carter wondered if any of these soldiers with Anselmo was actually the Hook Thief.

In his mind's eye, Carter replayed the discussion he and the Thief had exchanged. Even with the poor light in the carriage, Carter saw the only part of the Thief not covered by the mask: the man's chin. Something gnawed at the back of his mind. No, it wasn't the only thing he knew. The voice. Carter and the Hook Thief had talked. Carter heard the Thief's voice in his head, over and over, taking all the words and tonality into account.

And then realized he had heard it before. A second later, he comprehended he had seen the Thief's face before as well.

Carter turned and faced Jackson. "I know the Hook Thief's face."

Jackson, wincing as Anselmo cleaned the wound, said, "What the hell are you talking about?"

Starting to pace back and forth, Carter's mind raced. "Remember back in Austin when Hiram Colby was killed in the jail cell? You ran around to the east side while I went west. Well, I ran into a man. He was well dressed, yet had a scar on his cheek. I apologized to him, and he spoke to me." He stopped, turning on his heel. "It was the Hook Thief."

Jackson screwed up his face. "Are you sure?"

Carter chewed on his lip. "Pretty damn sure." His voice trailed off. He knew the Hook Thief's face, but not his name.

"Maybe you just got your head knocked around down here," Jackson said, moving his chin in the direction of Molina's compound. "Or all that damn smoke rattled your brain." He swore as the doctor picked up a needle and surgical thread. "That necessary?"

"You want to bleed out?" Anselmo said in a clinical voice.

"No."

"Then it's necessary." He pointed to a corner cabinet. Through the screened doors, various liquor bottles sat. "Pick your medicine."

Jackson's wry smile said it all. "When in Mexico, I'll take tequila. Cal, fetch it for me."

Carter had been lost in thought, but at the sound of his name, he came out of his reverie. He walked across the room, opened the cabinet, and selected the tequila bottle. The light brown liquid sloshed inside. He retrieved a cup from the top of the cabinet, poured two fingers, and handed it to Jackson.

The bigger man downed the liquor in one gulp. He wiped his mouth with the back of his hand, then grimaced when Anselmo pierced his skin. "Son of a bitch," he muttered.

Carter poured himself a little tequila and sipped it. Thoughtfully, he returned to the wall of photos. He focused strictly on the chins.

"Don't look too hard, Detective," Anselmo said. He didn't look away from his sewing.

"Why's that?"

"It's for your own safety. Knowing who he is can get you killed."

"You're still alive and you know him."

The doctor leaned in close to Jackson's arm, steadying his aim. He gingerly pushed the needle into the bloody skin and kept on about his work.

"*Si*," Anselmo said, "but he doesn't always operate in my country. True, he goes where he must after he's hired to recover that which has been stolen, but he's only been here a few times." He sighed. "No, it's no secret he lives in America, but your country is big, and he has many places to hide."

Carter grunted. Less than an hour ago, the Hook Thief saved them from Molina's men. He and the Thief had even agreed the mystery was more important than knowledge.

But that was before. Now, knowing he had seen the Hook Thief face to face, Carter wanted to know.

He turned and faced the wall again. He let his eyes glaze over, fixating only on the chins of the men in the photographs. The Thief had to be one of these men.

"Cal?" Jackson's voice. It contained a hint of worry that spun Carter on his heels.

Anselmo had stopped working on Jackson's arm. Now, one hand held the needle, ready to make the final stitch. His other hand grasped a pistol. The barrel was aimed at Jackson's head.

"I am a doctor, yes, and it is my duty to administer aid to the sick and injured. But I am also the keeper of a secret." He waited until Carter's eyes zeroed in on his. "I've been instructed to help you and let you go. But if you insist on probing my photographs, then I will have to make sure you both search for him no longer."

Jackson, with the pistol to the back of his head, muttered, "I'm good with not knowing." He winced again, likely a result of Anselmo tugging the thread in his hands attached to Jackson's wound.

Carter spread his arms out to his side, palms open. "Okay, okay. I'll stop." He shrugged. "Besides, he was good to us. Let's let his secret remain that way."

Anselmo motioned with his head. "If you don't mind, please sit over there." The spot was across the room with three chairs lined up against a wall. It was where he had placed the sword.

Nodding, Carter made his way to that area and sat. Looking down at the artifact, he said, "What makes you think I won't jump you as soon as you put the gun down? Or that Jackson won't punch you in the face when you're done?"

The doctor smiled, showing all his teeth. "Because, deep

down, you appreciate what he does and how he does it. The newspapers named him the Hook Thief, but he might as well be Robin Hood." With his thumb, he eased the hammer of the pistol down, then replaced the weapon into his doctor bag directly behind Jackson. "And because I'm the only one who has the antidote."

Carter froze. He turned sharply to Anselmo. "What antidote?"

"To the poison I put in the medicine I used to clean Detective Jackson's wound." Anselmo grinned again. "It's my personal insurance policy in case you don't take the hint about letting him go."

Sighing and rubbing his closed eyes with his thumb and middle finger, Carter said, "If my partner dies because of something you did, you'll need a whole lot more insurance from the likes of me."

"Good to know you still care," Jackson quipped. "Now shut up and let the man finish what he's doing and we'll be on our way." He held up a finger. "After...you give me the damned antidote."

❅   27   ❅

AN HOUR LATER, Carter and Jackson stood on the street, looking up at the Hidalgo Hotel. In this area of Vera Cruz, it seemed few were ready to turn in for the night. Lights from various cantinas spilled onto the street. Men and women walked up and down the sidewalks, darting into and out of the various establishments. It almost seemed like there was some sort of celebration and the two Americans were mere spectators.

Carter still held the hilt of the macuahuitl, but he had wrapped a sheet from Anselmo's office around the bulk of the sword. Still, it was pretty obvious the object would attract unwanted attention. Even the cabbie who had dropped them off seemed fascinated with it until Jackson swept his coat aside and revealed the holster and Colt strapped to his thigh.

"Want to just walk in the front door and see if anybody notices?" Jackson asked.

"Judging from the darkness of that back alley, it's prob-ably the safer bet." Carter stepped off the curb and started crossing the street. "You ask a question and distract the man at the front desk. I'll duck up the stairs."

"What do you want me to ask?" Jackson hurried to match pace with Carter.

"I dunno. Where's the best place for a tequila."

Jackson glanced up and down the street, spying the half dozen cantinas. "That's a stupid question. I'll think of something better."

He hurried in front of Carter, stopping just on the outside of the front door. He looked inside, then back to Carter. "It's empty. Give me ten seconds, then do your thing."

Carter nodded. He had grasped the sword higher on the hilt, inching the handle into his coat sleeve. It made for a shorter look, but the macuahuitl still extended from Carter's arm by four feet. He would just have to use his body as a shield.

Jackson ducked inside just as a figure rounded the far corner of the hotel from the darkness of the alley. The figure moved quickly to the front door, about thirty feet.

The hair on the back of Carter's neck stood on end. This man who approached could merely be walking fast to get to somewhere and have nothing to do with the Aztec sword. Or Molina. Then again, if word had spread about the fighting in Molina's compound, then Carter and Jackson, as Americans, stood out pretty bad.

Taking the door handle, Carter opened the door and slipped inside. Jackson hadn't reached the desk yet, but started talking as soon as he realized his partner was inside the hotel. Carter, keeping the arm holding the sword at his side, walked swiftly to the stairs across the lobby. The stairs were wide and painted white. They were meant to showcase the remarkable two-story lobby. In any other circumstance,

Carter would marvel at the architecture. Tonight, he was a sitting duck.

He ascended the stairs two at a time. From the hotel's bar came the murmuring of people talking and gambling. At one point, the opening of the bar and Carter's position aligned. He quickly crossed that threshold and breathed a sigh of relief.

Which died in his throat as he noted a man lean off the interior wall of the bar and cross the lobby. The man still wore his sombrero so Carter could not get a read on his face, but the rough clothes and the sight of holsters strapped to both thighs told the detective all he needed to know.

Carter cleared his throat and coughed. Loud. It was a signal to Jackson. But by this point, Carter had climbed high enough to where he had no line of sight between him and Jackson. He prayed his partner heard the message.

Reaching the second floor landing, Carter glanced down at the lobby floor. The man in the sombrero had reached the foot of the stairs and started climbing. Slowly, taking each step one by one. Maybe he was trying to look nonchalant. Maybe it worked for anybody else in this hotel, but Carter knew better.

The Hidalgo Hotel was a rough rectangle with the front door built at the corner. The better to showcase the entry from more than one avenue. To get to his and Jackson's room, Carter would have to make his way down the longer hallway to the end, then hang a left. In the time it would take Carter to even get to the left turn, the gunman would have reached the second-floor landing.

So Carter ran.

Thankfully, the hotel spent the money to lay long carpets along the center of the hallways so most of Carter's footfalls were as silent as possible. But the sound still carried, and as Carter rounded the corner, he shot a glance back at the main stairway.

The man in the sombrero topped the stairs and started running after Carter. One of his pistols was already in his hand.

Options flooded Carter's mind. On the one hand, he could charge down the short hallway to his room, fumble for the key, hope to get it inserted in time, and open the door before the gunsmith rounded the corner. Carter wasn't too sure about the police in this city, but he assumed the word of a local went farther than that of an American gringo.

Which left option two.

Carter slipped the sword out of his sleeve. It thunked on the floor. No time to unwrap the sheet and allow the centuries old blades to do their best work. Surprise would have to be his ultimate weapon.

Gripping the sword with both hands, Carter hefted the macuahuitl and brought it up to his shoulder. The gunman made no attempt to mask his approach so when Carter swung, he knew just where the man was going to be.

The gunman rounded the corner just as Carter ducked and swung the macuahuitl, blades out, at the man's legs. Despite the wooden sword still being wrapped in the sheet, the obsidian cutting structures still did sufficient damage to the man's thighs. The man yelled in surprise and pain. He fell forward. His momentum and the fabric of the sheet and the man's pants intertwining, ripped the sword from Carter's grip. He let go. In one smooth movement, he snaked his hand into his jacket and pulled out his Colt. He also followed the trajectory of the falling man as he sprawled face first onto the carpeted floor. One of Carter's boots stepped on the hand holding the gun. With his other boot, Carter reared back and kicked into the man's rib cage.

He wasn't rewarded with any cracking sounds, but he heard the air from the man's lungs whoosh out.

"*Suelta el arma*," Carter muttered in Spanish. Drop the gun.

Remarkably, the man complied. He extended his fingers, letting the pistol fall from his grip. Carter changed boots on the man's hand and kicked the useless weapon across the hallway where it clattered next to a closed door.

The man on the floor groaned. Carter knelt to the ground and slammed the handle of his pistol on the back of the man's head. The gunman's eyes slid up in their sockets and he passed out.

More footsteps hurried from around the corner. Carter stood and eased himself flat along the wall. The sword was trapped under the unconscious man so it was going to be a gun battle. Holding his arm at a ninety-degree angle, the Colt next to his head, Carter waited for the new figure to emerge.

The movement stopped.

Carter caught his breath, waiting for the other person to charge around the corner.

"Cal?" Jackson's voice. "You okay?"

"Yeah," Carter replied. "You?"

"Yup."

"Any problems downstairs?"

"Didn't see any, but we'd better disappear pretty quick. Need help cleaning up your mess?"

Carter holstered his Colt and walked to the gunman's body. He reckoned the man weighed about one fifty. Easy enough for both detectives to manage. "Probably. You get the legs. I'll get the arms."

Jackson emerged from the other hallway. He winced at the damage Carter inflicted. Blood now began to soak the carpet under the gunman's legs. "Damn effective weapon."

"Can you imagine a whole army using them?" With his boot, Carter moved the man's body, rolling him over onto his back. He fished the sword out from under the man's body, then placed it on the unconscious man's chest.

"Still no match for a gun."

"Maybe not, but this sword has a certain elegance to it." He stepped to the nearest door and tried the knob. It opened. Smiling, Carter returned and grabbed the man's wrists. Jackson picked up the man's heels and, together, they quick-stepped into the empty room. They deposited the body on the other side of the bed, then returned to the hallway, closing the door behind them.

Carter and Jackson both stopped, listening. From downstairs came typical sounds from a hotel and bar. Nothing seemed amiss. More importantly, no other gunmen approached.

"We're probably in the clear," Jackson muttered. He gestured to the sword. "Not sure how we're going to get that out of the country, though."

"We'll figure that out tomorrow," Carter said. "We'll wire Octavia and have her give us instructions."

Jackson produced their room key and held it up between them. He waggled it back and forth. He walked to their room at the end of the hall. He unlocked the door, and stepped inside. Carter followed close behind, until he bumped into Jackson, who had stopped dead in his tracks. His partner was rooted in place, his hands out to his sides.

"What the hell, Tom..." Carter said, and then he saw what Jackson had seen.

Sitting on the edge of the bed was Naomi Hendrickson, gun in hand.

$$\mathbf{\maltese} \quad 28 \quad \mathbf{\maltese}$$

THE VISAGE NAOMI presented resembled something akin to a cadaver.

Her right arm, the one Carter attacked with the sword back at Molina's estate, hung in a sling across her chest. The sleeve of her shirt had been ripped all the way up to her shoulder, laying bare her injured arm. The appendage already looked dead. The forearm seemed to be holding onto the upper arm by mere cartilage and muscle and skin. In between, where her elbow should have been, was empty space.

Someone had wrapped a leather cord around both her lower and upper arm. The cord both stopped the bleeding from each side, but also kept the two halves of the arm in close proximity to each other. The sling merely kept the arm in place.

Naomi's face was gaunt, drained of the precious blood she needed to stay alive. Her eyes had already sunken in, and her prominent cheekbones protruded from her face. Her hair was messed up. The room contained the distinct odor of smoke, proof that Naomi had to not only contend with her broken arm, but fight through the burning house to escape and make her way here.

The rest of the room looked like it had been searched all over. Clothes were scattered along the floor. Carter's makeup kit had been overturned, the jars smashed. The open window let in the warm sea breeze, fluttering the curtains. The wind washed over Naomi's torso, billowing out her shirt.

Two parts of Naomi looked unscathed: her eyes, which barely contained the fire within, and her left hand, which held the gun rock steady.

"Close the door," she commanded. Her voice, steely though it was, betrayed the pain she felt.

Never taking his eyes from Naomi, Carter kicked the door closed with his heel. The door thudded into place.

"Those goons your men?" Carter asked. With Jackson's body shielding his movements from Naomi, Carter slipped a hand into his coat and grasped the Colt.

"Don't," Naomi said, her voice still firm. "Or I might have to shoot your partner."

"I really wish you wouldn't," Jackson muttered. He kept his hands far away from his body and his own Colt.

Carter's mind raced. He had used all the magicians trick balls back at the Molina mansion. She already knew about his Colt and the pistol he kept strapped to his right forearm. Plus, no matter how much the team back at the detective agency worked, they could never create a silent spring-loaded trigger mechanism. As soon as Carter activated it, Naomi could kill them both before the small Derringer even landed in Carter's palm.

There was another option, Carter's ace, but he wasn't sure he could actually pull it off. Seeing no other option, even a bad option was better than none.

His hand pulled back from the Colt and grasped the

much smaller items and held them ready. He remained behind Jackson.

"Come to where I can see you, Calvin, dear," Naomi said. Her tone mimicked her mother's fawning voice from the previous week. "And don't try any of your tricks. I know them all."

"I guess you do," Carter muttered.

Carter, the hilt of the sheet-wrapped Aztec sword still in his hand, hoped she didn't know this last trick.

With the nail of his thumb, he flicked a Lucifer to life. The soft flame fizzed to life, igniting the other four matches Carter held in his grip. With the larger flame, he put it against the bottom of the sheet. It took a couple of seconds, but presently, a small flame started.

Dropping the matches to the dark carpet, Carter held up his hands. The one still behind Jackson held the macuahuitl, the blade angled to the floor.

"Both hands, Calvin," Naomi said behind gritted teeth.

The sound of the soft flame, the growing light as more and more of the sheet caught fire, and likely the feeling of warmth at his back caused Jackson to shoot Carter a look. It was subtle, but enough for Naomi to notice.

"What?"

Then Carter brought the sword up in his grip, letting the burning sheet hover high over Jackson's bare head. The light from the burning sheet brightened the room.

Naomi's eyes fell open in a wide O. Her mouth went slack jawed. "No!" she cried. Her focus shifted to the sword. Her gun barrel faltered.

But that was enough.

In a blur of motion, Jackson's right hand flew to the Colt holstered on his thigh. He cleared leather and fired from the hip. The loud sound boomed in the small room.

The lead slug caught Naomi in the center of her chest.

The force threw her backward on the bed. The gun leapt from her grasp and landed on the far wall. The movement must have loosened the leather cord because her arm started bleeding. That earlier wound had to contend with the gaping maw in her chest for what little blood remained in her body. Judging from the amount flowing from her chest, Jackson's death blow would win.

Carter quickly dropped the sword on the floor, stripped off his jacket, and muffled the flames. He hated losing such a fine jacket, but he hated the idea of losing a valuable artifact even more.

Jackson holstered his smoking gun and spun on his heels. "That the best you could do? Burn the thing we came all the way down here to fetch?"

Shrugging, Carter unwrapped the charred remnants of the sheet and examined how much damage his little stunt inflicted on the ancient weapon.

Only a partial burned area showed up on the tip of the sword. Otherwise, the macuahuitl came out of the little scrape unharmed.

Carter held up the sword. "See? Hardly any damage. And you're welcome for providing a distraction long enough for you to do your fast draw." He waggled his finger back and forth between them. "Team work. It's what we do best."

Jackson opened his mouth to reply, but his words died in his throat as two things happened in quick succession.

From the front door came the sound of the lock jamming in place. Shadows playing out along the thin strip of space under the door indicated someone in the hallway had just locked the two detectives in the room.

Carter was closer so he rose from his position and moved to the door. He gripped the doorknob. It was unmoving in his grip.

"Move," Jackson said. "Let me try. I'm stronger than you."

Carter let the slight jab go as he sidestepped and made way for his partner.

At that moment, a cloth was wedged under the door. All light from the hallway vanished.

"What the hell?" Jackson muttered.

Movement from the window caught Carter's peripheral vision. He turned just as four smoking objects flew into the room. Tossed was more like it. They were colored yellow, and the yellow smoke followed the trajectory of the objects, which turned out to be small balls. They bounced and rolled, coming to a halt at the detectives' feet.

Instantly, Carter knew what they were. Magician's trick balls. But he had never seen yellow ones before. But he recognized the red one.

He turned his face away from the red ball just as it exploded. He had brought his arm up and slung it across Jackson's shoulders, turning the bigger man to the door and away from the blast.

The explosion was loud in the small room. Carter's ears rang from the percussive sound, wincing at the pain it caused. The force of the blast was strong enough to push Carter and Jackson toward the door. They hit the door with their foreheads, but were otherwise uninjured.

Blinking away the red smoke from his eyes, Carter whirled to face the window. His hand plunged into his jacket, ready to draw his weapon, but the yellow smoke had now filled the room. He couldn't see anyone to shoot at, but he damn well knew who it was.

The Hook Thief.

It had to be.

Waving his hand in front of his face, working his jaw to stop the ringing in his ears, Carter charged across the room.

He got a face full of the yellow smoke. So angry was he that he never considered covering his face and nose from the smoke. He breathed it in as he crossed the smoke-filled room. He bumped his knee on the side of the bed, nearly falling on Naomi's corpse. It was then he realized the window had been closed.

Calvin Carter had enough time to wonder why someone would close the window before the blackness of unconsciousness crept along the sides of his vision and he fell to the floor.

❧ 29 ❧

CALVIN CARTER OPENED HIS EYES. He blinked away the morning sunlight streaming through the still-closed window. It took him a moment to get his bearings and make sense of what his eyes saw. He allowed his eyes to take stock of his situation without moving his head.

He was on the floor on his back. Something was under his head. A pillow? His arms were at his sides. He wasn't tied up in any way.

Still not moving, he listened. Outside the window, the sounds of Vera Cruz filtered in. Horses, men, women, and children went about their day as if nothing was wrong. Inside the room, nothing moved.

It was then his mind jolted to Jackson.

Carter sat bolt upright. His hand naturally flew to his holster.

The holster was empty.

Panic seized him. He got to his knees before the throbbing in his head overwhelmed him. He fell to all fours, shaking his head, trying to clear the pain. From this position, he noted the bed.

The body of Naomi Hendrickson was gone. Next to the large bloodstain rested his gun.

Made no sense.

Staying on all fours, Carter crawled to Jackson's body. His partner had been turned on his back. The other pillow from the bed was under his head.

Carter's fingers went to Jackson's neck. He felt the pulse and breathed a sigh of relief.

Jackson's eyes fluttered open. He saw Carter leaning over him and frowned. "You're not what I want to see when I wake up."

Carter grunted.

"What the hell happened?" Jackson said. His voice sounded like sandpaper.

Easing to a sitting position with his back against a wall, Carter grinned without humor. "We were knocked out. Those yellow balls must have some sort of tranquilizer in the smoke."

Jackson sat up, then groaned and held his head.

"It'll pass."

With his eyes still closed, Jackson muttered, "You're the only person I know who uses balls like that. Well, your magician friend, too."

"Wasn't him." Carter sighed as he kicked at the burned sheet.

The Aztec sword was gone.

"Then who?"

Carter's mind scraped at the last memory he had before dropping to the floor. It was through a haze of smoke, but he saw a figure clad in black outside the window, looking in.

"The Hook Thief."

Jackson exhaled air from his mouth. "Of course it was." Using the wall to help, he got to his feet. He surveyed the room. "She's gone, too. Who the hell could get a dead body out of a hotel room?"

"Evidently the Thief knows how." Carter stood next to his partner. He cocked his head at something on the bed.

Under his gun was an envelope. He walked over to the bed and picked up his gun, holstering it after verifying the rounds were still inside.

In neat, formal handwriting, Carter's name was written.

He picked up the envelope. It was expensive paper, thick like legal documents. He turned it over and noted a wax seal keeping the flap closed. In the middle of the wax was the impression of a hook.

Despite the situation, Carter smiled. Theatricality.

He broke the seal and opened the letter. Jackson came to stand next to Carter and they both read the note inside.

"Detectives Carter and Jackson,

"I hope you accept my sincere apologies for the methods I took to obtain the macuahuitl. I was fairly certain you would not have parted with it had I merely asked. But you see, I could not let you return it to Texas where it would languish in a museum or worse. This is a prized possession of Mexican heritage and it deserves to remain in this country. I have taken steps to ensure it finds a proper and honored location.

"You may feel compelled to search for it. Madame Hendrickson may even demand it. But I urge you not to undertake that expedition. It would prove ultimately futile and unhealthy. But rest assured, it will be well looked after and appreciated by those who know of its true value.

"As to Miss Hendrickson's body, please know I have taken care of it as well. She will find an honored place of rest. I do not envy you having to relate the news to Madame Hendrickson.

"You both are a good team. Each possesses traits the

other lacks. Colonel Moore did well when he paired you together. I am honored to have worked with you.

"Perhaps we can again in the future.

"To the mystery."

The area where a signature would typically go was blank.

Carter tapped the letter on his palm. He gazed out the window with a wistful look on his face.

Jackson shook his head. "You damn actors. Always leaving the stage in a blaze of glory." He crossed the room and opened the window. The freeze sea breeze blew inside, washing away the stale stink of smoke. He closed his eyes and breathed deeply.

Following his lead, Carter also walked to the window. The morning sun felt good on his skin. The salt air filled his lungs. He actually could feel his body reacting to the new stimuli. It was a new day, and he was alive to enjoy it.

He didn't relish informing Colonel Moore that they failed to recover the Aztec sword, and he dreaded even more telling Octavia about her daughter's death. How much would he say? Would he even bring up Naomi's other life as the mysterious Lacy? Probably not. What would be the point? Octavia now lost both her husband and daughter and the Aztec sword. That would be enough.

"I know what you're thinking," Jackson said. He kept his eyes on the expanse of water that was the Gulf of Mexico.

Carter nodded. "It'll be difficult."

Thomas Jackson turned to his partner with a huge grin on his face. He clapped a large hand on Carter's shoulder, turning him away from the vision of the water and pointing him north across the land. "But you'll have lots of time to think about how you'll say what you have to say."

Calvin Carter frowned. "Why?"

"Because when we go home, we're taking a train."

Keep reading for a sneak peak at the next Calvin Carter:
Railroad Detective novel…

BRIDES OF DEATH

Coming July 2019 from Quadrant Fiction Studio

The house sat not one hundred yards from the edge of the San Pedro River. The owner had built the home on top of a small, rocky slope, so when the river flooded—as it was wont to do every year during the spring thaw—the water would never rise high enough to reach the bottom step. The vast open fields between the house and the river were filled with lines of crops: potatoes, corn, and wheat. The tall stalks of corn wafted in the gentle breeze, bringing with it the fragrant sweetness of its fruit. The farmer who worked this land knew what he was doing. He had managed to get every last square foot filled with some sort of vegetation. It was likely the reason Jared Newell was as prosperous as he turned out to be.

But railroad detective Evelyn Paige didn't suspect Newell ever thought he would have to defend his land from invasion.

Even in the dim moonlight, she noted the worry lines along his eyes and mouth. The stump of an unlit cigar protruded from his clenched teeth. The muscles under his smooth cheeks flexed and rippled. He kept wiping the palms of his hands on his pants. The Winchester he held in his hands also got wiped down, this by the sleeve of his work shirt. He wore no hat, and Evelyn could clearly make out the beads of sweat along his brow.

The invasion was literally in the air. The low rumble of approaching cattle thrummed in the night. The river meandered around the rocks and a bend. Beyond the bend were the low hills that formed a semi valley. No bridge was necessary for the river wasn't too deep at that point and most horses and cattle could ford it.

Which was why the cattle rustlers had changed their tactics and chose the Newell farm as the new route up north.

"How long, you reckon?" Newell asked. His voice had grown thin and reedy, quite the contrast from the handsome man Evelyn had contacted a few days earlier.

The question wasn't directed at Evelyn. Despite her displaying her detective's credentials, Newell and his farm hands still didn't think she could possibly be a detective. No matter how many times she related how she had found herself assigned to the case out here in Fremont, Arizona, Newell's men considered her just a woman.

"Half a mile or so." These words came from Dan Horner. A large, beefy man with forearms as thick as Evelyn's thighs, Horner hunkered down amid the corn stalks. He, too, carried a Winchester, and had positioned himself twenty yards to Newell's left.

Evelyn trusted what Horner said. She could have easily countered, but the way the sound bounced off the rocks and hills made pinpointing the approaching herd problematic.

A horse blew, then the sound of hooves splashing in the river water met their ears. The lead rustler was getting closer.

Evelyn herself knelt a few feet away from Newell. He

had tried to get her to escape before the rustlers arrived, but she steadfastly refused. By her estimation, it was entirely possible that the same men who rustled cattle from Mexico were the same men who had killed man by the name of Joe Wilson. To the resident of Fremont, he was merely a cook in a local high-end saloon. To Evelyn Paige, Wilson was a fellow detective, a man she would now avenge.

She had discarded her ankle-length skirt for tight-fitting pants. Newell and his men simultaneously were horrified and filled with lust when they had laid eyes on her as she exited Newell's farmhouse. The carpetbag she had brought with her she left inside. Slung snug against her right thigh was a well-oiled holster made of black leather. Her cotton shirt was open at the neck and a jacket of thick denim kept out the evening chill. She also carried a Winchester and knew how to use it.

But even now, as confident as she was with her marksmanship and the task at hand, pangs of worry filled her gut. She had insisted on staying and helping. She hoped she would live not to regret the decision.

Further on past Horner were Newell's other farm hands. In all, there were five people defending the spread against an unknown number of rustlers. Her old friend and former lover Calvin Carter would have told her it was always a good idea to know one's opponents. In this case, Evelyn hadn't had enough time.

A shout by one of the rustlers came from around the bend. The splashing got louder. Evelyn had tried to coordinate the defense, but Newell brushed her away. He was a man, after all, and he knew best. The only thing he had agreed upon was concealment. That was why they all crouched amid the corn stalks and would rise at a given time and protect the farm.

The one thing Evelyn insisted upon was knowing just how many owlhoots they were up against, and not to fire prematurely. She hoped these stubborn men would at least do that.

A shadowed figure on horseback rounded the last bend. The rider angled the horse up on the far bank. His hat was made of pale material so it caught the moonlight well. The shine of sweat on the horse's rear flank also glowed dully. A few moments later, the cattle came into view. The small herd bumped up against each other, fearful of their night journey and likely wondering just how far they had left to go.

Evelyn wondered the same thing. Ever since she had arrived in Fremont to investigate the Wilson murder, she had quickly learned just how much was wrong in this town. Cattle rustling, it turned out, was merely the lesser evil.

Through the stalks of corn, Evelyn noted Claus Gile, the man closest to the river and the lone rustler, started fidgeting. "Keep it together, man," she whispered under her breath.

Newell jerked his head back to Evelyn. "Hush," he whispered harshly, "or you'll give us away."

Evelyn swallowed her pride and nodded in Gile's direction. "If he doesn't stop twitching, he'll be the only signal they need."

The rider turned his horse so it and he were head on with the cornfield. He didn't move, but the motions his body made told Evelyn he was likely peering into the corn stalks and the first place Newell and his men would hide for an ambush. Slowly, the rider reached to his side and pulled his gun out of his holster. His head cocked to one side, and then he brought the gun up and aimed it at the cornfield.

"Newell, I'll give you and your boys one chance to come out of there alive." The rustler's voice was deep and strong but laced with menace. "I figure y'all're in there or back at your house. If you're in the corn, show yourselves. I'll give to the count of ten."

Evelyn watched as new beads of sweat formed on Newell's brow. To calm him and to keep him from doing anything rash, she asked, "Who is that?"

"Colt Shaddock," Newell said. His voice was even lower than before. "He's the leader."

Nodding, Evelyn didn't need to be told about Shaddock. The outlaw ran his own gang down in these parts. It was likely him or one of his men that shot poor Joe Wilson in the gut. Witnesses said Wilson died in agony in the dirt. The grip on her Winchester tightened. She fought back the urge to get a bead on Shaddock and take him out with one shot.

Instead, Evelyn breathed evenly, calming her own nerves. Still, she tensed as Shaddock began counting down from ten to zero. He got down to three when Claus Gile stood, arms in the air, his rifle's barrel aimed high overhead, no threat to Shaddock at all.

The outlaw leader leveled his pistol and fired a single shot.

The bullet slammed into Gile, throwing him backwards into the stalks. The vegetation creaked and broke under the weight of the dead man. Within a second, the audible thump of a body landing on soil reverberated in the area. The next few seconds brought with them new sounds.

The rataplan of hoof beats pounded on the hard ground of Newell's land. But the galloping sounds didn't come from Shaddock's position or the river. They came from the opposite direction.

Evelyn jerked her head to the side and took in what she saw. A line of horsemen all charged forward. Her eyes counted nine. They were about three hundred yards away and closing fast. The moonlight showed only parts of their bodies and horses. What really revealed themselves were the muzzle flashes from their pistols.

Lead slugs chopped through corn stalks, ripping and rending their way through the plants. Evelyn and Newell stayed low. She hunkered down even more, allowing the first volley to subside. Then, without a thought to herself, Evelyn Paige chunked the butt of her rifle to her shoulder, stood, and opened fire.

Her first bullet took out the middle rider. He spun in his saddle, lost his balance and fell, face first, to the ground. She chambered the next round in a blur of movement. Her second bullet wedged itself in the chest of one of the horses. The beast whinnied in pain, but kept moving, albeit more slowly. The last shot she loosed before the other riders got a line on her took off the hat from the last rider on her left.

The bullets from the remaining riders poured into Evelyn's position. But she had already couched back to the ground and scurried over to Newell's position. She grabbed a handful of his shirt and kept him from standing. He ended up on his back. The cigar tumbled out of his mouth. He opened his mouth to speak, but she silenced him with a hand over his mouth. She brought her mouth close to his ear.

"We can make it to the barn, and from there to the main house. We have to go in waves. You and I will lay down fire while the other two run for it." She lifted her hand from his mouth.

"They'll never make it."

"*We'll* never make it if we don't try. You want to die here in your field or fighting like a man?"

She didn't wait for a response. In an unladylike manner, Evelyn crawled across Newell's body and called to Horner. "We'll cover your retreat to the barn. Then y'all cover ours." She waited a few seconds for Horner to nod then relay the information to Rufus Clarkson, the last man on the line. While she waited, she grabbed Newell's shirt and pulled him up to his elbows. "Get ready." Over her shoulder, Evelyn said, "Three, two, one."

Evelyn didn't dare stand and show herself. From the cover of corn stalks, she let her Winchester roar. Another rider fell before Newell, finally shaken from his lethargy, joined her. The riders reigned up and turned their horses away from the fuselage of bullets. Behind her, Evelyn heard the boots of Horner and Clarkson pound away.

New gunshots from behind her put an end to the retreat of Horner and Clarkson.

Shaddock, who had withheld fire while his men charged the cornfield, opened up with his own pistol. Two startled cries from Newell's farm hands were all the signal she needed to turn and aim her next bullets at Shaddock.

But the leader had already spurred his horse to movement. He made a wide arc, behind the now frightened herd of cattle. On the plus side, he wasn't shooting at Evelyn or Newell. On the down side, she couldn't get a clear shot off either.

She got her feet under her and yanked on Newell's shirt. She shifted the Winchester to her left hand and drew her pistol. "Come on. We're going to run for it. We'll take turns firing to give them something to think about."

"I don't know if I can," squealed the farmer.

"Then you cover me while I escape," Evelyn replied. She swiped her hand viciously across her forehead to get her raven hair out of her eyes.

Right before she started, however, the report of a scattergun boomed in the night. Buckshot lanced through the cornfield. A few pellets ricocheted and burned Evelyn's cheeks. She brushed them away absently. Newell, on the other hand, was spurred to action.

He got to his feet, lined up one of the riders in the sight of his Winchester, and loosed a bullet. The rider fell, screaming.

"Let's go!" he yelled.

Evelyn and Newell sprang to their feet. She risked a quick glance behind her to verify Shaddock still remained behind the cattle. He was. Satisfied, she leveled her Colt .45 with the cherry wood handles and fired two bullets into the now scattering horsemen. Newell shouldered his rifle and fired and levered two rounds. Then, both took off running.

The distance from the edge of the cornfield to the barn was approximately forty yards. Evelyn considered herself a fast runner and could have easily closed the distance in a few seconds. But the ground was completely open. She and Newell were sitting ducks if they ran in a straight line. So she ducked and weaved, trying to make it as difficult as possible to hit.

Newell must not have realized their predicament or the tactic to overcome it. The farmer ran straight for the barn, nearly passing Evelyn who had jumped out to a head start. They were not ten yards from the open barn door when Newell cried out in pain, stumbled, and fell face first into the dirt.

Evelyn took it all in out of the corner of her eye, but never stopped running. Only when she reached the relatively safety of the barn did she stop, turn, and reassess the situation.

Newell had dropped his rifle. His left hand was behind his back, desperately clawing at the dark wound on his shirt. He used his right hand and arm to crawl ever closer to the barn. His grunts were a mixture of pain and exertion.

Shaddock steered his horse from behind the cattle and

rendezvoused with the rest of his men. She and Newell had managed to subtract three from the total, but seven men still wanted nothing more than to put bullets into Newell and Evelyn.

She stood back in the darkness of the barn so that not even moonlight or starlight would reveal her position. She holstered her Colt and brought the Winchester to her shoulder. Three quick shots downed another rider.

Now there were only six.

"Surround the barn," Shaddock ordered.

Some of his men peeled away, two on each side. Shaddock and the man who remained by his side both angled their horses away from the open barn door and out of Evelyn's line of sight.

After a few moments, the only sounds she heard were of her own deep breaths and the painful grunts from Newell. The farmer still inched his way to the barn. Behind him laid a groove in the dry ground to show his slow progress.

Shaddock said something to the man with him. That man nodded and ran into the main house, to the north of the barn.

Evelyn fired her last bullet from her Winchester at the man. The slug thudded harmlessly into the ground, but Evelyn at least got a grim smile as she watched the man redouble his speed. She knelt on the dirt floor of the barn and pulled a leather pouch from an inside pocket of her jacket. She shoved her hand into the pouch and palmed a handful of bullets. Methodically, she began reloading the Winchester. She did it by feel as she slowly turned and took stock of her surroundings.

The barn was nice, but the dry Arizona summers had taken its toll on the boards. Some had shrunk while others had splintered. The end result was that she had slivers of sight on all sides. Not that it did her much good. All she could make out was the shadowed figures of Shaddock's men surrounding the barn.

Her heart slammed in her chest, but she managed to get her breathing under control. For a few moments, a wave of sadness overwhelmed her. She saw no way out of this situation. She would never again perform in a play, read great poetry, or taste the best wine. Nor would she ever see Calvin Carter again, or his partner, Thomas Jackson.

"Shit," she whispered.

Her voice cracked a little, but that small sound hardened her resolve. She set her jaw. She reached inside another pocket of her jacket and brought out a silver badge. It was her detective's badge. Following Carter's advice, she didn't always wear it in order to hide her identity until the proper time. It seemed this was as good a time as any. If she was going to die here in this barn, then she was damn well going to die with her badge on.

"Hello in there," Shaddock called. Since Evelyn couldn't see him, Shaddock's voice sounded disembodied. "By my count, there were only supposed to be four men with Newell. Didn't reckon on there being a fifth. Show yourself, and you might walk out of here alive."

Fat chance at that, Evelyn thought. She scurried over to a vertical wooden beam and got to her feet. Behind her, at the rear of the barn, she noted the shadows of Shaddock's other men. Might as well give them something to think about.

She sighted one of the men through one of the larger cracks. There was no way she could send a bullet through that sliver of open space and do any lasting damage. But it would certainly make her feel good.

Evelyn squeezed the trigger. The bullet tore a hole in the barn wood. The owlhoot cursed and ran away from the side of the structure.

"Hey, now," Shaddock called. "If you keep shooting, we're liable to shoot back. I'm giving you a chance to show yourself before you have to show yourself." A chuckle. "I'm a generous guy."

From the ground outside the barn, Newell managed to turn himself over on his back. He had pulled out his pistol and, with a loud cry, aimed it at Shaddock.

Three gunshots roared. Newell's body twitched with the impacts of the lead bullets. He dropped the gun and moved no more.

The man Shaddock had sent to the main house now hurried back to his leader's side. He held two things, one in each hand. Evelyn couldn't make out what they were, but moonlight glinted off them. When Shaddock lit a match with his fingernail, the light revealed what the man carried.

Two bottles, each with a cloth shoved in the neck.

Shaddock put the flaming match to the first cloth. The material flickered and caught fire. At a nod from Shaddock, the man threw the bottle at the outer wall of the barn. The glass smashed up against the wood, spraying flaming alcohol across the dry wooden wall. The flames found purchase on the wood and ignited it.

Desperate, Evelyn made another decision. "Shaddock, how do I know you won't just shoot me when I walk out?"

"Is that a woman? Well, I'll be damned." His voice was much closer now. The front wall of the barn was the only one with tools hanging from hooks. As such, Evelyn couldn't see out that side. "You wouldn't by any chance be that new lady in town, the one who works down at the rail station?"

So much for her cover.

"The same."

"What's your name?" Shaddock said.

The flames licked up the side of the barn. It now began to ignite one of the upper struts.

"Evelyn Paige," she called in a clear voice. "Detective Evelyn Paige."

The man who had thrown the burning bottle jerked his head as if hearing something for the first time. "Did you say Evelyn Paige?"

Confused, Evelyn didn't reply immediately. "Yes."

Unexpectedly, the man ran across her field of vision. The move surprised her so much she didn't react and try and shoot him. She waited, her eyes never leaving the growing fire.

"Detective," Shaddock finally called, "I want to let you know that you have my word that I won't shoot you when you leave the barn. In fact, there's someone out here who wants to see you."

Now that was confusing. She had never been to Fremont, Arizona. Only one time had she even passed through the entire territory, and that for a night's layover in Tucson. That a man allied with Shaddock apparently knew her confounded Evelyn. She hadn't been a detective that long to have amassed an enemies list. Besides, all the people she had brought to justice were either behind bars or under the ground.

But whomever it was clearly wanted her alive. With her eyes never wavering from the flames, she realized she possessed few options. She could burn to death, a thought that sent shivers down her spine. She could take her own life. Out of the question. Or she could surrender and see what happened.

The will to live, at least for now, prevailed.

"Okay, I'm coming out." She tossed the Winchester out the barn door. It flew, end over end, and landed in the dirt near Newell's body. She grasped her revolver and the thought of going out with guns blazing flashed across her mind. She shoved it aside as she tossed the pistol next to the rifle. Then, with her hands above her head, Evelyn Paige walked out of the barn.

As soon as she crossed the threshold, strong hands grasped her wrists and pinned her arms behind her. The hands belonged to the man who had thrown the bottle. She couldn't see his face, but she saw Shaddock. The outlaw leader walked up to her, regarding her with his head cocked to one side. The firelight danced over his face. He smiled, revealing a gap in his teeth. In his hand, he held the other bottle. He removed the cloth and took a long drink.

"My friend here tells me y'all've met before." He spat in the ground. "I'd love to hear the story."

Evelyn Paige turned as much as she could. The other man met her movement and tossed her to the ground. She landed on her side. Quickly, she pivoted, and got to her feet. She stood there, unarmed and defenseless, and gazed at the man.

Recognition flared in her memory. Her mouth dropped open and her eyes widened with the memory of the last time she had laid eyes on him. It was the first time she had realized she could make a good detective. She only knew the man by one name.

"Rance."

"Hello, Miss Paige," Rance said. "Glad you remember me."

"How did you…?"

"Escape? Not too difficult really. With all the confusion and shooting, I just slipped away. But not without some scars for the effort." He brought his hand up in front of his face. With the fingers of his other hand, he caressed a deep red, round burn. "You know the man who did this to me." It wasn't a question.

She nodded.

"Not sure if y'all still fancy each other, but I sure as hell expect him to come to your rescue when he hears you've gone missing."

The rest of Shaddock's men hurried to their leader's side. One of them, a thin rangy fellow, said, "What now, boss?"

"Tie her up. She's coming with us."

"You think that's a good idea?" the rangy man said.

Shaddock threw a gesture at Rance. "I owe him. If he thinks kidnapping this here detective will bring a man named Calvin Carter, then so be it." He pointed a finger at Rance. "As long as you deal with him."

Rance grinned mirthlessly. "Oh, I'll deal with Calvin Carter. With a bullet in his brain."

Outlaw Angus Morton and his gang have made a crucial mistake: they upped their crimes from robbing stagecoaches near El Paso to murdering a railroad agent and burning down a way station. Detective Calvin Carter and his partner are tasked with bringing Morton to justice.

One way or another.

When Carter arrives at Morton's last known location, he finds the town on edge. The bandit has the citizens terrified, wondering where next he'll strike. Even stranger are the rumors of a fire-breathing creature capable of utter destruction, a monster which could lay waste to the city.

As a former actor, Carter knows a tall-tale when he hears one. But he also knows a few things are not make believe:

Witnesses to the most recent attack turning up murdered.

Carter himself attacked.

And the deep, metallic churning sound of an infernal machine approaching...

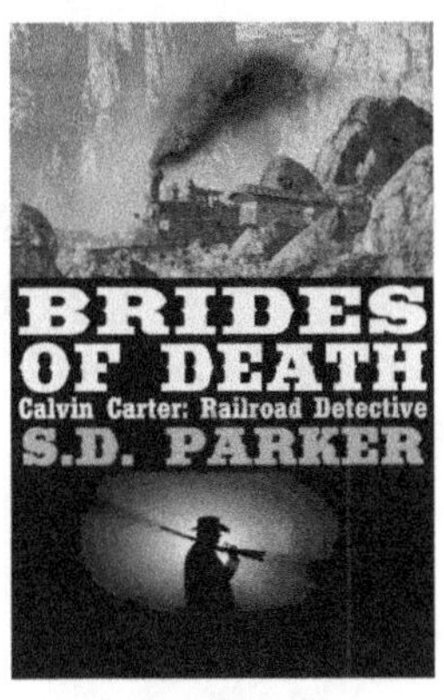

July 2019

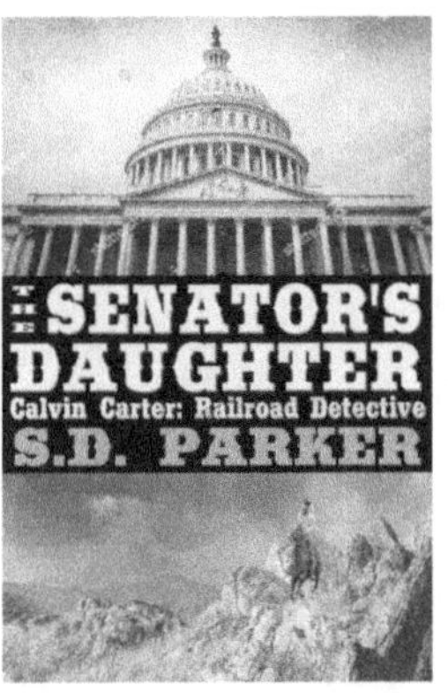

September 2019

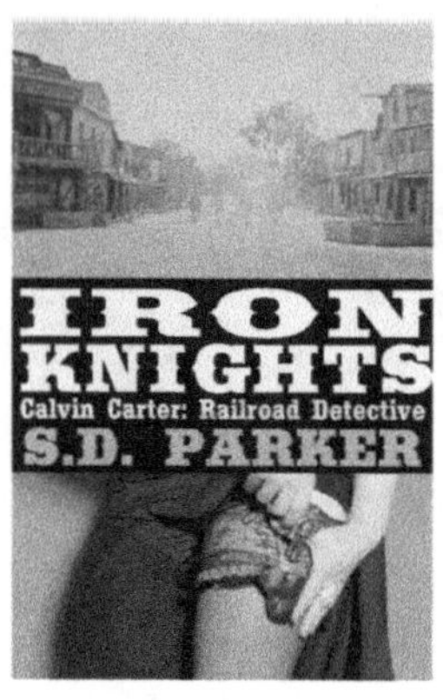

November 2019

What would you do if your spouse was murdered?

Isabella Gilmour woke one morning thinking it was just another day. It wasn't. It was the day the horrifying news thundered down on her: her husband had been shot dead by Bart Conway, the scion of the biggest cattle rancher of Junction City, Texas. In her moment of anguish, she invokes Mosaic Law: an eye for an eye, a life for a life. She makes a simple request of her father: "Go get Stephen's rifle."

Her desperate father begs her to let the legal system work. Will she, or will she let justice come in the form of a bullet?

A man shouldn't outlive his son. Neither should his killer.

In a searing new western from author S. D. Parker, you will discover all a father will endure to see justice done right by his murdered son.

Luke Russell was a cowpuncher, making an honest way in the world at one of the biggest ranches outside of Junction City. But he got himself in trouble over a girl, and he paid the ultimate price.

Now, a stranger's in town, asking after Pete Davidson, the man who put a bullet in Luke Russell's gut. This stranger is old, and folks realize it's Luke father, come to kill Davidson. The gunslinger is young and vibrant, just like Luke Russell was. The old man doesn't stand a chance.

Or does he?

Imagine you are a carpenter and a gunfighter asks you to build a coffin…for him. What would you do? And how many coffins would you have to make?

The answer comes in an exciting new Junction City novelette from author S. D. Parker in the style of Louis L'Amour, James Reasoner, and C. K. Crigger.

Emory Duvall practices his simple carpentry trade, knows everyone in town, and stays out of trouble. But when a young gunslinger pulls iron on him and makes an unusual request, trouble lands in Duvall's lap.

Now, the carpenter must figure out how to avoid getting shot… and how many coffins he will have to make.

This exciting new Western from S. D. Parker will have you asking a simple question: what would you do in Emory's position.

What would you do if your wife cheated on you with a dandy of a gambler?

John Hardwick answered that question for himself. Now, he's about to act on it.

John loves his wife like a Shakespeare sonnet: full, complete, and without equal. Unfortunately, John now finds himself in the crucible of infidelity. He knows the other man's name: Alton Raines, a professional gambler.

John is a good man, not prone to violence, but the images in his mind's eye—of his wife in Raines's bed—puts murder in his heart and a gun in his hand.

Sometimes a man hides something in plain sight. When that man is naked, what he's hiding is even more difficult to see.

Taking inspiration from movies Maverick and Butch Cassidy and the Sundance Kid, "The Naked Con" is the exciting new western short story from author S. D. Parker.

It's not every day that the passengers of a stagecoach in the Old West see a naked man cowering behind a rock. But the motley group of people bound for Uvalde, Texas, stop and question Finnegan McCall, naked as the day of his birth. He claims he's the new manager at the bank in town and a thief stole all his clothes and money.

But if McCall is telling the truth, then who is the stranger at the bank claiming he is the new bank manager? And why is this stranger asking the assistant manager to open the safe?

This humorous new Western from S. D. Parker will have you questioning who is whom and what it all means.

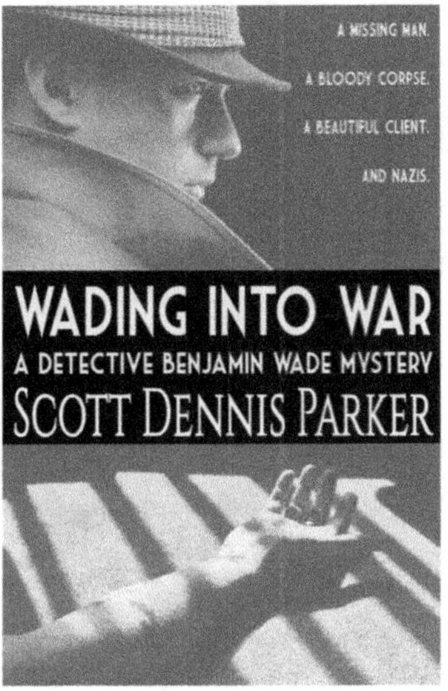

When bullets burst through a door, unarmed gumshoe Benjamin Wade knows his case just got a hell of a lot more difficult.

The smoke clears, the shooter escapes, and Wade finds a corpse. It's the man he was hired to find. His client would not be happy.

Beguiling and enigmatic Lillian Saxton asked Wade to locate a missing reporter who claimed to possess information she craved: whether or not her brother had died in Europe during the early days of World War II. The reporter vanished soon after his ship docked in Houston and she's desperate.

Wade, a laid back former cop, accepts cases so mundane he rarely carries a gun. Now, Wade must unravel the truth about the reporter's murder and the cache of missing documents that reveal a shocking story from Nazi-controlled Europe and an even more sinister secret on the home front.

The case made private eye Benjamin Wade laugh. Now, it might kill him.

May 1940, the last days of the Great Depression, and laid-back gumshoe Ben Wade isn't exactly rolling in the dough. He doesn't even have a secretary. He's so bad off, he can't refuse any case.

Elmer Smith is a local farmer. A few days after the police chased a hoodlum through Smith's farm, he receives a court notice: his chickens are infectious and scheduled for slaughter. Desperate to save his livelihood, Smith hires a lawyer to slow the process, but time is running out.

With his coffers nearly empty, Wade suppresses his pride and takes the case. Curiously, the police have no record of the incident. The nervous health inspector is suddenly evasive. And the inspector's beautiful secretary thinks she's being followed and seeks Wade's help.

To unravel the mystery, Wade obsesses on the central question:
What really happened the night police chased someone through
Smith's chicken coop? Wade isn't the only one asking the
question, but he might be the only one who dies for it.

Witnesses all said the same thing: the lunatic who jumped in front
of a moving car claimed the vehicle was a ghost. His death proved
him wrong.

Why would a man do this? That's the question ace reporter
Gordon Gardner asks. What started out as a basic police blotter
story initially depressed Gordon. As a reporter second to none,
how could a simple accident be worthy of his considerable
talents? Even his pairing with a beautiful photographer didn't
lighten his mood.

But when Gordon learns the truth about the crazy man's last
moments, he digs deeper and zeroes in on a fundamental question:
what made Victor Tompkins, a traveling salesman, leap in front of
a car?

The police don't care. They've already closed the case. His editor wants the piece yesterday. His rival reporter can't wait for Gordon to fail. Even his new partner, the beautiful Lucy Barnes, thinks Gordon is barking up the wrong tree.

Yet Gordon Gardner didn't earn his bulldog reputation by giving up and walking away. Too many oddities exist. Why would someone break into Tompkins's house after he died? What happened to Tompkins out in the country? Who were the killers who just gunned down one of Gordon's witnesses? As the footsteps approach his position, Gordon Gardner fears he'll never uncover the real truth of the phantom automobiles.

What if the only way you could discover who killed your brother was to lie to your commanding officer?

May 1940. Western Europe is on edge, wondering when the Nazis will strike. America is neutral, woefully unprepared for war, and President Roosevelt tries to steer the dicey waters of international diplomacy and keep the United States out of the conflict. Army Sergeant Lillian Saxton receives a cryptic message from an old flame who now lives in Germany: meet in Belgium and he will not only hand over the key to the Nazi codebooks but also information about the man who murdered her brother.

Lillian conducts all her missions with panache and confidence, even when bullets start to fly and enemy agents zero in to kill her. She's more uncertain of how she'll react when she sees the man who broke her heart or how she'll get out of Belgium when the Nazis launch their invasion.